GUARD
the
THRONE

Buy

for Melodrama

GUARD
the
THRONE

NISA SANTIAGO

Guard the Throne. Copyright © 2012 by Melodrama Publishing. All rights reserved. Printed in the United States of America. No part of this book may be used or reproduced in any manner whatsoever without written permission except in the case of brief quotations embodied in critical articles or reviews. For information, address Melodrama Publishing, P.O. Box 522, Bellport, NY 11713.

www.melodramapublishing.com

Library of Congress Control Number: 2011946163
ISBN-13: 978-1934157503
ISBN-10: 1934157503
First Edition: October 2012
10 9 8 7 6 5 4 3 2 1

Interior Design: Candace K. Cottrell
Cover Design: Marion Designs
Model: KAMERON DASH

Also By
NISA SANTIAGO

Cartier Cartel

Return of the Cartier Cartel

Bad Apple: The Baddest Chick

Coca Kola: The Baddest Chick

Checkmate: The Baddest Chick

Face Off: The Baddest Chick

Dirty Money Honey

PROLOGUE

The black Town Car came to a stop in front of Baisley Park Houses in Queens. It was a clear, warm Thursday afternoon in New York with blue skies. It had been a brutal winter, but the trees were starting to turn green again. Citi was ready to make it a terrific spring, starting today. It was her sixteenth birthday, and she was overwhelmed with anticipation and excitement. Today would be her special day.

She had left school an hour early to rush home to see what gift her father had ready for her. In Citi's mind, school wasn't that important. She barely went, and on the days she did go, it was only to floss her cream-of-the-crop wardrobe and show off the new jewelry her father had bought for her. She was the center of attention—queen bee bitch in her school and among her peers in the Queens hood.

Citi, short for Cynthia, was a beautiful young girl—a wet dream for many men. Her long, defined legs, ample hips, meaty thighs, and breasts that sprouted like a pair of balloons made her eye-candy in the hood. She had rich, brown skin and long, wavy hair.

Most of the men in the neighborhood only stared silently, keeping their impure thoughts about young Citi to themselves. They feared that her father, Curtis, would cut out their tongues or gouge out their eyes if they said something rude or absurd, or looked at his daughter's luscious figure for too long. Sometimes the men had to constantly remind themselves that she was only a teenage girl.

Citi made it hard for them to ignore her, with her sometimes scanty attire and flirtatious attitude. Curtis was disturbed by his daughter's antics and way of dress, but she was spoiled like left-out milk.

Citi swung open the back door to the cab and handed the African driver his fee. She stepped out of the car dressed in super-tight jeans and a tight pink tube top that accentuated her breasts. Her hair flowed down to her back like a stream, and her fresh white pair of Nikes were the color of fresh snow. Diamond earrings dangled from her lobes with style and screamed money, and the tennis bracelet around her wrist sparkled like an ice sculpture in the sun. She topped off her outfit with the most recent gift from her father—a diamond necklace that hung around her neck with precision. She was styled perfectly for her birthday, from head to toe.

Citi's father had promised her a car for her birthday—a Honda Accord. She loved that type of car, and knew she would sit like a dream behind the steering wheel, cruising the hood with all eyes on her. It would make her friends praise her even more, and her enemies envious. Citi felt she was too good to ride the city bus like the regular kids, so on the days that she did go to school, it was by Town Car only—forty dollars round trip, which her father could easily afford.

Curtis was a legend in South Jamaica, Queens. A natural-born hustler and once a part of the notorious Supreme Team back in the early '90s, he would turn forty in a few years. Among other things, Curtis had survived the notorious crack epidemic, avoided a lengthy prison sentence, and beaten the RICO Act—which had swooped up most of his allies.

He loved his kids greatly, but he loved his only daughter most. He treated her like a princess, giving her whatever she wanted. If any man dared to defile her, he had killers on standby to make them pay dearly.

Citi looked around the block as the cab drove away, searching for her birthday gift on four wheels. She was trying to see if her father had parked it anywhere close by on the street, but only the same old tired cars on the block were there—no sparkling Accord with a bow on it.

"He probably tryin' to hide it from me," she said to herself.

She strutted toward the towering project building. Baisley Projects was where she'd grown up and all she knew. Queens was her domain, and South Side was her playground, where she fought bitches with her girls, ran with her crew, and shoplifted for the fun of it. It was the place where she'd fallen in love with Randy, who had taken her virginity when she was only fourteen.

Citi walked into the building lobby with a bright smile. Her life was good, and she had no complaints or worries.

"Happy birthday, Citi," one of the young residents said as he passed by.

"Thanks, C."

"Damn! You lookin' nice."

"I know, right? You know a bitch gotta stay styling."

"Shit. I ain't mad at you."

"Anyway, you gonna see me cruising soon, C."

"Oh, word? Pops gettin' you that ride?"

"Yup."

"That's what's up. What he gettin' you?"

"You'll see."

"I can get a ride someday, right?"

"Nigga, why you beggin' a bitch already? You know ya bitch might get jealous if she sees you cruising wit' a fly bitch like me. I'm just sayin' . . . "

"Yeah, a'ight. I feel you, Citi, but I'm sayin', when you see a nigga around, stop by," C said, his eyes focused on her ample breasts and tight body.

"Stoppin' lookin' too hard, C. It ain't cute to be thirsty."

C laughed. "A'ight."

Citi spun on her sneakers and strutted toward the elevators, leaving C daydreaming about being with her sometime in the future.

Citi stepped into the smelly, pissy elevator and tried not to touch anything. She pressed her floor and it lifted slowly. The anticipation of receiving the keys to her new car and taking it for a spin around the neighborhood made her jovial. She stepped off the elevator and strutted to her apartment door with her keys in hand. From the hallway she could hear their high-end stereo system blaring.

Citi wondered why her father was playing music so loud. She walked into the lavish apartment and immediately began searching for her gifts.

"Daddy, I'm home," she called out with a smile, but there was no response.

She walked over to the stereo system that was blaring Hot 97 and turned it down. She then spotted a small box surrounded by birthday balloons and a card on the kitchen table. Her heart began to beat rapidly. This was the moment.

Citi snatched the black velvet box off the table and quickly popped it open. Instead of the keys to her Honda Accord, she saw a gold and diamond locket with her mother's picture inside.

"What the fuck is this?" Citi didn't care for another piece of jewelry at the moment, especially one with her mother's picture inside. She wished the bitch were dead. She tossed the locket aside and continued looking for more gifts.

"Daddy, where are you?" She was ready for her real gift, believing the locket with her mother's picture was only a gag. It had to be; her father never disappointed her, especially on her birthday.

Citi walked to her father's bedroom. Inside was silent. The door was ajar. Her brothers weren't home yet, but she knew her father had to be home. She figured he was ready to jump out and surprise her once she entered his bedroom. She smiled.

"Daddy, I'm comin' in. You better be decent and have no bitch in there."

Citi pushed open the bedroom door and saw blood everywhere. Her eyes widened with shock, and she began to tremble. Her father was duct-taped and lying facedown in the bed. He'd been shot execution-style. The place had been ransacked. The killer or killers were obviously looking for something important.

"Daddy!" she screamed. She rushed into the room and scooped her father's body into her arms. His mouth, wrists, and legs were duct-taped tightly.

"Daddy, Daddy, no, don't do this to me. Please, Daddy!"

Her father's blood began to stain her birthday attire. His body was still warm, but he was dead.

Citi ripped the duct tape from his mouth and stared into her father's dead eyes. She cradled him in her arms and cried.

Citi continued to grip her father tightly and comfort his dead body in her arms. She rocked back and forth. "It's my fault, Daddy. I'm sorry. I'm sorry. I'm sorry."

CHAPTER 1

THREE MONTHS EARLIER

Citi sat near her bedroom window and peered outside at the desolate neighborhood. The project courtyard and streets were empty for the moment. She could hear the wind blowing against the glass. The remnants of snow from the last winter storm lingered on the ground. Citi's insignificant bedroom window was encircled by the towering project buildings that housed murderers, drug dealers, and drug users, alongside civilized working-class residents trying to live in peace in a place that could sometimes feel like Baghdad.

She heard rap music blaring from the living room. The bass from her father's high-end stereo system was making the walls shake. It was Biggie playing, one of her father's favorite rappers. She could hear his raspy voice rapping about the hustle and streets of Brooklyn.

Citi lit up a cigarette and continued to look outside. At fifteen years old she was already a veteran to the criminal and street life. Her father hid nothing from his little girl. She grew up in a house occupied by only men—her father, her brothers, and her father's associates, who came through to cut work, talk business, and drink and play cards till the early hours of the morning. There were days when Citi would walk into the apartment and see triple-beam scales on the kitchen or living room table, cocaine lying around, and other drug paraphernalia in the place.

It wasn't unusual for her to walk into her home and see a strange woman on the couch or exiting her father's bedroom. Curtis was a playboy, and he had bitches in and out of his place on a continuous basis. Citi had seen more pussy come and go from her place than the "Playboy Mansion." She would always warn her father about the constant traffic, but he made it clear that he was the adult in the household and she was a child.

From a tender age, she had been exposed to a lot of things, but the one thing Curtis never exposed her to was murder or any other violent crimes. With his two sons, Chris and Cane, it was different. He was grooming them to take over his business when he was gone. He wanted his sons to see the truth in the streets and have the respect in the game and on the streets like he did. So he showed them bloodshed and advised them to never be on the wrong end of a gun.

Citi was blossoming like a spring flower. She had the image of a rose, but thorns were on her stem. Growing up in her environment, she adopted the rough, thuggish ways of her father and brothers, and she had the attitude of a pit bull from time to time. She began smoking at thirteen and fucking at fourteen. Curtis was so busy in the streets, he didn't have time to chaperone his daughter, so Citi pretty much got to do whatever she wanted.

Their project apartment was the nicest in the hood, furnished with all the amenities money could buy—flat-screens in every room, leather sofas, granite countertops, hardwood floors in the living room, and a stereo system that blared rap music. Stepping into their apartment was like walking into a lavish loft in SoHo. Security was like Fort Knox's, with a steel front door and a high-end security system containing small cameras at the door, along with an alarm. Guns were situated throughout the apartment, in case the wolves came sniffing around.

Citi continued to stare outside. She took a pull from the cigarette and became lost in her own thoughts for a moment. Hearing Biggie's lyrics about the finer things made her think about her approaching birthday in three months. Citi turned and focused on her room. Her bedroom was furnished with everything she had asked for: a canopy bed, laptop, designer clothing spilling out her closet and drawers, shoes and sneakers of every kind, along with a 40-inch flat-screen, and a vanity covered with high-end beauty products.

But the one thing Citi was missing was a car. She wanted a Honda Accord for her sixteenth birthday. Since last summer, when Citi saw Meeka pushing a sleek Accord with chrome rims and tinted windows, she wanted one too. She couldn't let a low-class ho with no style outdo her. Citi wanted to floss this coming summer, and that was only happening by having her own car. She had made up her mind on what she wanted for her birthday—a better and more stylish car than Meeka's.

As Citi stood by the window, she suddenly heard shots ring out. They came from outside and echoed near her bedroom. It was common in the projects.

Bak! Bak! Bak! Bak! Bak!

Citi didn't flinch. Even in the heart of winter, niggas still had beef, and people were still dying. The projects were the same, no matter what season it was. Lifestyles didn't change, people were still poor, and drug dealers still got their hustle on.

Her bedroom door opened up. "You okay, princess?" Curtis asked.

"I'm fine, Daddy."

Curtis smiled. The cigarette in his daughter's hand didn't disturb him. Everyone smoked. He nodded.

Citi looked at her father with a bright glow in her face. Curtis was very handsome, and Citi was proud to have come from such good genes. He was tall, pushing six-two, with an athletic build. He had black, curly hair, a dark, well-trimmed goatee, and rich brown skin. Curtis' piercing onyx eyes said that he was a man not to fuck with. His eyes exposed the dark, treacherous side of a killer. When he looked at his daughter, however, those same onyx eyes would illuminate with pride and joy toward his little angel.

"What's on your mind, princess? The shots didn't frighten you, right?"

Citi cut her eyes at her father and twisted up her face. "Daddy, we're cut from the same cloth. Why you tryin' to play me like that? That ain't nothin' new to me."

He laughed. "I know, but you know I gotta check up on you."

"I'm a big girl, Daddy."

"I know. That's what's scaring me."

"I'm okay."

Curtis nodded. "A'ight. You need anything?"

"Yes."

"What you need, princess?"

"It's not something now, but something relevant for my sixteenth birthday." Citi aimed a warm smile at her father.

He sighed. "Here we go. You're birthday is three months away, and already you're starting to put together a list."

"I don't need no list, Daddy, 'cuz I only want one thing."

"And what is that one thing?"

"A car."

"A car?"

"Yup. 'Cuz I need to upgrade."

"Upgrade?" Curtis walked farther in his daughter's bedroom and sat on her bed. "And how much is this car going to cost me?"

"Don't worry, Daddy. I'm not asking for a Lexus or a Benz."

"So what are you asking for?"

Citi took a seat on her father's lap and threw her arms around him lovingly with a beaming smile. "A Honda Accord."

"An Accord?"

"Yes, and I already know what model and color I want. You already know I'm gonna get my permit, and by the time I'm sixteen, I'm gonna have my license."

"You got this all worked out already, huh?"

"Yup. 'Cuz you know I get it from you."

"I see."

"So, we good on that, Daddy?"

Curtis smiled. "I'll think on it, princess."

"Okay."

Citi got off her father's lap, and Curtis stood up.

"Let me go back to my company, make sure these muthafuckas don't cheat me out of five grand on this game."

"Daddy, you always win."

"That's right. 'Cuz who the fuck remembers losers?"

Citi beamed. She was always happy when her father was around. He was a leader— an authority figure among his peers. He commanded respect and attention. He would always look a man and a woman in their eyes when he was talking to them, and he didn't take bullshit from anyone. He gave you respect if you deserved it, and demanded the same from everyone he surrounded himself with.

Curtis was a businessman first, a father second, and a lady's man last. Which meant he never put pussy over his business or his family. Bitches always come and go. The only woman he was still crushing over was Ashanti, the mother to his three kids, and the one woman who had his heart on lock.

Ashanti was pretty and curvy like a Victoria's Secret model, but rough around the edges. She was a bad girl with expensive taste. She lived in Harlem and grew up in the Alberto "Alpo" Martinez and Rich Porter era, while Curtis grew up under the Supreme Team. Ashanti refused to leave Harlem to live in Queens with her kids and Curtis. In her mind, Harlem was the place to live, where trends started and true hustlers got money. Queens was nothing but fabricated hustlers and confusing streets.

Despite their differences, she was Curtis' heart, and he loved her. But that same love didn't carry over to her three children, who all despised her for abandoning them and not trying to have a relationship with them. They didn't want anything to do with Ashanti. She was dead to them.

Unbeknownst to the kids, Curtis made it his mission to drive to Harlem on a regular to be with Ashanti. He paid her bills, updated her about their kids and their well being, and shared intimate moments and secrets with his wife. He trusted her. Even though Ashanti and Curtis had their affairs, they both pretended that their relationship was exclusive; that they were faithful to each other.

Curtis exited his daughter's bedroom and went back to his poker game. Citi knew the Accord was already hers; it was just a matter of time.

She heard the men chattering in the living room and decided to be nosy. She peeked in on her father playing high-stakes poker with his associates. Curtis gambled big, and he won and lost big. The table was cluttered with poker chips, beer cans, burning cigarettes, cards, and money. Cash was spread out across the table like a bank vault had exploded.

Citi smiled when she noticed Maino seated at the table clad in a wifebeater with a hulking gold chain around his neck. Maino was Curtis' partner and right-hand man. He was from Brooklyn, and was another man you didn't want to fuck with. Curtis and Maino had known each other for years—well before Citi was born. Maino was savvy and ruthless like Curtis. The two men had Queens and Brooklyn on semi-lock, and their names rang out like a Hot 97 party horn. Having been through war and hell together, and having seen the evil each other could do, their friendship was cemented. In fact, they called each other brothers.

There were stories about Maino easily beating a man to death with his bare knuckles for the slightest infraction, and hunting and killing three men after they attempted to murder Curtis a few years earlier.

Maino was stocky and fit. He had a bald head, black beard, and beady eyes that intimidated any man with his intense stare. When he stood up, he was just as tall as Curtis, and he tipped the scales at 255 pounds. He was a bear.

Maino was temperamental, easily triggered, and always ready to act. He regularly carried a Ruger P95 and a sharp blade in his back pocket. Maino was a beast. It took a lot to gain his trust and respect. Curtis was one of the few men he respected and trusted.

Maino was one of Citi's favorite people in the world. He always talked kindly to her, and, like her father, he was always bearing gifts. Citi knew that with men like her father and Maino having her back, nobody in Queens or Brooklyn had the courage to disrespect her, because the word was out that if anyone did, it would be some biblical shit storming down on them.

"Yeah, muthafucka!" Maino threw his cards across the table, revealing his winning hand. "Straight flush, niggas!" He was ready to collect the pile of cash.

Tito tossed his hand on the table in frustration. "Muthafucka!"

Curtis shook his head, laughing. He puffed on a cigar, and the smoke lingered around the table. It was a masculine evening of shit talking and beer drinking. It was the one time Curtis got to relax and chill with his people.

Maino was all smiles. He took a pull from the burning cigarette between his fingers and leaned across the table to pull his winnings in.

"You cheatin'-ass nigga," Dre unexpectedly uttered, clearly upset.

Maino stopped collecting the cash and glared at Dre. "What the fuck you say to me?"

"Nah, I ain't say nuthin'," Dre replied calmly. "Go ahead and collect."

"You callin' me a fuckin' cheater?"

"I ain't callin' you a damn thing, Maino."

"Nah, you called me a fuckin' cheater, nigga."

Dre sighed. "You buggin' right now, Maino."

"So I'm a fuckin' liar now, huh? I'm hearing things come out your fuckin' mouth."

Dre didn't respond. He took a sip from his beer and locked eyes with the terror that sat opposite him. One of Curtis' street lieutenants and best hustlers, Dre was always quick to talk shit without thinking first, so his mouth constantly got him into trouble.

"Dre, repeat yourself, nigga," Maino said through clench teeth. He stood erect over the table and glared at Dre.

"Why you buggin', Maino? I was just jokin' wit' you."

"Nigga, you think I'm fuckin' joking?"

"Maino, just chill," Curtis chimed.

"Nah, fuck that! Curtis, you know this nigga talk too fuckin' much and think everything is fuckin' funny. I'm tired of that bitch-ass nigga!"

"Fuck you, Maino! Fo' real, you think everybody scared of you. Nigga, I pack my gun too."

"What? That's a threat, Dre?"

With the blink of an eye, Maino snatched the Ruger from his waistband and pointed it at Dre.

Curtis and Tito jumped up from the table, shocked.

"Nigga, what the fuck you doin'? Put that shit away, Maino," Curtis screamed.

"Maino, it ain't that fuckin' serious," Tito shouted.

"It is that serious."

Dre could only sit still at the card table and stare down the barrel of the gun that was trained on him. He tried to keep his cool as he locked eyes with Maino.

"You got somethin' smart to say now, nigga?"

"We cool, Maino," Dre said. "Ain't no disrespect to you."

"I know it ain't gonna be."

"Maino, my fuckin' daughter is in the next room. Chill the fuck out."

The room had become tense. Maino, his outstretched arm clutching the Ruger and his finger slightly on the trigger, glanced at Curtis. Maino was unpredictable. Dre knew there was a possibility that his life could end in a second.

"Put it away, Maino," Curtis said sternly. "I don't want my daughter around this shit."

All the while, Citi was behind the corner watching the entire incident silently. She felt her heart race.

"Yeah, you right, C," Maino said. "I'm wilding right now." He lowered the gun and smiled. "I was just fuckin' wit' you, Dre."

Dre exhaled, somewhat relieved. "You fuckin' crazy, Maino," said Dre.

"I know."

Then, abruptly, Maino raised the gun at Dre and fired.

Bam!

The bullet ripped through Dre's shoulder and pushed him back and out of the chair. He tumbled to the floor and cried out in pain. "Ah, shit! This nigga shot me!"

"What the fuck is wrong with you, Maino?" Curtis screamed.

"I just gave that nigga a flesh wound," Maino said coolly. "He gonna be a'ight."

"Yo, what the fuck!" Tito shouted.

Dre squirmed around on the floor, grasping his shoulder. He couldn't believe Maino had shot him.

Curtis screamed, "Maino, I got fuckin' neighbors, and you do this shit? I don't need cops comin' to my place."

"My bad, Curtis. I just needed to teach this young nigga a fuckin' lesson."

"By doin' this?"

"He got the message, right?" Maino said, stuffing the Ruger in his waistband.

Curtis shook his head and looked down at Dre. "Tito, take him to the hospital. Y'all know the routine."

"A'ight."

Maino was a twisted fuck, and Curtis knew it. His evening with the fellows was put to an abrupt end. He needed to clean the blood off his floor and get rid of any evidence, just in case the cops were called and came knocking on his door.

Curtis shot Maino an unpleasant look. "I don't need this shit right now, Maino."

Maino shrugged.

Curtis turned and saw Citi staring at them. He sighed. "Citi, get back in your room," he shouted. "You don't need to see this shit."

"I already saw it."

"You okay?" he asked her.

Citi nodded.

Curtis looked at his princess, and she didn't seem disturbed at all. He knew, no matter how hard he tried to hide any violence and murder from his daughter, it was inevitable that she would witness it. His world was hard, ugly, and cruel.

CHAPTER 2

Citi woke up on a Saturday morning to her brothers arguing in the next room. She heard Cane scream, "Yo, fuck those niggas! I don't give a fuck!"

Citi sighed. Cane was always the loudest one in the room. She glanced over at the time, and it was almost noon. She'd wanted to sleep in late. She didn't like mornings, especially during the winter months. Snug under her covers, clad in her panties and bra, she couldn't help overhearing the conversation.

"Yo, why you trippin?" Chris said.

"'Cuz them niggas is fuckin' faggots, yo. I'm ready to fuck 'em up."

"You need to chill, Cane. Don't be trippin' over that bullshit."

"What? You need to stop actin' like a fuckin' bitch."

"I'm a bitch?"

Cane said, "Yeah, nigga, we come from the same blood, and you actin' like you scared to put in work out there."

"Fuck you, Cane. Who you think you talkin' to like that? I'm the nigga out there tryin' to get shit done and make it happen."

"Yeah, whatever, nigga. All I know is, you need to act like you a fuckin' Byrne sometimes."

Citi couldn't take their yelling anymore. She jumped out of her bed and hurried to her bedroom door. She swung it open and shouted, glaring at them, "Can y'all two just fuckin' chill and shut the fuck up? Dammit!

Y'all actin' like a bunch of babies."

Chris and Cane turned to look at their sister.

"What? We woke you or somethin'?" Cane asked. "Wake ya ass up then!"

"Where's Daddy?" she asked.

"I don't know," Cane replied.

Citi sighed heavily and slammed the door.

"Sorry, sis," Chris shouted.

"What you apologizing for?"

"Shut up, Cane!"

▲

Cane was sixteen and the hothead in the family, quick to react without thinking. He loved the streets and took full advantage of the perks of being a Byrne. He grew up idolizing men like Maino and his father, having heard stories about his father and the Supreme Team. Cane walked around the hood feeling like he was untouchable. If you pulled a knife, he was ready to pull a gun. And if you pulled a gun, he was ready to shoot first. And if you shot first, you better hope he was dead, because he wasn't the type to forgive. He thought he knew it all.

At seventeen, Chris was the eldest of the three siblings. He was the business-minded one, the one to think things through and analyze a situation. He wanted his father to go legit with their drug money. He kept his ears to the streets and was well informed, reading The Wall Street Journal and staying focused on the news.

But the two were both flashy in their jewels and attire. They both had nice cars, Cane, a BMW, and Chris, a convertible Benz. Curtis indulged his sons to whatever they wanted and needed. He had schooled his sons on the streets and the business continuously since they were toddlers, so they knew their father's life and his trade like they knew the latest rap song.

Guard the Throne

Citi could no longer sleep after her brothers' racket. She looked out the window. It was another cold day in January. She sighed when she heard the strong winter wind blow against her window. She turned on her stereo and listened to Mary J. Blige sing her heart out.

She locked her bedroom door and stripped down naked, admiring herself in the mirror. Citi was so proud of her body, a grade-A figure she'd inherited from her mother. It was the only thing she was grateful to receive from her mother, and the only thing her mother had passed on to her.

Citi spent her Saturday afternoons in the Korean nail shop in Rochdale Village or Kandi's Beauty Salon on Linden Boulevard. Then on Sundays, she would go shopping in the malls or in the city, splurging hundreds of dollars on outfits, shoes, and makeup. She loved getting dolled up and pretty for her nights out. Like clockwork, her Saturday nights were spent in the clubs or hanging with her girlfriends, where she showed off her new attire and gleaming jewels. She loved the attention, especially the attention she got from men, both young and older. Everyone knew who she was, and she flaunted her status like she was the daughter to the president of the United States.

It was one in the afternoon when she decided to get dressed and make some phone calls. Her day didn't start until three, but her brothers had disturbed her beauty sleep. She picked up her phone and decided to call Dana, her best friend. It wasn't fun going to get her hair and nails done alone. She needed a friend to accompany her; someone to talk to and gossip with.

Dana lived in the project building across Guy R. Brewer Boulevard, and was one of the few teens in the projects with her parents married and living in the same home. The girls had been friends since the sixth grade and were willing and ready to do anything for each other. They had similar tastes—fashion, dick, and attention. Dana's parents were both city workers and could afford to provide their only child with almost the same luxuries that Citi had, but Citi was able to afford more than her friend because her father had a lot more bank than Dana's parents' combined income. But Dana was a booster, shoplifting from department stores like it was an art, and whatever she didn't want for herself, she passed on to Citi.

Citi dialed Dana, and it rang a few times before she picked up.

"What, bitch?"

"Get dressed," Citi said. "I'm ready to go get our nails and hair done."

"You treatin'?"

"Of course."

"A'ight. Knock on my door when you ready to leave," Dana said.

"One hour."

"Where we goin'?"

"The Koreans in Rochdale. They always do me right."

"Yeah, they be on point."

"One hour, Dana."

After Citi hung up, she walked over to her closet and opened the door, and clothes spilled out like the closet had thrown up, leaving mountains of name-brand attire scattered everywhere. She started to pick through her clothes, trying to put together the perfect outfit to sport for the day. She couldn't look too cute because of the cold, but she was ready to show off her winter attire something fierce. She had outfits for every season and every occasion, and she always made sure her coordination was precise, from her underwear to the coat matching her boots or shoes.

She glanced at the time. It was going to take her more than an hour to get ready, at least two hours minimum. She took a nice, long shower, shaved her valuable parts, and styled her hair into a long ponytail until she could get it done professionally later in the evening.

Citi stepped out of her bedroom looking genuine in her Seven jeans and parchment-colored faux-wrap top underneath a Moncler winter coat.

She sported a pair of beige winter boots and platinum hoop earrings. She walked into the living room to see both her brothers watching TV and smoking weed. They paid her no mind and stayed focused on the college football game.

"Where Daddy at?" she asked.

Cane shrugged. "I don't know. Go look for him."

She sucked her teeth. "Fuck you, Cane! Well, can I get a ride to Rochdale from one of y'all?"

"Take the bus."

"You know I don't do buses, Cane, so stop playin' yourself."

"Walk then."

Chris laughed at his brother's remark.

"Fuck y'all! Y'all both ain't shit!" Citi screwed up her face and turned to walk away. "I can't wait till my birthday."

"Why's that?" Chris asked.

"'Cuz I'm gonna get Daddy to buy me my own damn car."

The brothers laughed.

Chris told her, "You ain't even got your license yet."

"So you think that's gonna stop me?"

Chris looked at his sister and saw the determination in her eyes. He took a pull from the burning haze between his fingers and exhaled.

"Let me get some of that," Citi said, reaching for the blunt.

"You put in for this, sis?" Cane asked.

"No. You think that's gonna fuckin' stop me?" Citi sucked her teeth and snatched the blunt from her brother's hand and took a few tokes. Then she asked them for a ride again.

Chris told her, "A nigga tired, Citi. Shit, we been out all night, and I ain't tryin' to leave this pad unless it's an emergency. You tryin' to go outside to get all pretty for whatever. It ain't that important right now."

Citi sighed. "Fuck it! I'll get a cab."

"See? Problem solved," Cane chimed.

Citi exited the apartment and strutted down the narrow corridor toward the elevator. When she approached, the elevator doors opened on cue, and out stepped a leggy brunette dressed in a short skirt and short leather jacket.

She eyed the woman and knew exactly where she was headed. Before the woman could pass, she uttered, "He ain't home."

"Excuse me?" the leggy woman replied.

"If you're lookin' for my father, he ain't home."

"And who are you?"

"I'm his daughter," she replied sassily.

"Oh."

Citi instantly pegged her as a gold digger. It bothered her greatly that Curtis always had a string of women in and out of the apartment. In fact, she hated most of them. Bitches were always trying to be in her father's pockets. Citi was the main girl in her father's life, and knew none of those hoes could come between her and her daddy. She would argue with them and was quick to put them in their place, making it very clear to them that they were only temporary. The ladies weren't with her father because they were trying to find love and warmth—they all had an agenda, and she would pick them apart little by little until they became frustrated.

The woman stopped in the hallway and peered at Citi. She was beautiful and was dressed like a model straight out of Paris. She was exactly her father's type—leggy, long hair, curvy, full hips, and a face like Beyoncé's.

Citi glared at the woman like she was the Antichrist.

"Well, let me knock and see anyway," the woman said.

"I said he ain't home," Citi repeated sternly.

The woman rolled her eyes. "Little girl, what's your name again?"

"I never gave it."

"Well, look, I'm Victoria."

"And?" Citi stepped closer to Victoria. "My father's out, so I'll tell him you stopped by."

Victoria sighed. "I don't need this."

"So leave!"

"You're rude. Your daddy needs to teach you some manners."

"He don't need to teach me shit!"

Victoria forced a smile. "I'll come back."

"Do that."

Victoria spun on her heels and headed toward the elevator.

Citi glared at Victoria and muttered, "Bitch!" She watched her step into the elevator. Citi then went down the four flights of stairs and made her way toward Dana's place.

▲

"I told that bitch off, yo. She think she could just come bustin' into my daddy's crib like she lives there," Citi told Dana. "Fuck that fake-lookin' bitch!"

Dana laughed. "You a trip, Citi."

"I just don't like fake fuckin' bitches."

Citi and Dana were taking it easy in the soft leather recliners in the Korean nail shop in Rochdale, getting pedicures in the half-empty salon.

Citi sat in the chair like a queen on her throne, watching the Korean immigrant scrub the bottom of her feet. "They couldn't pay me enough to do this," she said to Dana.

"Hey, someone gotta make us look good," Dana replied.

"As long as that someone isn't me. I rather stay on this end of her job."

Tonight was party night at the club on Jamaica Avenue. It would be a young, vibrant crowd with plenty of cuties for Citi to flirt with. She planned on showing up looking flawless, and that started with a manicure and pedicure. Afterwards, the girls got their hair done at Kandi's Beauty

Salon on Linden Boulevard and hit up the stores on Jamaica Avenue for a few outfits.

▲

Citi walked out her bedroom dressed in a studded off-the-shoulder mini-dress that showed off her curves and exposed her gleaming legs in a pair of spike pumps. She also sported a pair of double-stone drop earrings and rhinestone bangles around her wrist.

The apartment was empty; her brothers were gone, and her father was nowhere around. They were either out on business or with their whores somewhere. Citi would cherish the solitude in the spring, but the winter months made being alone in the apartment eerie. She yearned for company, but her father didn't allow any boys into his place, so she always went out.

She met up with Dana in front of the building. Dana decided to show off her sexy figure in a dusted sequin racerback dress and a pair of sexy peep-toe pumps that gave her six more inches in height. Both girls looked like they were ready to work the track instead of go to a club.

As they waited for their cab to arrive, Citi said, "I can't wait till I get my fuckin' car."

"Shit, we gonna be styling over the summertime."

"Hell, yeah. You know it."

They slapped each other high-five.

Citi's cab arrived, and the girls climbed into the backseat and instructed the driver to head toward Club Dawn on Jamaica Avenue.

Citi couldn't wait to see Cold Lay mix and cut up the records in the club. Though he was six years her senior, she had a small crush on him, and wherever he was deejaying, she made it her business to be in the crowd to watch him do his thing.

CHAPTER 3

The line outside Club Dawn stretched down the block. Citi gave the driver his fare and strutted toward the place. Both girls instantly caught the attention of everyone as they stepped out of the cab. Eyes lingered on their long legs and sexy attire. The young men made catcalls at them, and the ladies couldn't help but to stare.

Citi smiled. She and Dana paraded past everyone in line to get inside the club and headed toward a side entrance. Going through the front was for losers, and Citi didn't have time to wait on that line like she was regular. She was Curtis' daughter, and his princess didn't wait on any lines. She was always VIP.

They rounded the corner and moved down a side alley that was cluttered with parked cars. There were a handful of people by the side entrance, and the heavy steel doors were shut tight. The people in the alley were getting restless also, all waiting around for some kind of hookup, so they could avoid the hectic crowd around the corner.

Citi moved through everyone and knocked loudly. She looked up at the overhead camera angled down at them, wanting whoever was behind the door to see her face clearly.

Moments later, the door was pushed open from the inside, and a man dressed in all black emerged. He smiled at Citi and her friend.

"Damn, Ditty! What took you so long?" Citi asked.

"It's a busy night," he replied. "This your friend?"

"Yeah," Citi answered.

Ditty nodded. He looked the two young girls up and down and couldn't help but to smile. Ditty was a young thug who used to work for her father. He was tall like a basketball player and pushing 240 pounds. He was an intimidating man who grew up to love violence and guns.

Ditty had caught a few charges and was on probation, and he gave up the streets and became a bouncer via a friend he knew at the club. Working there allowed him to take out his aggression on unruly troublemakers inside.

Ditty had respect and love for Citi because of who her father was, and he had a crush on her.

"We in there, right?" Citi asked.

"Yeah, of course."

Ditty opened the door more, his back against it, and motioned the ladies through.

Others loitering in the alley could only gaze at the ladies in astonishment.

"Yo, what about us?"

"C'mon, man, we tryin' to get in too."

"Y'all muthafuckas is gonna have to wait, so step the fuck back!" Ditty shouted. No one dared try him. The scowl on his face to match his powerful size was all he needed for crowd control.

Citi and Dana strutted through the dim, narrow hallway, and could hear the thunderous bass playing from the club. The girls giggled like schoolgirls and hurried toward the party with eagerness.

The girls emerged from the side tunnel and stepped into a whirlwind of revelers partying like it was New Year's Eve. Inside the club was like an all-out all-star parade of revelers, ballers, women, and craziness. "She Will" by Lil' Wayne and Drake blared throughout the club.

Citi began dancing to the track—she loved Lil' Wayne—and cut loose on the floor, reciting the lyrics like she'd written them herself.

She looked up and could see her boo, DJ Cold Lay, mixing it up above in the DJ booth that was elevated over the large crowd. He was surrounded by admirers and his crew, and looked extra sexy with his backwards Yankees fitted. His wifebeater exposed his heavily tattooed arms, and his gleaming diamond chain swung around his neck with an eye-catching pendant—a turntable encrusted with black and white diamonds. Cold Lay was flashy, and the ladies loved him. Citi wished she was up there next to him.

"I need a drink," Dana said.

Citi agreed. The girls couldn't take two steps toward the bar without some random dude trying to snatch them up for a dance or trying to holler at them. The attention was what the girls were looking for, especially from the cute ones with swag.

The girls approached the crowded bar and looked for some sucker to buy them a drink. They didn't want to deal with the hassle of showing their fake IDs to the bartenders and being questioned about their age. It was easier to show off their cleavage, smile, and flirt with some willing male to get free drinks all night.

Citi looked around, and she saw many willing applicants. The men in the club were like hungry wolves, and two young things like Citi and Dana were what they craved.

It didn't take long for Citi to be in a nigga's ear and have him smiling. It took a simple hand on his thigh, a laugh, and some enticing words. He soon waved the bartender over and paid for the girls' drinks without problems.

Citi thanked him for the Cîroc. He wanted a little more of her time, but Dana was more interested in him than she was. So she passed her friend over to him, and stared up at the DJ with gleaming eyes.

As the night progressed, the music seemed to get louder, and the party was livelier, with the DJ mixing it up like he was Funkmaster Flex on Hot

97. Citi and Dana were in the midst of the crowd on the dance floor, gyrating their hips and rubbing across the men wildly, like they were in a strip club. And the men didn't have a problem giving the young ladies the attention, copping cheap feels and grinding behind Citi in her mini-dress.

Maino, flanked by his goons, stood in the VIP booth in a flashy black mink coat, his jewels shining heavily. He was watching his partner's daughter wild out in the club like a whore. His beady eyes narrowed in on Citi. Her mini-dress was riding up her thighs, exposing the color panties she had on, and the men were all over her like ants at a picnic. He scowled, placed the champagne glass on the table, and headed toward the dance floor to confront Citi, hurrying down the short flight of steps and pushing his way through the crowd. No one dared to argue with him. He looked like a bear with his mink coat clinging to his back and the glare on his face.

He zeroed in on Citi dancing with an older gentleman, her booty shaking like an earthquake. Her dance partner's hands were all over her, like he was doing a medical examination. Lust for Citi was evident in his eyes.

The man licked his lips, embraced Citi snugly, and allowed her ass to rub against his crotch as they moved to a Kanye West song. Sporadically, Citi would glance up at DJ Cold Lay, to see if she'd grasped his attention, but he was into spinning his turntables and shouting into the microphone. She was just another regular girl on the dance floor.

Citi took a few sips from the drink in her hand. Dana wasn't too far from her. She backed her ass up into a young man's crotch and stimulated a hard-on for her to feel rubbing against her butt.

Maino continued to plow his way through the crowded dance floor like he was treading water. He approached Citi and didn't hesitate to snatch the man dancing with her by the back of his collar. Maino yanked him back with immense force, almost lifting the man off his feet like he got hit by a gust of wind, and made him collapse on his ass. He shoved him to the side like a bug.

The man was stunned for a short moment. He didn't know what had attacked him. He jumped up on his feet with his fists clenched and was ready for a fight.

Maino pivoted on his shoes and shot such an intimidating stare at the poor clown, he made the guy curl up like a frightened pup. Maino outweighed him by a hundred pounds.

"What, muthafucka? Get the fuck off her like that," Maino exclaimed through clenched teeth. "I'll fuck you up, nigga!"

He then turned to Citi and barked, "What the fuck is wrong wit' you, Citi?" He towered over Citi and glared at her.

"What the fuck, Maino! Why you trippin' for?" she shot back.

"I'm trippin' cuz you actin' like a fuckin' whore in here."

"You ain't my daddy, Maino."

"I am tonight." Maino grabbed Citi by her arm and pulled her away from the dance floor.

Dana, noticing the disturbance, followed behind her friend.

Citi tried to resist, but Maino's grip around her slender arm was too strong. It felt like she was caught in a bear trap. He continued to drag her toward his booth in the VIP section, everyone looking on.

Citi glanced up and noticed that she finally had DJ Cold Lay's attention while she was being embarrassed. She felt like crying.

Maino pushed her into the seat. "You need to chill here."

"Maino, why you doin' this to me? I'm fuckin' grown!"

Maino looked her up and down, taking in her complete attire, and chuckled. "You wanna grow up too fast, and act like a whore, and I guarantee you, these niggas out here will treat and devour you like one."

Citi folded her arms across her chest and let out an irate sigh. She coldly looked up at Maino as he towered over her.

"You don't disrespect your father like that," he said.

"Fuck you!"

"Watch your tongue against me, little girl."

"There ain't nothin' little about me. I know you can see for yourself, Maino," Citi countered with a smirk.

Citi was the only one Maino allowed to curse at him. If it was anybody else, they wouldn't have left the club alive. He shook his head. "Daddy's little girl."

"Fuck you!"

Citi continued to look at him with contempt. She always had respect and love for Maino, but tonight she wanted to cut his throat for embarrassing her.

Dana came and sat next to her friend. "Everything okay, Citi?"

Citi sucked her teeth. "Niggas is fuckin' trippin' in here. Fuckin' faggots, that's what y'all all are! Fuckin' faggots!"

Maino downed his champagne and looked at Citi like he was ready to give her a serious spanking. His goons couldn't keep their eyes off Citi. They were glued to her long, shapely legs and her big breasts.

Maino caught a few of his goons gazing at Citi too hard. "What the fuck y'all niggas lookin' at?"

The men quickly diverted their attention from Citi.

Citi smiled as she crossed her legs slowly. She knew could have any nigga she wanted. Maino kept her and Dana hostage in the VIP area with him until he was ready to leave, ruining their night and her hopes of flirting with DJ Cold Lay.

An hour before dawn was to crack open the sky, Maino escorted Citi and Dana out of the club and made them climb into the backseat of his Yukon. Citi still had an attitude. He remained nonchalant and drove the girls home.

Citi jumped out of the truck, slammed the door like a mad woman, and marched into her building.

Maino sat behind the steering wheeling pulling at his cigarette and smiled. He respected the feistiness in Citi. She was definitely daddy's little girl. His eyes lingered on her ass too long as he watched her storm into the lobby, never turning to look back.

He had watched her grow up, and Maino felt that she was growing up too fast. She was becoming a wildcat, and he knew Curtis had a handful with her.

But he respected the attitude. Citi was going to create attention in whatever room she stepped into or wherever she was—she had to be the center of attention. It was in her blood.

CHAPTER 4

Citi sat by her bedroom window and took a few pulls from her cigarette. She still couldn't get over the embarrassment from Maino at the club the night before. She woke up in a foul mood, which worsened when she saw it was snowing outside. Citi hated the snow. It was always inconvenient. The snow and cold weather were a burden on her fashion. She couldn't flaunt her cute skirts or tight shorts, or prance around in her open-toe sandals and show off the body that God had blessed her with. Spring couldn't come fast enough for her.

Citi wanted to go back to bed, but her growling stomach convinced her to make her some breakfast. She extinguished the cigarette in the ashtray and headed to the kitchen, on a mission for some pancakes and sausages.

Citi noticed her father's leather coat hanging over the back of the chair, and his shoes were in the corner. The leather coat was always an indication that he was in his bedroom. His bedroom door was closed, but Citi wanted to knock and greet him with a good morning—or good afternoon. She figured he'd had a late night and needed his rest.

She removed the pan from underneath the kitchen cabinet, took out the eggs and milk from the fridge, and started the process of making herself a hearty breakfast. She'd learned to cook from Ms. Eloise next door. It was a skill that Citi was proud of. Ms. Eloise had become a surrogate mother to Citi when her own mother, Ashanti, didn't have the time to raise her daughter. Without her own biological mother around, Citi had to learn a few girly things on her own, from her first period to wearing her first training bra.

There had been times when Curtis tried to get the many women who were in and out of his life to help Citi become a young lady, but Citi hated the bitches her father brought around. She saw them as gold-digging bitches who didn't care for her father like she did.

The delightful aroma from the pancake batter cooking in the pan began to fill the kitchen. The kitchen came to life with Citi's cooking. The pancakes were becoming fluffy, and her smoked sausages were looking juicy. When her brothers didn't come out their bedrooms to stuff their faces, she knew they weren't home. Chris and Cane were greedy, and whenever Citi took to the kitchen to make one of her dishes, they would always be the first ones around to devour her cooking.

Citi began setting a place for herself at the table. Her stomach growled. She hadn't eaten in hours, and the liquor from last night still churned in her stomach.

As Citi sat to eat, she smiled to see her father exiting his bedroom, shirtless and wearing sweats. He carried a warm smile walking into the kitchen.

"What you cooking, princess?" he said with a smile.

"Pancakes. I made enough."

Curtis looked around the kitchen and took in the aroma that filled his nostrils. "Where are your brothers?"

"Don't know. I know they ain't home, 'cuz they ain't stampeding around the kitchen trying to eat up everything."

Curtis chuckled.

Citi jumped from her chair, ready to fix her father a plate of pancakes and smoked sausages. She reached for another plate from the dish basket. But before she could place a lick of food onto his plate, a scowl crossed her face. She instantly went from happy to livid within the blink of an eye.

"Good morning," Victoria greeted with a smile. She stepped out of Curtis' bedroom barefoot and clad in one of his T-shirts. It was clearly too big for her, falling down to her knees and covering her nakedness. Her disheveled hair and satisfied smile were a clear indication that she had been fucked right.

Citi glared at her father's company. "What the fuck is that bitch doin' here?" she spat.

"Citi, apologize."

"No. Why is she here, Daddy? She doesn't know you. She just fuckin' you for a come-up, or some money."

Curtis shouted, "Citi, what the hell is wrong with you?"

"I'm tired of these bitches coming and going."

"Young lady, you need to watch your mouth," Victoria chimed.

"Fuck you, bitch!"

"Curtis, that's your daughter, but you need to check her. That little brat is spoiled, and she needs somebody to spank her ass."

"I dare you to come over here and lay a fuckin' hand on me." Citi clenched her fists as she continued to glare at Victoria.

"Citi, go to your damn room now!" Curtis shouted.

"Tell that bitch to leave, Daddy."

"She's not going anywhere. She's my company."

Citi looked like she was ready to cry.

Victoria stood behind Curtis and smirked at Citi, angering her even more. Victoria then said, "If you were my daughter . . ."

Before Victoria could finish her sentence, Citi sent a porcelain plate flying at her head. "Fuck you, bitch!" she screamed.

Victoria moved her face from the hurling plate just in time as it smashed against the wall behind her. Remnants of the plate struck her in the face.

Curtis lost his cool and went chasing after Citi like a cat after a mouse. But Citi was fast. She sprinted from her father's grasp and out the kitchen.

Before Curtis caught up with her, Citi ran out the apartment in her bedtime attire and went running off to the apartment next door. She banged on Ms. Eloise's door. Eloise opened the door, and Citi went flying into the old lady's apartment like a gust of wind.

Curtis watched from the doorway of his apartment. He figured Citi needed to cool off. He looked at Ms. Eloise and said, "You keep her for a moment, and teach that girl some respect, Ms. Eloise."

"She'll be fine, Curtis. I'll talk to her." Eloise's wrinkled smile lit up the hallway like a beacon.

Curtis nodded. Then he shut his door and went back to entertaining Victoria.

Citi sat slumped on Ms. Eloise's couch looking like she had lost her puppy. Her arms were folded across her chest, and tears streamed down her cheeks.

Eloise entered the living room and peered at Citi with her warm smile. She stood only five two and weighed no more than 110 pounds, but she had a heart that outweighed everyone else's in the projects. Her hair was pinned up in a bun, and her kind eyes focused on Citi like a worried mother. Clad in a rainbow housecoat that covered her frail frame like a shroud, she approached Citi with concern.

"What is wrong, chile? Talk to me."

"I'm okay, Ms. Eloise."

Eloise sat next to Citi and tried to console her. "I know you're not okay, chile. What's wrong? You know you can always talk to me, Citi."

Citi wiped the tears with the back of her hand and sighed deeply. "I'm tired of my father bringing these bitches over. I thought we were going to have a great breakfast. He dissed me for her."

"You know Curtis cares about you a great deal, but he is a man, and a

40

man will always be a man. But you, Citi, you will always be his princess. I've known your family for ages, and your father will always put you first, like he's always done."

"Well, I didn't feel first in his life this morning."

Eloise smiled. "You are, with him and with me."

Citi managed to smile.

"C'mon, I'll make you some hot chocolate and fix you a piece of chocolate cake."

The mention of a piece of Eloise's chocolate cake put an even bigger smile on Citi's face. Eloise was known for her cooking, but she was even more famous for her baking.

Citi followed Eloise into the kitchen. She tried to forget about her father's bitches. When she was at Eloise's place, it felt like time stood still and she was in good hands. She and Eloise talked like they were mother and daughter.

▲

Curtis stepped out his door clad in black slacks with a stylish button-down underneath his woolen pea coat. He wanted to look like perfection. He planned on seeing Ashanti today in Harlem, and every time he went to see her, he dressed like he was the Dapper Don. Everything on him was precise. Even the cufflinks on his shirt sparkled like diamonds.

He had gotten rid of Victoria earlier. She was the finest bitch in Queens, but she couldn't compare to Ashanti. She didn't even come close. Curtis' feelings for Ashanti were unmatched.

He walked down the hallway and stopped in front of Eloise's door. He knocked and waited. Eloise opened up and smiled at Curtis.

"How is she?" he asked.

"She's fine, Curtis. We're just sitting here talking over some hot chocolate and cake."

Curtis smiled.

"You want to speak to her?"

"Nah, that's okay. I'll give her some time. She needs it."

"Okay."

"Tell her I'm making a run. I'll be back tonight."

Eloise nodded.

Curtis reached into his pocket and pulled out a large bankroll of fifties and hundreds. He peeled off three hundred-dollar bills and attempted to pass the cash into Eloise's hands.

"Curtis, there is no need for that," Eloise said, rejecting the money.

"Take it, Ms. Eloise."

"I'm okay, Curtis. You keep your money."

Curtis sighed. He hated when she turned down money from him.

"Go run your errands, and I'll keep Citi here with me. It'll be like an afternoon sleepover with us girls," Eloise said with a smile.

Curtis smiled. "What would I do without you?"

"I don't know."

Curtis said good-bye, and Eloise closed the door. Curtis lingered in front of her apartment for a short moment with the cash still in his hand. He crouched near the door and subtly slid the three hundred dollars under the crack of the door. He was going to give Eloise something whether she liked it or not.

Curtis got behind the wheel of his flashy Mercedes-Benz. He started the ignition, and the engine purred. He pulled down the sun visor and checked his reflection in the mirror quickly. He looked handsome. He pulled out of the parking spot and headed toward the Van Wyck Expressway.

Curtis navigated his Benz through the busy Harlem streets. It was early afternoon, and 125th Street looked like a farmers' market, with the shoppers strolling up and down the cluttered sidewalks, and traffic at a crawl. Curtis smoked his Newport as he sat reclined in his ride, R&B

playing in his ear. He was thinking about Ashanti. He wouldn't admit it publicly, but he missed her. He was looking forward to their rendezvous at her apartment on Amsterdam Avenue.

Curtis found parking and stepped out of his car looking like the mack he was. He quickly caught eyes, as locals peered at the fashion that adhered to his athletic frame, and the jewels gleaming underneath the cold afternoon sun. He made his way toward the towering project building smoking the cancer stick.

Ashanti opened the door with a smile and a cigarette in her hand. Curtis stood in front of her with a glowing smile. Sade was playing in the apartment.

Curtis gazed at Ashanti's outfit. Her tight leggings highlighted her thick, curvy hips and legs, and her skimpy T-shirt exposed her pierced belly button. She was voluptuous up top. Her midnight hair flowed down to her shoulders with grace, and her slanted eyes were hypnotizing. Ashanti's body was to die for, and Curtis never got tired at looking at her from head to toe.

"You're early," she said, blowing smoke from her mouth.

"You ain't glad to see me?"

She stepped to the side to allow Curtis into her lavishly decorated apartment. He locked eyes with his woman and entered into her domain. She was living like a queen in the projects, thanks to him.

Curtis reached into his pea coat pocket and pulled out a wad of hundreds. He passed Ashanti her monthly allowance—five grand. Ashanti took it from him and placed it on the living room table.

"I got you living nice, huh?"

"'Cuz you know I was the best piece of pussy you ever had, nigga. And you still can't get enough of this."

Curtis chuckled.

The queen-size sleeper sofa by the window, the Hiro living room table set, the Lisbon dining room set, the Hana-ki floor lamps situated exactly so around the apartment, and the Luxor entertainment center seemed to come straight out of *Elle Decor* magazine.

"You always had taste, baby," Curtis said.

"In my fashion, furniture, and in my men," she replied with a grin. "You thirsty?"

"I'll take a drink."

Ashanti sauntered over to her makeshift bar and began pouring Curtis a shot of Jack Daniel's. She knew it was his favorite. Curtis' eyes lingered on her thick thighs wrapped snuggly in her leggings. He had a strong craving for her that ate away at him like a sickness.

She handed him his drink, and he took a few sips.

"So, you gonna ask about your kids?"

Ashanti took one last pull from the cancer stick and rubbed it slowly out into the ashtray. Looking at Curtis, she exhaled and said, "I know they're okay. Their daddy is gonna always take care of them. But what's the update on them?"

Curtis took another sip of whiskey and placed the glass on the table.

"Me and your daughter got into it this morning."

Ashanti chuckled. "Over what?"

"Nothing serious. She's definitely got your attitude and temper."

"That's my girl. And Chris and Cane?"

"My little niggas are about their business. They're learning, especially Chris. He's like me. But, Cain, you know he's a wild one. He got into it the other day with some rivals. He knocked these two niggas out cold on the street. I had that beef squashed, though."

Ashanti smiled. "Like father like sons."

It was cool to hear about her kids, who were now teenagers. She hadn't seen them in years. She didn't want to be a mother, and didn't want to raise any babies, but Curtis continued to get her pregnant. Ashanti had tried the domestic life with Curtis, but it was short-lived. Her heart was in the streets, and she didn't have time to be slowed down with three children on her back.

The two came to a resolution: Curtis would raise their children without any interference from Ashanti. The two clearly still loved each other. Whenever Curtis got around his woman, he felt the urge to throw her against the wall and spread her legs.

"You lookin' good right now, Ashanti."

"Don't I fuckin' always?"

"Yeah, but you lookin' somethin' extra right now." Curtis approached her.

"You tryin' to fuck? You tryin' to deliver something more than cash to me?"

Curtis took Ashanti by her hands and pulled her into his arms. The taste for her showed in his eyes. He slipped his arms around her sensuous curves and took in her sweet, alluring fragrance. Chanel No. 5 filled his nostrils.

Ashanti wanted to purr in his grasp. Curtis always had that effect on her. No matter how many miles away he was, when it came to sexing, Curtis had her open.

"It's been a while, baby. You miss it?" she whispered in his ear.

"Every day."

Slowly, he bent her over the dining room table and pulled down her leggings to her ankles. She had no panties on. Her pussy started to pulsate for his penetration.

Curtis quickly unbuckled his pants and dropped them to the floor. He cupped Ashanti's tits and neared his dick to her goodies. He eased his dick into her and let out a pleasing moan, feeling her warm juices from her tunnel tickle him. Their bodies became electric as he fucked her from the back.

Ashanti curved over the dining room table with her legs spread into a downward V, feeling Curtis place a strong grip around her slender neck and taking hold of her waist with his other grip. He rammed her sensuous tunnel with zeal.

"Fuck me, baby," Ashanti cried out.

Curtis aimed to please the mother to his three kids. They took their passionate act into the bedroom, where Curtis had her body contorted under the sheets. They clasped hands as he ground himself deeply into her rich opening, with Ashanti's moans bouncing off the bedroom walls.

In next to no time, they rested against each other in a tight embrace, both pleased with each other's performance. Despite their separation from each other, they pretended to be exclusive, neither one confessing their infidelity. It was evident on Curtis' face and in his actions that he was truly in love with her.

Ashanti lifted her head from Curtis' sweaty chest and reached for her pack of Newports on the end table near the bed. She lit a cigarette and took a deep pull.

The two were silent for the moment. Curtis closed his eyes for a moment and took in the tranquility in his her room. The sounds of Harlem seeped into the bedroom, making it the only noise in the room to disturb the stillness. The bedroom felt like a safe haven from the trouble outside.

Ashanti took a few more pulls from the cigarette and then turned her head slightly to catch a glimpse of Curtis, whose muscular upper torso gleamed with sweat. He looked relaxed.

Ashanti, her naked frame perched at the end of the bed, had the gaze of a person with something on her mind. She sighed. "You know Alonzo is coming up in the game. Your friend just made a serious come-up off some Haitians in Brooklyn. He ain't scared to make moves. That nigga sees what he wants and takes that shit. He's doing his thang."

"Alonzo? When you saw him?"

"He be around Harlem, and he was lookin' fresh. I saw him driving around in a new Bentley down One Hundred and Twenty-Fifth Street. That nigga had them bitches' pussy leaking when he stepped out that nice-ass Bentley coupe. You shoulda seen the look on muthafuckas' faces. Alonzo ain't playing. I can't front. That nigga's ambitious. He's doing it lovely."

Hearing Ashanti speak about his longtime Dominican friend so highly put a slight scowl on Curtis' face. Alonzo and him came up together, along with Maino. They once were like the three amigos. They had street dreams and put their dreams into action.

Alonzo was handsome with his boyish looks, hazel eyes, and trimmed goatee. He had a stable of bitches willing to work and please him in any fashion. Though his stature was slim, he was able to hustle and kill like the best of them.

Alonzo's family was connected, and he used that connection to advance himself in the drug trade. Curtis and Maino were once his partners, but over time, he became their connect. They'd remained friends and trusted each other, to some extent.

Ashanti continued to glorify Alonzo to Curtis, not realizing that the details had him burning with fury. Curtis remained silent.

"He asked about you."

"What the fuck you tell him?"

"I don't speak your business, baby. You do your business with him, and I respect that. I know that's your longtime friend, but I ain't tryin' to tell your business out there. But you know what? Alonzo has that and then some, and maybe the table needs to turn, and it should be the other way around. You're smart, baby—really smart. Alonzo should have been the one copping from you, not the other way around. Shit, you know the only reason he came up the way he did was because of his uncle. You need to come up stronger, Curtis, and get yours."

Curtis didn't reply. The way Ashanti spoke so highly of his friend had brought on suspicion. He came to the realization that Alonzo was fucking her. Alonzo was known to sleep around and fuck with men's wives, sisters, mothers, and daughters. It didn't matter a woman's status or his friendship with the husbands and family members. He had no limitations on who he put his dick in. Alonzo took whoremonger to a whole new level. When it came to sex, he didn't have any moral obligations. And he loved money just as much as he loved pussy, and Curtis knew this about him.

Ashanti added, "Baby, you need to get grimier out here with these niggas."

"You sayin' I'm slippin?"

"Shit, niggas know not to fuck wit' him, especially after goin' after the Haitians for a sweet score. Alonzo definitely can get ugly with it."

"And what the fuck are we to you? Mickey Mouse or somethin'? You forget who the fuck I am?"

"I mean, you and Maino, y'all do ya thang, fucked a few niggas up and caught some bodies back in the days, but you ain't gettin' extreme wit' it like how y'all used to be back in the days. You still get money, but why the fuck is Alonzo pushing a Bentley coupe, and you ain't? I want extra, Curtis, and for you to make that shit happen, baby, you gotta get ugly with it. Let these muthafuckas know you still ain't nobody to fuck with. Yeah, you got your rep, these niggas out here respect you and Maino, but I need my house in Miami. You know how I feel about that."

Ashanti wanted to live like a basketball wife. She wanted more than just a beach house in Miami and some throw-around money. She wanted to be the queen bee bitch. She wanted the red-carpet treatment. She wanted to drive around in her own Bentley and flaunt million-dollar diamonds around her neck and wrists. Gucci, Prada, Coach and money were what she craved. The few thousand dollars a month was okay for the moment, but she yearned for more. She was seething with jealousy because she knew that Alonzo's baby momma was getting the benefits from his score off the Haitians.

She walked around the bedroom butt naked, taking drags from her cigarette. She was in Curtis' ear like a snitch, because she wanted him to step up. She thought her little pep talk would help him take his business to the next level.

She continued to praise Alonzo like he was God Almighty.

Curtis sprang up from the bed and charged her. He pushed her against the wall and placed a firm grip around her neck. "Why you keep glorifying this nigga's name, huh? You fuckin' him?"

Ashanti gasped. The cigarette dropped from her fingers, and she locked eyes with him. "Can you please remove your fuckin' hand from around my neck!"

Curtis quickly came to his senses and took a few steps back from her.

"Like I was sayin, step your game up, Curtis, 'cuz I want out of the fuckin' projects."

Curtis started to get dressed. Their rendezvous was over.

CHAPTER
5

Curtis sat in his Benz under the cool moonlight in his Queens hood. He had a lot on his mind after leaving Ashanti's place. Her affair with his friend and drug connect had him troubled. He felt disrespected and betrayed. Alonzo was his close friend for many years, and Ashanti was the love of his life, and for the two of them to be intimate with each other was like plunging a hot needle into his eye. It was an agony that was swallowing him up, and it was hard for him to forget, or forgive the sin.

Ashanti never admitted to the affair, but Curtis knew it happened. The look in her eyes when she spoke about Alonzo and her silence gave her away—along with Alonzo's scandalous past. His notorious reputation with women preceded him. For a long time, he had a thing for Ashanti.

The hood was quiet, but Curtis' inner thoughts were ear-shattering. He was seething. Business was good in his eyes. His respect passed through from borough to borough, but Ashanti saw otherwise.

He was getting older. He and Maino were becoming two OGs in the hood, and in time, he saw retirement coming his way. He was ready to pass down the business to his two sons. Curtis was thirty-six years old and had survived the streets by being smart and always being one step ahead of his enemies and the police. He'd had many close calls with both, but he'd escaped death and extensive imprisonment. He had defied the odds against him and won. He'd made tons of money and was ready for an investment into something promising. In his mind, it was time to get out and do it right—before death or prison came his way.

He and Maino were set to meet up with Alonzo the next day to re-up and talk business. But now, Curtis didn't trust Alonzo. Alonzo's dick in Ashanti had thrown a monkey wrench into things. Alonzo had been smiling in his face and conducting business as usual while fucking his woman. It was the ultimate betrayal. Curtis felt like a fool. He hated to be played.

Curtis smoked his cigarette and hung back in the driver's seat of his Benz, his mind spinning with wild thoughts and accusations. He peered out the window and rested his eyes on the front entrance to his building. For years, it was the place he had called home; where his kids were growing up and where his sons were becoming men. He wanted Chris and Cane to maintain his legacy.

He looked at the lobby and remembered serving crack fiends in that same lobby when he was only twelve years old. He was hustling under the Supreme Team umbrella. He had learned the drug trade quickly and soon moved up the ranks in the drug organization, and by the time he was nineteen, he was running his own corner and had his own crew.

Curtis thought back to when he and Ashanti had first met. She was a beautiful young girl with a magnetic style and smile. She was a Harlem-born wild child who had men chasing behind her like groupies. Her aura was unforgettable. She used to come to Queens to visit her cousin, and they would hit up the clubs with a fierce appetite to party and flirt with the men, especially the ballers and shot-callers from the hood. Ashanti was heavily into bad boys, and when she met Curtis in the Q club one night, she was instantly drawn to his bad-boy swag.

Curtis, Alonzo, and Maino were surrounded by their heavily jeweled crew in the VIP area—popping bottles and capturing the attention of every woman in the club. They partied like they owned the place and had the respect from everyone in the club.

Guard the Throne

When Curtis and Ashanti first laid eyes on each other, it was like love at first sight. Curtis invited Ashanti and her cousin to join them in VIP, and they quickly accepted the offer. The female cousins became the center of attention among the fellows in VIP, and right away, Curtis was drawn to Ashanti's lively behavior. She was a party girl with a lust for the street life. The two began talking, and their chemistry was undeniable. He snatched Ashanti's attention easily, and within six months, she was pregnant with Chris.

Curtis put out the cigarette in the ashtray situated in the center console and exhaled. Alonzo had been his friend for so many years, but a line had been crossed. It was an unwritten rule—Keep your hands out of another man's candy jar—but some men just couldn't control their sweet tooth and had to taste certain forbidden sweets.

The time on the dashboard read fifteen minutes after midnight. Curtis had been sitting in his Benz for over an hour pondering. He was about to get out the car when his cell phone rang. It was Maino calling. Curtis already knew what he was calling about.

"What's good?" he answered.

"Yo, that thing for tomorrow, we still on it, right?" Maino asked. "That thing wit' A?"

"Tomorrow's no good. Something came up with my daughter, and I gotta go handle that."

"I can go solo and handle that business, and you go take care of that business wit' yo kids, you feel me? We need to hand that business ASAP."

"I already talked to A about it, told him we'll meet him the day after to definitely handle that. And, besides, I wanna kick it with him for a moment. Pull his coat to something important."

"You already talked to A?"

"Yeah, earlier today, and he cool with it."

"A'ight. What you need to holla about wit' him?"

"Nigga, not over the phone," Curtis reminded Maino.

"Yeah, you right."

"Get at me tomorrow."

"Fo' sure."

Curtis ended the call and continued to scowl. He'd lied to Maino. The meeting for their re-up with Alonzo was still scheduled for tomorrow afternoon, but Curtis wanted to go alone and have a one-on-one talk with him—confront him about his affair with Ashanti. He didn't want Maino in his personal business. The pain that lay heavy in his heart had him thinking about doing the unthinkable to a once close friend.

Curtis stepped out of his ride, with his pistol tucked snugly in his waistband, and walked toward the lobby. The cold feeling he felt inside wasn't going to go away until his issue with Alonzo was resolved.

He entered his apartment and saw Citi asleep on the couch with the TV on. She was wrapped up in a blanket, and junk food was scattered across the glass coffee table. He removed his winter jacket, tossed it onto the back of the chair, and approached Citi. He watched his baby girl sleep for a moment. She looked so peaceful. Citi resembled her mother in so many ways, from her natural beauty to her persona. Her sudden explosion earlier would have easily matched her mother's. Both women were so temperamental, but he loved them both.

Curtis perched on the couch near his daughter's toes, which peeked from underneath the blanket. She was curled up in the fetal position, looking like a sleeping beauty, while MTV played on the 60-inch flat-screen. It seemed like she was alone in the apartment. Curtis made a mental note to talk to his sons. He hated when they left Citi alone in the apartment at nights. She was still a little girl in his eyes, even though she was going to turn sixteen soon.

Curtis carefully picked up his daughter, still wrapped in the blanket, and carried her off into the bedroom, where he laid her gently in her bed.

"Daddy," Citi whispered softly.

"Just sleep, princess. I'm here," he said, stroking her hair.

"I'm sorry, Daddy. I didn't mean to get so angry with you earlier," Citi said drowsily.

"It's cool, princess. You know I still love you."

Citi closed her eyes and fell back asleep. Unbeknownst to Curtis, she was really high and had been drinking. She had fallen asleep on the couch just an hour before his arrival, and the bottle of Grey Goose she'd been sipping on had rolled underneath the couch.

Curtis watched her fall asleep in the comfort of her canopy bed. That eased his mind somewhat from the pain and dismay he was feeling earlier.

He lingered in Citi's bedroom for an hour and then stepped into the living room. His sons were just arriving home. He glared at Chris and Cane, and barked, "How you leave your little sister alone for hours?"

Cane replied, "She ain't a little girl anymore, Pop."

"I don't care!" Curtis approached his sons closer with his scowl. "You two are her older brothers, so start fuckin' acting like it!"

"We out there handling business, Pop," Chris chimed. "We ain't got time to be lookin' after Citi. She a big girl now."

"I'm not asking you to babysit her, Chris. But you have to understand, I have enemies out there. People I've done harm to, to climb up in this business or to make an example out of, they're quick to do harm back to me or mines, which includes coming after my children, and they won't hesitate to use y'all to get to me.

"I'm teaching you the streets to be smart and to stay ahead of your enemies and close friends too. You keep this family close, and you protect your sister. This shit here, it ain't one big party. You always keep your guard up and pay close attention to the slightest infraction or disrespect against you. 'Cuz if you don't, within time, something you thought was simple can become a major fuckin' problem. Y'all hear me?"

"Yeah, we hear you, Pop," the brothers replied simultaneously.

Curtis stared into his two young sons' eyes. The respect for their father showed in their teenage faces. Curtis was the big dog in town, and he was training his young pups to become pit bulls in the streets and to follow in his footsteps.

Chris took in his father's words more seriously than Cane. Chris wanted to become like Curtis. He wanted to have the street smarts along with the business sense to take his father's business to the next level. Cane, on the other hand, was like a wild animal ready to tear the streets up and take advantage of the name he was born under. He was more reckless than his older brother.

Curtis turned and went into his bedroom. He had a lot on his mind and needed to get some sleep. Tomorrow was going to be an interesting day for him.

▲

Late the next afternoon, Curtis came to a stop in front of the towering steel structure in Midtown Manhattan. The beautiful exterior, decorated with aluminum plating illuminated by the sunshine, was a fortress of luxury for the wealthy and elite. The building gleamed like a mirror, reflecting the concrete jungle.

New York in the winter months was brutal. It was a chilling fifteen degrees outside with gusty wind, causing New Yorkers to bundle up tightly in their winter attire. A few residents looked like Eskimos, clad in their thick winter coats, ski hats, and long scarves, their faces covered like they were ready to commit a bank robbery.

Curtis stepped out his Benz wrapped warmly in his black pea coat with the beanie ski hat. He wore wool gloves, and his pistol was concealed in its holster underneath the stylish coat. He was sharp as always. He moved like the world was his to control. He rushed for no one. He blended in with the Midtown crowd like he was born with a silver spoon in his mouth.

He tried to teach his sons the ability to fit into a crowd. He warned them not to always dress and act like a hood nigga from the projects. A man who didn't know how to adapt in his ways or style would soon become a marked man in life. Curtis could move with the wolves and not be harmed, and he could also move with the sheep and not be suspected as a predator.

He walked into the grand lobby decorated with large crystal ceiling lamps and marble crystal pillars. He headed toward the elevators, pushed for one of the two doors to open, and waited. The lobby was quiet. He was the only soul in the place, a plus for him.

The elevator doors opened, and Curtis stepped inside with his cool manner. He pushed for the penthouse and waited. The lift ascended like a rocket taking off in a crisp push upward. Curtis reached the top floor and stepped out into the plush hallway decorated with precious plants and elegant paintings. He strode to the double doors, adjusted his appearance, and casually knocked twice.

Dino answered. He stood six-six and weighed over 300 pounds. He was a grizzly-looking muthafucka and could easily break a man's neck with his thumbs alone. He was Alonzo's personal bodyguard.

"Dino," Curtis greeted with a deadpan gaze.

"Curtis, what's good?"

"Where Alonzo?"

"He'll be down soon." Dino stepped to the side and allowed Curtis entry into the penthouse. The butt of a holstered Desert Eagle peeked out from his suit jacket.

The place was immaculate with its marble flooring and marble crystal ceiling lamps. The tall and completely transparent French windows that opened up to the balcony offered a spectacular view of Manhattan from thirty-one floors up. There was a full bar and grand piano by the windows. The beautiful steel and glass aquarium, filled with exotically colored tropical fish, was the perfect addition to the living room in the penthouse.

Dino stood behind Curtis. He trusted him, so there was no need for a patdown. Alonzo had been expecting him.

"Where's Maino?" Dino asked.

"Something came up."

Dino didn't think otherwise about it. He moved his wide frame over to the bar and began making himself a quick drink.

A short moment later, Alonzo came down the spiral staircase with a smile aimed at his longtime friend.

"Curtis, what's good, my friend?" Alonzo greeted with open arms.

"Alonzo," Curtis replied halfheartedly.

The two men hugged each other. Alonzo was happy to see his friend. He was dressed in a long white bathrobe and some swimming shorts, indicating he'd just come from the pool in his upstairs bedroom. A diamond chain with a diamond-encrusted cross around his neck and a diamond pinky ring were small indications of his wealth.

"Yo, where's Maino?" Alonzo asked, looking around.

"He couldn't make it," Curtis said. "Something came up."

"It's cool. It's cool. We can all link up some other time."

Curtis remained nonchalant, but he kept thinking about Alonzo and Ashanti together—the two of them fuckin' their brains out and laughing at him behind his back. When he looked at Alonzo, Curtis felt nothing but rage. He was ready to tear Alonzo apart for the violation he committed.

Alonzo continued to be all smiles. Money and power had gone to his head. He wanted to be Tony Montana AKA Scarface with a passion. He was the rising king of Harlem.

"You want a drink, Curtis?" Alonzo asked.

"Nah, I'm good."

"You sure, my friend?"

Curtis nodded. "I just wanna take care of business."

"Yeah, business is good out there. We all making money," Alonzo said as he walked toward the bar to prepare himself a drink. "Just think, Curtis, when we was growing up, did you ever think it would be like this for us? Living large like muthafuckin' rap stars? Damn, we some rich niggas!"

Curtis didn't reply.

"I mean, you, me, and Maino . . . shit, we like the new Supreme Team out there. I feel fuckin' untouchable." Alonzo walked behind the bar gloating about his success.

Dino moved to the side and sat in one of the plush chairs that decorated the living room.

Alonzo removed a few bottles from underneath the bar and poured himself a shot of Goose.

"I heard you came up, though," Curtis mentioned.

Alonzo lifted his head from the bar and locked eyes with Curtis. He smiled and chuckled. "People talk, huh?"

"Everyone's talking."

"Shit, you know a nigga gotta hit the streets out the blue sometimes and put in that work, like how we used to do back in the days." Alonzo took a sip from his drink and removed himself from behind the bar. He stood across from Curtis, jovial about the stickup he'd committed on the Haitians from Brooklyn. He had no problems revealing to Curtis that he was the culprit.

He continued the story with, "Yo, got a tip from this bitch I was fuckin', some functioning addict named Marisol from the Bronx. Bitch snorts more coke than Tony Montana. But she bad, though. So, she's into me for ten stacks. I got the bitch scared shitless over her debt to me, and she's willing to do anything to pay it off. Well, come to find out, her ex-boyfriend's cousin runs an operation out in Flatbush, and she knew the ins and outs of the nigga's operation, mostly some off-brand muthafuckas wit' some come-up. Bitch pulled my coat to it and I couldn't resist. Niggas were sloppy with it, Curtis. They lived overtop a bodega in Flatbush and we caught them slippin', me and Dino here. We went overkill on them niggas. Shit, it was either them or us. But it was a good score. I felt refreshed after jookin' them banana-boat muthafuckas. Came out with more than we expected."

"You still like to be on that cowboy shit, Alonzo."

"Shit, it keeps the blood flowing in me. You feel me? It keeps my name ringing in these streets, and my reputation fierce out there for any muthafucka thinking about trying to get at me, to think twice."

"But, anyway, we here on business, right?" Curtis took a few more sips then placed the glass on the granite countertop and walked over to the window.

Curtis continued to be a bit standoffish. He assumed Alonzo didn't know about him knowing about the affair with Ashanti. He was itching to snatch the pistol from out his holster and start shooting up the apartment. But he kept his composure and listened to Alonzo talk.

"What you need, though, Curtis?" Alonzo asked. "You know I'm here for you, my dude."

"Three ki's," he replied.

"Just three? Damn, nigga. Upgrade, muthafucka! You know I got you. If you need more ki's on consignment, just ask. But three? Shit, Curtis, as long as you and me been friends and been in this fuckin' game, shit, you should be moving at least twenty bricks a month or something."

"Nah, just three," Curtis repeated coolly.

Alonzo shook his head. "What? You trying to play it safe or something?"

"I just don't need the headaches right now."

"Headaches? Shit, nigga, what the fuck you so stressed over?"

"When you have a teenage daughter, you'll understand."

Alonzo laughed. "Muthafucka, get a nanny. I got one. C'mon, nigga,

I got your three ki's. Dino, we'll be right back."

Curtis followed Alonzo down the corridor into a room nestled at the end of the hallway.

"How's Ashanti?" Alonzo suddenly asked.

Curtis' blood started to boil. Alonzo had some nerve asking about her. The question irritated Curtis like nails scraping against a chalkboard. But he held his tongue and calmly replied, "She's a'ight."

"Tell her I said hi."

Alonzo walked toward the back room, his back to Curtis. Curtis' hand was near the holstered pistol on his left side. It would have been so easy to open fire and take him down. Alonzo wouldn't even have seen it coming. But then he would have had to worry about Dino. Hearing the shots would send the big bear charging at him.

The men entered the room. It was sparsely furnished, with no windows and bare eggshell-colored walls. No life or art was displayed anywhere in the room. It was Alonzo's safe room. There was a large safe embedded into the wall—the elephant in the room.

Curtis stood by the doorway as Alonzo opened the safe. The drugs and cash stashed in his vaulted safe equaled $450,000 and thirteen ki's.

Curtis saw the mother lode and he wanted it. It was the cash and drugs that Alonzo had taken and killed the Haitians for.

He removed three bricks for Curtis and then closed the safe back up. "Three bricks," he said, handing the drugs over to Curtis.

It was a done deal. The men went back into the main room where Dino was behind the bar once again.

Alonzo glared at his bodyguard. "Muthafucka, I don't pay you to drink my damn bar dry. Shit!"

"Sorry, boss," Dino replied.

Alonzo shook his head and focused his attention back on Curtis. "We okay here?"

"Yeah, we're fine. I need to use your bathroom though."

"Nigga, you know where it is. Stop actin' like you a fuckin' stranger in this crib. Shit, fuck you asking for? What? You need a nigga to hold it for you too?"

Curtis managed to chuckle. "Nah, you can't lift that much."

Alonzo laughed. "You got jokes, nigga."

Curtis turned and went to use the bathroom on the first floor. He shut the door and immediately removed the 9mm from his holster and screwed the silencer onto the tip of the pistol. He took a good look at himself in the large mirror. His eyes were cold. He sighed heavily, knowing what was about to transpire.

Alonzo had crossed that line, and now it was time for him to pay the consequences in fucking with his man's wifey. It was going to be painful to do. They'd been friends for twenty years, and now because of pussy, their friendship was about to end violently.

Curtis gripped the pistol tightly. He continued to stare at his reflection. He had killed before. But this, by far, would be the hardest murder that he would ever have to execute. It was like killing his brother. But his brother had violated their friendship when he'd put his dick into the mother to his three kids—the love of his life.

Curtis exited the bathroom with the gun down at his side and hidden slightly behind his right leg. Alonzo would be completely caught off guard by the attack. When he entered the room again, Alonzo was posted by the bar with another drink in his hand. Dino stood by the French windows that peered out at the vast city.

Curtis locked eyes with Alonzo, who was still all smiles. He walked into the room with a grim expression. Alonzo lowered the glass from his lips and started to pay closer attention to his longtime friend.

"What's up?" Alonzo asked. His eyes dropped down to where Curtis' right hand was situated behind his leg, concealing the pistol.

Curtis went into action like a strike of lightning. He swiftly brandished the 9mm, outstretching his hand and trained it at Dino. The husky bodyguard was caught off guard. He opened his eyes wide in shock, and before he could react, two shots went off.

Dino's head jerked back violently from the bullets piercing his skull, and he slammed into the windows with a powerful thud. His blood sprayed across the glass like paint. He was dead instantly.

"Yo, what the fuck, Curtis!" Alonzo shouted. He was frantic. "You lost your fuckin' mind?"

"No! You fuckin' lost yours," Curtis retorted.

Alonzo was defenseless. He gazed at Dino's body sprawled out across the rich marble floors. A thick crimson pool grew across the floor where Dino's body lay.

Curtis stepped closer to Alonzo and aimed the gun at his head. There was no turning back now. "Let's go, down the hall and back to the safe," he instructed Alonzo.

"Yo, you fuckin' robbing me now, nigga? You fuckin' serious?" Alonzo wasn't budging. He stood his ground with a hard gaze at Curtis.

Poot!

The shot whizzed by Alonzo's ear, nicking him, and smashed into a few bottles behind the bar.

"Muthafucka!" Alonzo screamed, grabbing his ear where the bullet grazed him.

"I ain't playin', muthafucka."

Alonzo looked into his friend's cold eyes. "So it's like that, huh?"

"Let's not make this difficult, Alonzo."

"Nigga, shit already is."

Curtis forced Alonzo back into the safe room at gunpoint. He remained a few steps behind him. If Alonzo even flinched wrong, he was ready to put three shots into his back.

Alonzo reluctantly opened up the safe and then pivoted on his heels to stare at the friend betraying him. He glared down the barrel of the gun and through clenched teeth said, "Twenty years we go back, muthafucka, and you pull this shit. You were my friend, nigga!"

"Friend? You should have thought of that before you fucked her."

"What?" The realization suddenly set into Alonzo. "She came at me, Curtis."

"Nigga, you knew she was off-limits. You fuckin' knew how much I love that girl. She's the mother to my kids!"

"So, you gonna rob and kill me over a piece of pussy? We go back before her."

"You just don't get it, Alonzo. Ashanti is more to me than just another notch on my belt. But you don't know shit about that."

"Nigga, like you a fuckin' saint! How many times you cheated on that bitch? Y'all ain't even together anymore, from my understanding."

"You just don't get it. Ain't no fuckin' boundaries with you, Alonzo. There never been. Ever since we were kids, you did shit your way and ain't give a fuck about anybody else. I'm tired of you."

"You do this to me, Curtis, and I swear, it's gonna be hell on earth for you and your fuckin' family," Alonzo said through clenched teeth.

"I don't give a fuck anymore."

Poot! Poot! Poot! Poot! Poot!

Curtis slaughtered Alonzo at close range, and his body crumbled at Curtis' feet like dirty laundry. Blood was everywhere. Curtis stared down at Alonzo's body for a moment. Then he stepped over it and reached into the safe, pulled out the bundles of money and drugs, and began dumping them into a black duffel bag.

He rushed from the penthouse, keeping his face lowered to the floor and head turned away from the security cameras. He knew the building like the back of his hand. He made his exit out the back entrance of the high-rise, racing underneath the parking garage, and emerging from the back door into a narrow alleyway.

He walked casually to his car, carrying $450,000 and thirteen ki's of pure cocaine in a small duffel bag.

CHAPTER 6

Curtis woke up to the constant ringing of his cell phone. He had slept in his clothing and could almost not sleep last night. The scene at the penthouse kept replaying in his mind.

Alonzo had killed the Haitians for the drugs and loot, and now Curtis had returned the favor, violently striking the hand that was feeding him. Alonzo was a high-profile player in the game, and his people would be searching desperately for the culprits responsible for his death. His men would be looking to kill everything in sight—anyone who could be considered a suspect was walking on thin ice. The streets were about to become flooded with blood.

Curtis knew he had to play his cards right and tread lightly. Not only was his own life in jeopardy, so were his children's.

The chime in Curtis' ear was giving him a slight headache. He set his phone on vibrate and tossed it across the room. His bedroom was dark, even though it was almost noon. The curtains were black and closed tightly, not letting a degree of sunlight seep through. His pistol was close to his reach. It was on the bed, cocked back, the safety off and ready for any danger. If anyone besides his kids came through that bedroom door, Curtis was ready to open fire.

The advantage Curtis had was, no one had seen him come or go, and no one was aware that he had a meeting with Alonzo. As far as Maino knew, Curtis had cancelled their meeting, so Curtis' alibi was that he never went. It had been postponed until the next day; even Maino could be a witness to that.

Alonzo had enemies everywhere he turned. Even though he was respected and feared, not everybody liked him. There would be a lot of fingerpointing—the Haitians, a jilted lover, a jealous boyfriend, or a rival crew.

An hour later, Curtis decided to finally tune himself back into the world. He couldn't hide from the trouble brewing. He had gotten his thoughts together, knowing he had covered his tracks carefully. He checked his cell phone. Fifteen missed calls showed on his display screen. Most of the missed calls were from Ashanti and Maino. He got out the bed and moved toward the window. He pulled back the curtains and peered outside for a moment. Armageddon hadn't happened yet.

The phone rang in his hand. It was Ashanti again. He decided to answer this time.

"Hey, babe," he said coolly.

"Curtis, I've been trying to call you all morning. Something happened to Alonzo." Ashanti was frantic and sounded like she was in tears.

"What the fuck you talkin' about, Ashanti?"

"They found him murdered in his penthouse."

"What?"

"They killed him. Shot him and Dino to death," she cried out.

There was a short pause.

Ashanti then asked, "Baby, did you have something to do with it?"

"What? What the fuck you talkin' about!" he barked. "You fuckin' accusing me of it, and over the damn phone? Bitch, you must have lost ya damn mind! My friend is dead, and you fuckin' blaming me?"

"I just thought—"

"You thought wrong!" he screamed.

"I'm sorry, baby. What's gonna happen?"

"I'm gonna find out what's going on, but stay off the damn phone, and be careful who you talk to," Curtis advised in a cooler tone.

"Be careful, Curtis."

"Just hang up," he said sharply.

After the phone went silent, Curtis stood by the window and sighed heavily. He turned to look at the bed, underneath which was the duffel bag filled with drugs and cash. It wasn't the most suitable place to hide the booty, but until he could think of a better place to stash it, his bedroom was the only place he could trust.

It was about to be a busy day for Curtis. His cell phone continued to ring again. He glanced at who was calling, and it was Maino. He had to take the call. He figured Maino had also heard about Alonzo's death already and would be ready to go to war.

"Maino," Curtis answered softly.

"Where the fuck you at right now?" Maino exclaimed. "I've been tryin' to call you all fuckin' morning, and you ain't pickin' up. We need to tool the fuck up, Curtis. I know you already heard about Alonzo."

"Yeah, I heard."

"He dead, yo! Alonzo is fuckin' dead!" Maino screamed.

Curtis could feel Maino's deadly temper through the phone. His aggression was evident as Maino growled at him.

"Where they get him at?" Curtis asked.

"At his penthouse in midtown, him and Dino."

"Damn."

"Yo, we need to meet right now, Curtis."

"Where?"

"I'll come to get you. Be at your place in a half-hour."

"A'ight."

Maino hung up and left Curtis in his room pondering. Shit was about to hit the fan. He needed a shower and a change of clothes, after being in the same attire for twenty-four hours.

Curtis pivoted on his heels and looked at the bed again. He had a small fortune hidden underneath. He'd already made up his mind not to share the wealth with Maino nor confide in his friend. The truth would die with him. It would be his secret. The first thing Maino would want to know was where the money and drugs had come from. Curtis couldn't think of a reasonable explanation to give to Maino, so it was best to live the lie. Maino wasn't a stupid man. He would put two and two together if the contents of the duffel bag were ever exposed to him. He didn't know what Maino's reaction would be if he knew the truth. Maino was unpredictable, and Curtis wasn't willing to take a chance.

He crouched near the end of the bed and pulled out the bag. It was unzipped, and the bundles of money and ki's of cocaine were almost spilling out of it, like an overflowing bathtub. It was a sexy thing to see. Curtis gazed at it for a moment. It was a sweet score—blood money that no one could know about. Not even his kids.

He started to wash up and change clothes. The apartment was quiet. His sons were gone, and Citi had been cooped up in her room all morning.

An hour later and Maino was still a no-show. But Curtis wasn't rushing. It felt unreal to Curtis—that he'd just killed his friend of twenty years. There was no turning back from it, though. The wicked deed had been sealed. He was a richer man because of it, and it was proof that the game had no loyalty.

The duffel bag remained snuggled in the corner between the bed and the wall, out of view from the doorway. It was going to take hours to count it all. It would have to be done when no one was around. Curtis needed privacy. He didn't want to worry about being interrupted when he placed the bills in the counting machine. He didn't want to be questioned by a damn soul.

He knew a drug crew in Yonkers and another crew in Long Island to unload the product on. It would be a healthy profit in return, but he'd have to make the deal under the radar. Neither Maino nor any Alonzo's people could catch wind of him doing any side deals with different crews. It would bring on suspicion.

The cell phone started to chime once again. It was Maino calling. "What up?"

"We downstairs," Maino said.

"A'ight, be down in a minute." Curtis zipped up the bag and pushed it back under the bed. He stuck the pistol into his waistband, donned his thick leather jacket, and exited the bedroom, closing the door behind him.

Before he stepped out the front door, Citi emerged from her bedroom and greeted her father with a smile.

"You leaving, Daddy?" she asked. She stood in front of her father clad in a pair of tight shorts, a wifebeater, and a multi-colored scarf tied around her head.

Curtis turned to gaze at his beautiful little girl. She was growing, and growing up fast. Her natural beauty filled the room. His eyes lingered on his daughter's curvy body. She was a father's nightmare.

"I gotta make an important run with Maino," he said to her. "Go put some clothes on. I might have company coming by later on."

"Okay." She turned to go back into her room.

"Citi," Curtis called out to her.

She turned and looked at him. Curtis approached his daughter. His eyes showed the love he had for his little girl. The murderous gangsta that he was on the streets dissipated once he was around her. Citi waited for him to say something.

"You know I love you, right?"

Citi nodded.

"You're the best thing in my life right now. And, no matter what happens, I will always love you."

"Daddy, you're scaring me. What's wrong?" Citi asked with a worried gaze.

"Ain't no reason to be scared, and there's nothing wrong. I'm coming right back, princess. I just wanted to say that to you." He smiled, then turned and made his exit.

Citi followed him to the door and watched her father fade into the elevator. Despite her father's words, her heart was telling her that something was wrong, but she didn't know what it was yet.

Curtis stepped out of the lobby with a poker-faced gaze at Maino seated behind the steering wheel of his Yukon. As he approached closer, he saw Maino wasn't alone. Tito was riding shotgun. Tito attempted to step out from the front seat and climb into the back, but Curtis shouted, "Nah, I'll get in the back."

"You sure, boss?"

"Nigga, stay where you at," he ordered.

Tito shrugged.

Curtis climbed into the backseat and the greeting between them was somber.

Maino was clearly upset. "I'm ready to ride on whoever did this shit, Curtis," he said. "I'm ready to murder whoever, nigga!"

"We gonna find out," Curtis replied. "Just chill."

"Chill? Nigga, Alonzo's dead. How the fuck I'm supposed to chill?"

"We need you at a cool head, Maino. Don't get hotheaded and end up doing something stupid. We need you levelheaded right now on the streets."

"A'ight, I'ma be fuckin' chill—until I stick my fuckin' gun in someone's mouth."

"Emanuel wanna meet up wit' us," Tito mentioned.

"In Harlem?"

Tito nodded.

"Let's roll then." Curtis looked at Maino. He looked like a boiling pot that was ready to spill over.

The ride into Harlem was a somber and heavy ride. Each man had something troubling on his mind. Alonzo's death weighed their hearts heavy. Retaliations against whoever was responsible for Alonzo's tragic death were a definite obligation.

Emanuel had called an emergency meeting. If Emanuel Martinez was in town, then the game was about to take a serious turn. Emanuel was the next to step up and take charge behind Alonzo's death. The two were first cousins. Emanuel was a brutal man who didn't play games. He rarely smiled and took killing and torture to a whole new level. He made Maino look like Mickey Mouse. He grew up being an enforcer for a Colombian cartel and had moved up the ranks by spilling blood by the gallons, torturing any poor soul who crossed him. Having Emanuel in New York meant people were about to die.

Maino drove over the Triborough Bridge and entered Harlem, where the streets were cluttered with afternoon traffic and daytime shoppers. He navigated down 125th Street and then turned onto a side street and parked in front of a vintage barbershop. The three men went indside, where only two barbers were on staff with one customer seated in the chair. The place was retro, with hydraulic, reclining barber chairs with cracking leather, nice wooden-framed mirrors, and aged framed photos of famous celebrities coming into the place for a haircut—even one with Sammy Davis Jr. and Fred Williamson.

The mixture of talc, hair tonics, Barbicide, and cheap coffee created a manly smell. Classical jazz played inside. This place was known for having that old-school feel, so there weren't any flat-screens or modern technology.

Maino and Tito followed behind Curtis as they walked toward the back, bypassing the activity in the shop and moving through a door that led to the basement. Downstairs, they met with a group of six men and Emanuel Martinez. The room was filled with heavy cigarette smoke and chatter.

When Curtis entered, the room fell silent. Curtis looked around. All eyes were suddenly on him like he was an alien. His heart started to beat rapidly, but he held his composure. He looked across the room and spotted Emanuel standing erect in the room. His dark, steely glare locked in on Curtis as he smoked his cigar.

Emanuel Martinez only stood five-nine, but he was a strong presence in the room. He was dressed sharply in a three-piece Armani suit and glittering diamond pinky ring, and his thick goatee was trimmed precisely.

"Curtis," Emanuel called him over.

The men standing between them in the concrete room parted like the Red Sea. Curtis moved through the crowd with confidence, penetration, and a deadpan expression. Maino and Tito followed closely behind him.

When Curtis came near, Emanuel reached his arms out to him and pulled him into a hug. It was a tight embrace. Curtis knew he didn't suspect a thing. He would walk out of the meeting alive.

Emanuel sighed heavily and then asked Curtis, "You heard anything?"

"I just found out this morning. I'm just as shaken up about it as you, Emanuel."

"Muthafuckas, they killed him. Shot him down like some dog in his own fuckin' place," Emanuel exclaimed gruffly.

"We on it," Curtis assured.

Maino stepped up, and Emanuel greeted him with the same tight embrace. Everyone had known each other for years. Tito was the only unfamiliar face to Emanuel and the others.

Every swinging dick in the room was a killer. Collectively, the six men Emanuel had around him had over sixty murders under their belts. They were all casually dressed in button-downs and slacks with indentations of holstered weapons under their suit jackets. Their thick accents indicated they were from out of town.

"Yo, Emanuel, we fuckin' on this shit, ASAP, you hear me? Alonzo was like a fuckin' brother to us. And you have my word, when we find these niggas, I'ma make sure they die slow and painful," Maino said.

Emanuel nodded. "You were always the two men I could count on."

"It either gotta be these Haitians out in Brooklyn or some bitch had him set up," one of the men in the room chimed.

Everyone had speculations. Everyone in the room was itching to kill anyone responsible. Curtis remained cool and appeared upset like everyone else. He was the least suspected. He continued to talk to Emanuel. They had leads as to who could have possibly done the murders, and whoever the finger pointed to was about to be in for a rude awakening.

"I need to feel better right now. Hector, bring that bitch out," Emanuel growled.

Hector, his right-hand man and contract killer nodded. He pivoted on his wing-tip shoes and walked toward the back of the room and approached a locked door.

A short moment later, he was dragging a naked and bound woman roughly. She was blindfolded. She squirmed in Hector's grasp and fought with him, but the pistol to the back of her head made her fold up like a lawn chair and cooperate with the proceedings.

"Who the fuck is this bitch?" Maino asked harshly. "She got somethin' to do wit' Alonzo's death?"

"Nah, she fucked me over from another personal incident. And now it's time for this bitch to pay the price," Emanuel said.

The men in the room stared at her like she was a sheep trapped in a wolf's den. They were all ready to tear her apart, not caring she was a woman. She was a little portly with swinging tits and dark nipples. Her hair was disheveled, and she showed signs of abuse and having been tortured already. Her body was covered in bruises and cigarette burns, and her face was bloody.

When Hector removed the blindfold from around her eyes, they were black and puffy. Someone had worked her over really badly.

Hector pushed her down into a chair. She was crying and scared.

Curtis and Maino already knew Emanuel and his ways. He didn't care who you were. Man, woman, or child, if you crossed him, became an enemy to him, you would surely die in a horrific way. Hector, liked to get creative with death. He was a towering goon, standing over six-six, and was brawny like a prizefighter.

Emanuel walked over to the frightened girl. She was in her late twenties. She was tied to a metal chair with her arms bent behind her. Her eyes darted around the room like a pinball.

Emanuel slowly walked circles around the woman in the chair. "You see this bitch? She's a thief and a fuckin' liar. You take twenty grand from me, and think I won't find out. You think that I've forgiven for that infraction against me?"

The men in the room looked on. Everyone was quiet. When Emanuel spoke, everyone hushed.

The lady was trembling greatly. She finally decided to speak. "Baby, Emanuel, I'm—"

"Shut the fuck up!" Emanuel struck the woman in her jaw with his closed fist. "Did I tell you to talk?"

It was a mighty blow that almost sent her flying out the chair, but the ropes digging into her wrists and ankles kept her seated upright. She spat out blood and coughed.

Curtis and Maino watched as Hector began preparing to torture the woman. He removed a blowtorch from a bag and lit it, letting the hot blue flame come to life. He looked at Emanuel for the approval, and Emanuel nodded.

Hector smiled and moved the hot blue flame toward the woman's nipples. She squirmed and pleaded in the chair with tears streaming down her face. She was helpless.

Hector didn't hesitate. He pressed the flames into her nipples, and a piercing scream filled the room.

"Shit!" someone uttered.

Hector continued to assault the woman with the blowtorch in places unimaginable until burning flesh was reeking in the basement room. Her skin was boiling with blisters, and her hair had caught on fire. It was a slow and agonizing death.

Curtis couldn't believe what he was seeing. He had seen death before, but the way Emanuel and Hector killed someone was just plain brutal.

"Yo, I'm out," Curtis said.

"What? You leaving already. Shit, they about to get to the good part." Maino was sadistic just like the rest of them.

Curtis made his exit, and Maino and Tito followed behind him.

When they reached upstairs into the barbershop, Emanuel had called out, "Curtis."

The men turned around.

Emanuel came closer. He stood in front of Curtis and said, "Alonzo was family to you and Maino. He loved you like a brother. I want you and Maino to keep these streets close and find these muthafuckas! You understand?"

"We on it," Curtis replied.

"The business you had going with Alonzo will now continue through me," Emanuel stated. "Whatever you need, you come talk to me directly."

"A'ight," Curtis replied coolly.

Emanuel took a pull from his cigar, and stared at Curtis for a moment, his dark eyes cold and callous. If Emanuel suspected him, it didn't show. It was still love and business between them. He turned to head back into the basement, and Curtis, Maino, and Tito left the barbershop and climbed into the Yukon.

Maino and Tito were ready to execute business in Alonzo's name. Curtis was thinking of an exit strategy.

CHAPTER 7

The screams coming from the fifth-floor apartment were quickly muffled. The men who were torturing Loony for information didn't want his neighbors to hear the commotion and call the police, so they stuffed a towel into his mouth. The place had been ransacked, and Loony was sprawled out on the wood floor bleeding profusely. He had a swollen jaw, cracked ribs, and two bulletholes in his knees, courtesy Maino's .45 with silencer.

Tito, with brute force, kicked him in the side, causing Loony to wince.

Maino yanked the bloody towel from his mouth and crouched down over him. He shoved the pistol into Loony's mouth. "Tell me somethin', muthafucka!"

Loony mumbled.

Curtis stood by the windows and watched his men work Loony over something serious. He had to bury his conscience. He was the only one who knew Loony was speaking the truth. Loony was just the unfortunate one who was at the wrong place at the wrong time. Someone linked him to being around Alonzo's penthouse palace around the time of his death.

Maino decided to follow up on the lead and try to get Loony to confess to something. He removed the deadly tool from Loony's mouth and said, "Speak now, or forever hold your peace."

"Maino, c'mon, man, I don't know shit!" Loony desperately cried out.

"Oh, well." Maino pointed the gun at his head and was ready to fire.

"Wait! Wait!" Loony screamed out, his hands stretched out in front of him. "The only thing I can tell you is, maybe Juliette might have something to do wit' it."

"Juliette?" Maino questioned.

"Yeah, Alonzo's baby mother," he answered.

"I know who the fuck she is. Nigga, you lying to live," Maino barked.

"Nah, man. I seen her around pushing this sweet candy apple red BMW. And from my knowledge, her and Alonzo weren't on good terms lately," Loony said.

Maino glanced over at Curtis. "What you think?"

"I just don't see it," Curtis replied. "She loved him."

"Curtis, you and I both know Alonzo was the biggest dog in the streets. He fucked everything moving, and Juliette ain't take too kindly to his infidelity, especially when he was fuckin' her best friend," Loony explained.

"Yeah, it do make sense," Maino replied.

"It do. Believe me, man. I know she had somethin' to do wit' it. She's been hanging around a few shady cats lately. She had to set him up," Loony exclaimed.

"You know what? We'll pay that bitch a visit too," Maino said.

"You believe me?" Loony asked, looking somewhat relieved.

"We'll see." Maino then fired two shots into Loony's head.

Curtis, Tito, and Maino left Loony's apartment for the neighbors to smell him a week later. No one would lose any sleep over his death.

The three men climbed into Maino's truck. Maino turned to look at Curtis and said, "Yo, you know what? It do make sense now."

"What the fuck you talkin' about, Maino?" Curtis asked.

"I ain't been seeing that bitch around lately. She pushing a new Beamer, and since Alonzo's death, she's been MIA. And, c'mon, who else would be able to get close enough to Alonzo like that? In his penthouse suite, and get the drop on him? Someone he trusted."

"I just don't see it, Maino. Juliette ain't that smart or cold to pull it off. Loony was lying to save his own ass."

"Nah, fuck that shit. She guilty of something, and if she ain't pull the trigger her damn self, then she got someone to do it for her. Probably some nigga she fuckin'! You know Alonzo would be doin' the same for us. And I ain't gonna rest till I murder every last one of them muthafuckas involved."

"Let's ride then, nigga," Curtis said halfheartedly.

▲

Maino pulled up to a posh brick building on Harlem's West Side. It was early morning, and the neighborhood was quiet with the chilling cold keeping the majority of the residents off the streets.

Tito and Curtis sat in the truck smoking. Maino reached for the pistol under his seat and cocked it back. "Yo, let's see this bitch!"

Curtis was still reluctant, but he knew it was best to go along with the program. Even though he was the boss man, he had to follow every lead they heard on the streets to avoid bringing suspicion upon himself. Emanuel and his men were looking for victims to slaughter, and he had to divert attention away from himself and his family.

"Let's just do this shit," Curtis said.

The men exited the truck and coolly walked to the front of the five-story building that towered over the still morning streets. Their guns were concealed under their winter wardrobe, and their faces were stone cold. Maino and Tito followed behind Curtis. They had gotten information about Juliette's whereabouts and apartment number through an informant. She was steadily moving around Harlem from one apartment to the next, but a few hundred dollars spread out through Harlem streets was able to root up what they needed to know.

The men moved through the tiled lobby with one mission on their minds—revenge. They stepped into the elevator and rode it to the fifth floor in silence. Stepping out, they quickly began looking for apartment 5D. It was located down the hall, snuggled between the other two apartments like a cozy little secret.

"Here we go," Maino said quietly. He was anxious to kick down the door and start blazing, but that would attract too much attention from the neighbors.

"You two, stay out of sight and let me do the talking," Curtis said. He knew seeing three thugs outside her door would intimidate Juliette and prevent her from opening up.

Curtis took a deep breath. He took one last glance at his goons poised for action and nodded. The knocking was loud, and at first, there was no answer. It seemed like no one was home.

Curtis knocked again, and this time he heard movement behind the door.

"Who is it?" a female voice shouted.

"Juliette, it's me, Curtis. Open the door, so we can talk."

"Go away, Curtis," she yelled. "I don't want or need you here."

"Juliette, I just wanna talk to you."

"Fuck off, Curtis. You think I'm gonna trust you or anybody else after what happened to Alonzo? Get away from my fuckin' door!"

Curtis sighed and contained his frustration. Juliette wasn't budging.

"Why are you being so stubborn? I'm only worried about you. Alonzo was a brother to me, and I know he would want me to check up on you."

"You ain't come alone. I know you got Maino with you. I can fuckin' smell him from behind my door. And if you don't leave from my gotdamn door in one minute, I'm callin' the police."

Curtis knew it was pointless to keep arguing with her. Juliette was obviously spooked.

Juliette suddenly shouted, "And if you even think about chargin' through that door, I got shotgun in my hands and won't hesitate to kill anyone who comes in this muthafucka!"

Chk-Chk!

"Fine. I'm leaving. When you stop actin' like this, come and holla at me so we can talk. I ain't the fuckin' enemy, Juliette. I owe it to Alonzo."

"Tell me whatever, nigga!"

Curtis stepped away from her door, and Maino and Tito followed behind him. Stepping into the elevator, Maino cursed, "Stubborn fuckin' bitch!"

"We'll just come back," Tito said.

"Hells yeah," Maino said. "When she least expects it."

Curtis remained silent. He knew what was going to transpire once they finally caught up to Juliette. Maino was ready to tear her apart. He was a savage muthafucka who shot first and didn't give a fuck about the repercussions later.

The men got into Maino's truck.

Maino looked at Curtis. "Yeah. That bitch is guilty about something. Why she ain't open the fuckin' door to you? She got somethin' to hide."

▲

The next day was colder than before. The early-morning residents had gone off to work, and the streets were empty. Maino was relentless. He and Curtis sat parked outside Juliette's building, waiting, knowing she had to leave her apartment sooner or later. They smoked cigarette after cigarette, as minutes turned to hours, and morning started to transition into the afternoon.

"This bitch gotta come out soon," Maino said.

"Just be easy."

"Fuck being easy! I can't wait to lay hands on this bitch."

"You forget she's Alonzo's baby mother?"

"Nigga, Alonzo is fuckin' dead, and if she had anything to do with it, then so is this fuckin' bitch!"

Curtis had no response. He leaned back in the passenger seat and took a pull from the cancer stick.

A few building residents came and went. The men sat with little conversation between them. Parked across the street, they were watching the lobby entrance like two hawks.

A short moment later, Juliette emerged from the lobby pushing a young toddler in a posh stroller. She was bundled up in a stylish winter coat and a long scarf, trying to look inconspicuous.

"There that bitch go," Maino spat, reaching for his gun under the seat. He was ready to rush at her.

"Yo, chill, nigga. What you gonna do? Attack her in public and get us both locked up? Think, nigga. She's gotta come back."

"Yeah, you right."

"We get at her on the inside. Less eyes and less attention on us."

Maino nodded.

They watched Juliette push the stroller up the block and turn the corner. It seemed she was going to be gone for a moment in their eyes. They planned on being patient.

Curtis and Maino departed the Yukon and calmly walked toward the front entrance. They walked into the building unseen by any resident and without any hassle. This time, they took the stairs up to the fifth floor. They inspected the area. The sprawling, ritzy structure was silent—no loud music coming from any apartments, no neighbors screaming at each other, and no foul odor lingering in the hallways like in the projects. It was the Upper West Side of Manhattan, where the two Queens thugs would stand out. So they were clad in long trench coats and polished wing-tip shoes, looking more like detectives than thugs.

Juliette arrived back to her place an hour later. She moved hurriedly into her building. With the .380 concealed in her purse, she wasn't taking any chances, especially with her infant son. But when she stepped off the elevator, Maino's .45 was quickly placed to her head.

Maino roughly grabbed her by the arm. "Don't fuckin' scream, bitch!" he whispered sternly in her ear.

Juliette became frozen with fear.

Curtis loomed into her view with his pistol aimed at her son in the stroller. "Let's not make this difficult, Juliette. We just wanna talk to you," he said calmly.

Juliette glared at Curtis. "Get that gun outta my son's face. You dare point a gun at Alonzo's child?"

"It's the only sure way to get your attention."

Maino told her, "Shoulda opened the fuckin' door yesterday, and we wouldn't have to pop off like this."

Maino gripped her arm tightly and forced her into the apartment. Once inside, he struck her in the back of her head with the gun, a powerful blow that sent her cringing to the floor.

"Maino, relax. We came here to talk," Curtis exclaimed.

Maino smirked. "Now we can talk."

Curtis shook his head. Sometimes it was hard to keep his pit bull on the leash.

"Y'all niggas get the fuck out my house!" Juliette screamed, still hugging the floor.

"We ain't goin' no fuckin' where!" Maino replied.

Juliette all of a sudden went scrambling for her purse on the floor. It was a desperate attempt to retrieve the .380 inside.

Maino kicked the purse out of her reach, and it went sliding across the room. "What the fuck you reaching for? A gun, bitch?" Maino shouted.

With the baby asleep in the stroller, Maino snatched Juliette by her hair and dragged her across the hardwood floors into one of the bedrooms. To shut her up, he hit her again, and then they placed duct tape over her mouth and tied her to a chair.

Maino had the pleasure of stripping her naked. He lusted over her curvaceous body and wished he could fuck her. Her perky tits and smooth brown skin had him somewhat aroused.

Curtis noticed the way his friend was staring at Juliette, and he had to remind him that they were only there for business.

"We just want to talk," Curtis said. "You gonna chill out when we remove the duct tape from your mouth?"

Juliette refused to answer.

"I need an answer, Juliette."

She looked up at Curtis and reluctantly nodded.

Curtis smiled. "That's my girl."

He gestured to Maino, and the duct tape was ripped away from her mouth.

"What the fuck y'all niggas want?" she cried out.

Maino went straight to the point. "Who killed Alonzo?"

"I don't know!"

"Bitch, you lying. You know somethin', and we ain't leaving here until we get the truth from you," Maino exclaimed.

"Fuck you, Maino! You was always an evil muthafucka!"

"Oh, word? You feel that way? You cunt bitch. Then you gonna see how evil I can get today."

Out of the blue, a sharp blade appeared in Maino's hand, and it went slashing across Juliette's face and opened up her skin like a zipper. Her screaming pierced the room as blood trickled down her face.

Curtis quickly stuffed a rag into her mouth to muffle her loud scream. He looked at Maino and said, "Nigga, what the hell is wrong with you?"

"Muthafucka, I ain't come here to play nice wit' the bitch."

Curtis seemed to be dumbfounded by the unexpected attack. He stared at the pain in Juliette's eyes. The tears streamed down her face as the blood coated her once pretty skin.

Maino stood over Juliette with a scowl, the bloody blade still clutched in his hand. "Now, we gonna talk about this fuckin' car you've been driving in the hood, a brand-new candy red BMW. How the fuck you get a car like that?" He snatched the rag out her mouth to allow her to talk.

Juliette's restraints were too tight around her wrists and ankles. She couldn't free herself. And she was concerned about her baby still sleeping in the next room. "Please, my baby—"

"Fuck that little nigga!" Maino shouted. "I swear, if you don't start talkin' and tell us what we need to know, I'ma cut his little ass up too."

"You touch him, and I'll fuckin' kill you. I swear to it!"

"Bitch, you ain't in the position to threaten anyone right now." Maino neared the bloody blade to her exposed nipple. "I'll start cuttin' away, bitch. You wanna fuckin' test me?"

"It was a gift from him, you stupid muthafucka!"

"A gift? Bitch, you lying. I know you and him were beefing. Why the fuck would he want to buy you a car? You ain't suckin' his dick that good. Huh, bitch?"

"Fuck you!"

Juliette's smart-ass remark caused her to receive a powerful blow from Maino's closed fist. It struck her right temple and shook her up for a moment. She became dizzy. If she hadn't been tied to the chair, she would have collapsed against the floor.

"You wanna talk shit, bitch?" Maino yanked her by her hair violently, jerking her neck back like a whip being snapped. He looked like he was ready to break her neck. He pressed the blade against her neck and nicked the flesh of her throat until he saw blood.

"Talk to me, Juliette. I can make this easy on you."

Curtis stepped up to Juliette, his eyes a little easier on her than Maino's.

"I'ma do this bitch and her son right now, if she don't fuckin' talk," Maino barked.

"Fuck you, Maino!" Juliette growled through clenched teeth. "The only people that could have gotten close to Alonzo and kill him like that were you and Curtis. I know he had a meeting with y'all on the day of his death."

"Bitch, you talkin' crazy. That nigga was like a fuckin' brother to us. And we ain't had no meeting wit' Alonzo. The shit got postponed," Maino replied.

"I warned Alonzo not to trust y'all."

"Bitch, who the fuck you think you is, accusing us of his murder? You done lost your damn mind! You know what"—Maino pulled out his pistol and shot Juliette in the head, and she slumped over in the chair, her blood pooling around the chair.

"What the fuck is wrong wit' you, Maino?" Curtis spat.

"She was outta pocket, Curtis. Gonna talk that shit about us. You was gonna let that shit slide?"

"You were a little extreme."

"Man, fuck that bitch! She lucky I don't body her son too."

"Every neighbor around probably heard the shot."

"So fuck it! We out."

The two men walked into the living room where Alonzo's son started to cry. The gunshot had awakened him. They gazed at the crying child for a moment and decided to leave him there alone with his mother dead in the bedroom. Curtis would call in the homicide once they were far away from the crime scene.

CHAPTER
8

Curtis sat locked in his bedroom, counting the money in privacy. He had stacks of it piled on the bed. He moved it through the counting machine, and the bills spilled out, totaling into the hundreds of thousands. Ten-thousand-dollar stacks decorated his bedroom like furniture.

Curtis took a seat in a chair, stared at the cash, and sighed. He tried to free his mind from the guilt he was feeling. He knew Juliette was innocent, and it ate away at him the way she was tortured and killed. But the game was always ugly. It was one of those cost-of-doing-business situations that he had to deal with.

It had been two weeks since Alonzo's murder, and the Harlem streets were running red with blood. With Emanuel in town, it felt like Iraq for hustlers and rival dealers. His reach was everywhere. Contract murders were being carried out like it was a franchise business, and people were scared.

Queens wasn't immune to the turmoil going on in Harlem. Three men implicated in the escalating beef uptown were shot dead on Linden and Guy R. Brewer three days earlier. Curtis' number one priority was the safety of his family.

The thirteen ki's were an added bonus, and a problem too—a catch-22. Curtis had to dump the bricks of cocaine on a crew quickly. It was too much of a risk to keep it in his place, and an even bigger one to unload it on the streets with the wrong crew. There were too many snitches and too many big mouths talking in New York, so dealing with the wrong person could either mean a bullet in the head or police kicking down his door. His actions had to be swift and stealthy.

Curtis thought about calling Shot, a major player locking down Hempstead, Long Island. He and Shot went back several years. Shot was a stand-up dude—an original gangsta. They both grew up in the same era, when the '80s produced real millionaires from off the streets and real gangsters didn't snitch on you at the drop of a dime. He was one of a few hustlers on the streets Curtis could sell the ki's to without having word get back to Maino.

Curtis picked up his cell phone and dialed Shot.

"Yo, who this?" Shot answered in his gruff tone.

"It's C," Curtis replied, not wanting to shout out his whole name through the phone.

Shot instantly knew who it was and replied excitedly, "What's good, my nigga? It's been a minute."

"I know. Listen, I need to make this call short."

"A'ight. You got some business for me?"

"Snowman like a muthafucka."

"Yeah, that's what I need to hear. Shit's been kinda crazy out here lately. But get at me, C. Let's see if I can make this shit melt."

"A'ight, tomorrow afternoon. Where at?"

"You already know where," Shot said. "Shit ain't changed from before."

"A'ight."

Curtis hung up feeling a little relieved. Shot was a businessman like himself, and he knew he had the clout and clientele to move thirteen ki's of hard white in his hometown without a problem. Hempstead was far enough away to be off Emanuel and Maino's radar.

Maino knew of Shot, but he didn't fuck with any Long Island niggas. Maino felt that Long Island was the country, and full of snitches. He had bad blood with the hustlers out in Long Island, especially with the Terrace Boys, a ruthless drug-dealing crew who attracted too much attention with murders. But it was like the pot calling the kettle black, when it came to Maino. He had traded gunfire with the Terrace Boys on a few occasions. Eventually, they stayed out of his neighborhood, and he stayed out of theirs.

Curtis stashed the money away neatly in two separate bags and slid it underneath his bed. It had been a long morning, but he'd finished up some much-needed business and was ready to relax for a moment. His mind was spinning with so many things.

Knocking at Curtis' door suddenly caught his attention. He figured it had to be one of his kids looking to get his interest. "Who knocking?" he shouted.

"Daddy, it's me," Citi replied. "Why you got the door locked?"

"Hold on, princess."

Curtis moved quickly, hiding any cash in the room from plain sight. He placed the counting machine on the floor in the closet and snatched the .45 off the bed and hid it under his pillow. He did a fast check around his room, and everything looked normal. Even though his daughter knew about his business, he didn't want to explain to her where all the extra money had come from.

He donned a T-shirt and unlocked his bedroom door. Citi walked in, beaming at her father. She was always a prize in his eyes. It'd been three days since he'd seen his kids.

"Hey, princess," Curtis greeted her with a warm smile.

"Daddy, why you hiding from us?" Citi joked.

"It's just business I'm taking care of, princess."

"I know, Daddy."

Citi, looking like an R&B princess in her sweat pants and T-shirt, hugged her father closely. She always felt protected under his wing. When she was around, she always brought a glow and daughterly love, and Curtis' world suddenly became a different place. The stress and problems would temporary fade away, and he seemed to become a new man.

Curtis smiled at his daughter. "What you came in here to bother me about? Your birthday gift?"

"No, not just that, Daddy. I had to see if everything is okay with you. I'm not that spoiled."

Curtis laughed. "Uh-huh, tell me somethin' different. You're spoiled enough."

"'Cuz you love me this much." Citi extended her arms.

"You need to spread your arms out a little much more," Curtis joked.

"I wish I could. I would spread wings for you, Daddy, and then we can soar in the air together."

"I'm ready to fly, princess. Just point us in the right direction." Curtis pulled Citi into his arms and smiled. He said to her, "You know what, princess?"

"What, Daddy?"

"I'm gonna get you that car for your birthday. An Accord, right?"

Citi pulled back from her father with a huge smile. She howled. "Daddy, fo' real? Are you serious? Ohmygod, Daddy! I love you so much!" She leaped into her father's strong arms and embraced him.

Curtis smiled from ear to ear. The joy and sparkle on his daughter's face was why he did what he did on the streets—Blood and drug money made his family live in the lifestyle of the rich and hood-famous. Curtis was never cut out for a nine-to-five job, making minimum wage, and his kids weren't made for welfare checks and hand-me-downs. But he also understood that you reap what you sow; that for every action there was an equal and opposite reaction.

Citi couldn't stop beaming. She was so joyful that she steadily jumped up and down in the bedroom. She couldn't wait to hold her set of car keys in her hand and take her new car for a spin around the hood in style. She ran out of her father's bedroom shouting, "I'm gettin' my new car! I'm gettin' a car for my birthday!"

She danced and jumped around the apartment like she was in a Broadway show, while her two brothers, who were in the kitchen fixing a snack, looked at her dumbfounded.

Curtis emerged from his bedroom with a wad of hundreds in his hand. He was ready to celebrate and splurge a good amount of money on his kids.

"Yo, Pop, how you buying Citi a new car and forget about us? Shit, we need an upgrade too. That ain't right," Cane argued.

"You don't need a new damn car, Cane. You're driving a Benz now."

"I'm a Byrne, Pop. We always travel in style and stay upgrading our shit," Cane replied. "I had that Benz for seven months now, and it's gettin' old."

"I'm with Cane on this, Pop," Chris chimed. "How you come out your room balling with a fistful of cash and then get stingy with it? I mean, can we get some love, too?"

"Y'all some haters! It's *my* birthday comin' up, not yours. Why y'all tryin' to ruin shit for me?"

Cane shot back, "Ain't nobody tryin' to ruin shit for you, Citi, and ya damn birthday is a month and a half away."

"That's right, and I'm just asking for one thing. It ain't fuckin' fair for y'all two to be the only ones driving and not me. I'm tryin' to shine too."

"I just know she better not get a better car than me, Pop," Cane said.

"Everybody, just shut the fuck up!" Curtis exclaimed, his voice booming through the room. "Y'all really are starting to act like some fuckin' rugrats right now. Cane and Chris, y'all are not gettin' no new car right now. Are y'all two serious? Earn your keep around here and stay focused on your education and business. Fuck a Beamer or a Benz! Ain't y'all supposed to be men? A man doesn't look for another man to buy him shit that he can get himself."

The boys took the tongue-lashing from their father quietly.

Cane scowled. "We holdin' shit down out there for you, Pop. Why you gotta treat us like we kids?"

"You and your brother are men, Cane, so act like it. I don't want my sons looking for a handout from anybody, even from me. Y'all go out there and get your own."

"And we are, Pop," Chris replied.

"I love y'all. But I'm not gonna always be around for y'all to do business under my wing. The wolves are out there and they're fuckin' ready to devour what y'all have, and they ain't tryin' to leave you with any scraps. You hear me, Chris and Cane?"

His sons nodded.

"You carry yourself out there with your heads up and stay sharp about the choices you make. Y'all hear me? We family, and you never turn your back on family. I don't give a fuck what happens."

Citi's eyes stayed glued to her father as he talked. The gleam in her eyes showed the love and admiration she always had for him.

"Let me tell y'all somethin'. Y'all are my kids, and that carries much fuckin' weight in the hood, but you don't trust any muthafucka. Sometimes blood and friendship can fuck you over when it comes to money. Niggas is greedy and jealous out here of a nigga on a come-up, and believe me, those two ingredients can definitely get you pushed over the edge when a nigga gets to play you close enough."

Curtis started to have feelings that karma was gonna come for him soon and snatch him away violently like it did Alonzo and Juliette.

After his stern speech, Curtis peeled off three grand from his huge wad of cash and gave his kids a grand apiece. "Spend that wisely," he said to them.

His children noticed the extra cash but didn't question him about it. "Thanks, Daddy," Citi said with a smile.

Curtis turned to walk back into his bedroom, unable to shake that feeling of karma getting ready to take shots at him and knock him down on his ass. He assumed it was a long time coming, since he'd always escaped death and prison by the skin of his teeth.

Chris stared at the stack of hundreds in his hand. He thought about an investment. He was ready to prove to his father that he could hold down the throne.

Cane smiled and blurted out, "Shit, I'm goin' fuckin' shoppin'!"

It was a cold, breezy afternoon as Curtis navigated his way through the Long Island streets in his gleaming Benz. Hempstead was almost a replica of Queens, with its sprawling homes, vacant lots, and rundown corners, not to mention bodegas, liquor stores, and churches lining the streets and boulevards. Cops did their steady patrol of the area, but the streets were too cold for the corner hustlers to be outside.

Curtis steered his ride into the narrow driveway of a ranch-style home on a tree-lined street. He parked in the backyard and stepped out, expecting Shot to greet him in the backyard, where high fencing, thick shrubbery, and towering trees gave the men the privacy they needed.

"My nigga, Curtis!" Shot yelled from the back door of the home.

He had a broad smile and skin like tar. His braids made him appear young, even though he was reaching forty, and his height and weight made him look like he could be a linebacker for the New York Giants. He greeted Curtis with a strong bear hug and looked his longtime friend up and down.

"Shot, it's good to see you again," Curtis replied.

"Same ol', Curtis. I see we both ain't aging fast. Looking like you could still be a teenager yourself."

"What can I say? A good diet and some good pussy keeps me fit."

Shot laughed. "You still chase them young whores?"

"Never chased the whores. The bitches chase me."

"And you ain't got a problem letting them catch you either," Shot replied, patting his friend on the shoulder.

Curtis smiled. "Sometimes I can be an easy catch."

"I hear that. So what you got for me?"

Curtis went to the trunk of his car and unlocked it. He opened it up and removed a small duffel bag. He went up to Shot and said, "I'll feel better if we can continue this inside."

"Yeah, of course, let's go inside. It's fuckin' brick out this bitch," Shot replied.

Curtis followed behind Shot into the stash house. It was furnished with leather couches and flat-screens, and high-end security cameras watched every area outside the place. Three teenage girls sat at the kitchen table in their underwear, packaging crack into small vials for street distribution.

Curtis' eyes lingered on one of the girls a little too long.

Shot said to him, "Careful, Curtis. She's only seventeen."

Curtis shook his head. "How you do it, man?"

"What? You mean these young bitches in their underwear workin' for me? Shit, I'm giving them a job. These bitches ain't got anywhere to go. Before workin' for me, they were out there broke, giving pussy away for free, and ain't had a pot to piss in. Now, they're making five hundred a week easily. Let's just say, I'm like the Red Cross around this bitch."

Curtis stared at the pretty young seventeen-year-old in her pink panties and white bra. She reminded him of his own daughter. Curtis knew Shot was fucking the girls. Word on the streets was, Shot was also a part-time pimp. He got his money any way he could. But it wasn't Curtis' business. He followed Shot into the next room and placed the duffel bag on the table.

Shot removed a cigar from his pocket and lit it. He took a few heavy pulls from it and looked at Curtis as he unzipped the bag and removed thirteen ki's of hard white.

"Nice."

"Give me ten thousand a ki, and we good," Curtis said.

"Ten stacks." Shot took another pull from the cigar. "What's the catch? Why you cheaper than the others right now?"

"Ain't no catch, Shot. I just need to unload some weight, giving it to you for a decent wholesale price right now."

"I see. But, listen, I can only take five ki's off your hands right now."

"Only five?"

"Yo, the game ain't the same out there like it was years ago. Between the young boys fuckin' it up and the snitches and the police on a nigga's ass, I gotta slow things up for a moment."

Curtis was disappointed that Shot wasn't taking it all from him, but he kept his poker face and nodded. "A'ight, I understand that."

"But if this is some quality shit, nigga, we gonna be in business for a long time."

Shot snapped his fingers at one of the young kids lingering around in the living room playing video games. "Yo, Mike, go get that for me."

The young boy jumped up and dashed into a neighboring room.

Curtis had a small chitchat with his friend. Curtis' nerves were on edge. He wanted to make the transaction quick. With the .45 tucked into his waistband, his eyes were on alert. Even though he and Shot were always cool with each other, he always followed the advice he gave his own children—You never know when a nigga will get greedy on you and set you up.

The teenage kid came running out the room holding a small plastic bag filled with money. He handed it to Shot and went back to playing video games.

Shot passed the plastic bag to Curtis, who peeked into the bag, which was filled with five ten-thousand-dollar stacks—all hundreds.

"We good?" Shot asked.

"Yeah, we good."

Shot threw his arm around Curtis and embraced him closely. With the cigar clutched between his fingers and a smile on his face, he said to Curtis, "You know, if you wanna fuck one of them bitches in the kitchen, go ahead, nigga. They gonna be cool with it."

"Nah, I'm good."

"You sure? You missin' out on some of that golden pussy, my nigga, especially the one you was lookin' at earlier. Her pussy is like ecstasy, Curtis . . . have you trippin' in it."

"Nah, I got places to be," Curtis replied dryly.

"A'ight, business first. Gotta respect that."

Shot walked with Curtis outside. Before Curtis got into his ride, Shot said, "Yo, I'm sorry to hear about Alonzo, man. I knew y'all were close."

"The game is fucked up right now."

"Yeah, anybody can get got, if they got Alonzo. Damn!"

Curtis didn't want to speak about it any longer. He wanted to erase Alonzo's murder from his mind, but no matter where he turned, people were always bringing it up.

He had phone calls to make. He backed out of the driveway, and before he could turn the corner, he was back on his cell phone making calls to New Jersey. He knew of a crew out in Trenton that probably could take the rest of the drugs off his hands.

CHAPTER 9

Citi and Dana strutted up Jamaica Avenue like divas. They turned heads with their tight jeans forming perfect bubbles in the back and their pretty faces glowing like the sun in the cold weather. The avenue was bustling with shoppers and traffic. The Easter holiday was approaching soon, and everyone wanted to take advantage of the discounts a few clothing stores were advertising and buy a few nice garments to show off when the spring weather finally touched down in the city.

Citi had $1,500 cash and was ready to spend the majority of it on shoes, earrings, and a spring jacket. She wished she had more cash on her, because the shoes she had her mind set on were eight hundred dollars alone. The girls went in and out of stores on the avenue like a pinball game and racked up on shopping bags of pricey attire and laughing and flirting with a few cute boys. Most of the thugs and roughnecks instantly knew who Citi was, and they gave her much respect, knowing not to push up too hard on the urban princess. Her daddy had eyes and ears everywhere on the streets.

The girls were lounging around the food court at the Coliseum and saw a few young hoods from their buildings. Dante, a young worker coming up under Maino's crew and the alpha male of the group, locked eyes with Citi and smiled. Citi smiled back at Dante. His swag and apparel had Citi intrigued. At seventeen, he was tall and built like an athlete, styling long braids that coiled down to his shoulders and a long, icy chain around his neck. His skin was bronze, and his teeth were like a Colgate advertisement.

The girls remained seated at their table and watched Dante and his crew stirring up attention from security in the building as they were loud and disorderly. They intimidated a few shoppers in the mall and acted like they owned the place.

"Ain't that ya boo?" Dana said, pointing to Dante.

"He's cute, right?"

"You fuckin' him yet?"

Citi smiled. "No."

Dana laughed. "Your father would kick his ass."

"My father don't know shit, and he ain't gotta know shit. It's my business. I'm grown." Citi rolled her eyes at Dana.

"Uh-huh. You know damn near all of these niggas on the streets are on his payroll."

"Dante's different."

"You think?"

Citi pushed Dana playfully and then turned her attention back to Dante. He was walking over with Booboo by his side. The young boys approached the ghetto princess with their sagging pants and a security about themselves.

"Citi, what's up, love?" Dante greeted with a smile.

"Hey, Dante." Citi smiled back.

Dana stared up at Booboo, a handsome street thug with an aquiline nose, long cornrows, and steely look.

"Ladies, y'all lookin' so damn fine right now," Booboo proclaimed.

"We always lookin' fine. Nothin' less, but always at our best," Citi replied, her eyes on Dante.

"I feel you, ma. What y'all doin'?" Dante asked. "Shoppin'?"

"I'm tryin' to look good," Citi said.

"You ain't gotta try, ma," he returned.

"Yo, y'all goin' to the club tonight, right? I'm performing," Booboo informed them.

"I ain't even know you rap, Booboo," Dana said.

"Shorty, I'm nice on the mic . . . gets it in on stage. Niggas out here ain't fuckin' wit' me."

Dana and Citi smiled.

"Yeah, he do his thang," Dante added.

"A'ight, we might come through tonight. If we ain't busy," Citi said, her eyes still focused on Dante.

Booboo said, "Yo, we definitely wanna see y'all there. It's gonna be poppin' tonight, ya feel me?"

"We feel you, Booboo." Dana smiled.

The girls continued to flirt with the young thugs, who didn't have a problem showing how interested they were in the girls.

Dante took a seat next to Citi and placed his arm around the back of her chair. They sat so close to each other, it looked like they were ready to kiss.

Citi was ready to rape him with her tongue. His touch made her skin tingle with excitement. The only thing she could think of was his strong arms wrapped around her and his lips tasting and kissing every inch of her.

"So, I'm gonna definitely see you tonight?" Dante asked her.

"Of course."

He smiled.

Booboo and Dana had no problem showing their affection in public. The two locked lips with each other as Dana sat on his lap with her arms around him.

"Look at these fools," Dante joked.

"Get a room!" Citi said.

Dana threw up her middle finger at Citi and Dante.

Guard the Throne

The two couples exited the Coliseum together, with Citi feeling the need to hang out that night and get closer to Dante.

▲

Citi walked into her apartment to find Cane seated on the couch cleaning a TEC-9. Two .45 pistols and a Ruger P89 rested on the coffee table. Cane looked up at his little sister and smiled.

"Where you get these guns from?"

"I just bought them. Ain't they sweet?" he replied, playing with the TEC-9 in his hands.

Citi stared at the weapon in Cane's hand. It was a scary piece to see up close. She could only imagine how many lives it had cut down.

She cringed a little when he playfully pointed it at her. "Don't point that shit at me!" she yelled at him.

"Chill, sis. It ain't loaded."

"I don't care!"

Cane shrugged her off and continued cleaning the gun. He looked like a kid with a new toy.

"Where's Daddy and Chris?" she asked him.

"They ain't here," he replied, being short with her. His focus was more on his newly acquired gun than his little sister.

Citi walked into her bedroom and shut the door. She wanted to get ready for tonight. She tossed her shopping bags on the bed and opened up her closet door to add to her stylish collection.

She had a few hours till the club time, so she rolled up a joint, came out of her clothing, and listened to a few CDs before nightfall.

▲

Club Speed in Hollis, Queens was teeming with young revelers dancing and throwing their hands up to Lil' Wayne's track, "She Will." The outsized club jumped from wall to wall with ballers and thugs, sexily dressed ladies, and wannabes.

Citi and Dana walked into the dim building like superstars. Citi was looking fabulous in her miniskirt and four-inch heels. The men marveled at her beauty and tried to get her attention, but she completely ignored them and looked around for Dante. But he was nowhere to be found in the dense atmosphere.

The girls hit the bar and quickly had one of their admirers buy them a drink.

Hips started to sway to the Jamaican tunes that blared throughout the club. Citi hit the dance floor with her drink in hand and her body oozing sex appeal for the niggas to drool and gaze at. She backed her ass up into the men that poised behind her, stimulating hard-ons that poked her.

Dante and Booboo approached the girls shortly after their arrival. Dante grabbed Citi's attention, taking hold of her thick hips from behind and grinding his pelvis into her, swaying with her.

Citi turned to see who had grabbed hold of her waist in such an aggressive manner. She smiled and hugged him tightly. "I was lookin' for you, boo," she said.

"I'm here now."

The two continued to dirty-dance like they had privacy, while Dana and Booboo hugged each other and locked lips on the dance floor.

The night continued with the girls hugged up on their thugs in the back of the club, their entourage of goons close by. The girls got tipsy from drinking Grey Goose and smoking haze. They tried to keep the burning blunt from the eyes of security that walked around the club.

The night was a success without any incident. Citi moved through the crowded club with Dante like the ghetto queen she was. This was what life was about for her, the life she lived, and the only life she knew how to live—partying, flaunting her father's wealth, the clothes, and mingling with the thugs from her hood.

▲

Guard the Throne

The four of them exited the club after three a.m., jumping into Dante's '98 money-green Maxima that sat on polished chrome rims and tinted windows. Citi sat shotgun while Dana rode in the backseat, hugged up with Booboo. The night was still young, and the girls weren't in any rush to go home.

"Yo, where y'all wanna go?" Dante asked.

"Shit, a bitch is fuckin' hungry," Dana said.

"Word," Booboo added.

"So, what, y'all wanna head to the chicken spot on Liberty?" Dante asked.

"Yeah, that will do. I can go for a three-piece right now," Citi said.

"Fuck a three-piece. I need a whole fuckin' hen right now," Dana joked.

Dante started the ignition and peeled out of the parking spot to show off for the girls. He whipped the car down the block doing sixty and made a hairpin turn at the next corner, tires screeching.

Citi and Dana laughed.

Dante pulled into the parking lot of Kennedy Fried Chicken. He pulled on a blunt and passed it to Citi. Rick Ross blared throught the speakers, and the thunderous bass rattled the vehicle. The streets were quiet, and the parking lot was empty of cars. The chicken spot was twenty-four hours, so it was the place to go right after a night of clubbing.

Dante stepped out of the Maxima first, his stomach growling. He had a taste for some chicken and biscuits. Citi climbed out and strutted toward him with a smile, her eyes red from the weed.

Dante took one last pull from the burning haze and passed it to her for the last time. She took it and inhaled like a thorough weedhead.

"Yo, y'all comin' in?" Dante asked Dana and Booboo. The two were nestled together in the backseat like a vine and kissing intensely.

Booboo took a second to pull himself from Dana's sweet grace. "Nah, y'all go ahead."

"What you want then, nigga?" Dante asked. "A three-piece meal or somethin'?"

"Nigga, fuck a three-piece. Bring back a fuckin' bucket of chicken or somethin'," replied Booboo. "I'm hungry like a muthafucka."

Dante shook his head. "Nigga, you gonna starve fuckin' around wit' some pussy."

"I ain't gonna let my baby starve. I got somethin' for him to eat right here," Dana said, gesturing between her thick legs.

Dante laughed. "Y'all crazy."

"Ya know it," Booboo said.

Dante threw his arm around Citi, and the two walked into the empty Kennedy Fried Chicken spot, with the thick partition separating the workers from the customers. Citi remained snuggled closely against her boo as he ordered twenty dollars of chicken and biscuits.

Dante pulled out a wad of twenties and tens to pay for the order. "So, what's up wit' you, ma?" he asked.

"What you mean?"

"I mean, ya pops ain't gonna mind me having his daughter out all night? 'Cuz I ain't tryin' to have any problems wit' the nigga."

Citi sucked her teeth. "Please, nigga. I'm fuckin' grown."

Dante smiled. He took Citi by her hand and twirled her around in a 360, focused on her thick backside. "Shit, I can definitely see that. And ya growin' in all the right places too."

Citi chuckled. "Shut up. You so silly."

"I know, right? But, real talk, I don't need any trouble wit' ya pops and definitely not Maino."

"There ain't gonna be any trouble. Whatever happens tonight is just between you and me. And I know Dana ain't gonna say shit, and Booboo ain't no snitch, right?"

"Nah, that nigga cool. He a ride-or-die nigga fo' real."

"He must be, 'cuz Dana is lovin' ya boy."

"And what about you?" Dante asked her.

"And what about me?"

"You lovin' the kid?" He smiled.

Citi pressed herself against him a little more tightly and brushed her hand against his crotch. "It depends."

"It depends on what?"

She could feel the butt of his gun tucked into his waistband poking against her slightly.

"Depends on how good you continue to treat me tonight." Her hand squeezed the bulge in his jeans, and she was impressed.

"Shit, I plan on treatin' you better than ya pops do," Dante said convincingly.

Citi laughed. "I don't know about that. My daddy treats me very, very well." She lifted her wrist to show off her sparkly diamond tennis bracelet. It was last year's birthday gift from Curtis.

"Damn, that shit is nice."

"I know," she returned smugly.

Dante adjusted the pistol in his waistband and then banged on the partition. He shouted, "Yo, what the fuck is takin' so fuckin' long back there?"

"Five more minutes," the worker quickly replied. "We're making fresh chicken right now."

"Well, hurry the fuck up. A nigga is fuckin' hungry in this bitch. Y'all shoulda been had that chicken ready." Dante turned his attention back to Citi. "You good?"

Citi nodded. She glanced down at his waist. "Why you got that on you right now? You should have left it in the car. You in some beef right now?"

Citi was well aware that the police constantly patrolled the area at night because of past shootings, harassing every black male within proximity.

She didn't want to get into any trouble, and she wasn't in any mood to spend the night in Central Booking. She was too cute to be in jail.

"You ain't know? Niggas is on edge right now, ma. Shit has been hectic on these streets since Alonzo got bodied."

The news of Alonzo's death hit Citi like a brick to the face.

"What?"

"Niggas is warring in Harlem over that shit, and some of that beef uptown is trickling into our hood. I'm keepin' my gat close. I ain't tryin' to get caught slippin' out here."

Hearing about Alonzo's death had Citi tripping a little. She knew he was a significant figure in her father's life. She'd met Alonzo a handful of times, and always thought he was cool and very handsome. But he had always been a mystery to Citi. His death had to be bothering her father. His behavior during the past two weeks was strange. He wasn't home mostly and he had become withdrawn from his family in some way, but now it was making sense.

"Yeah, everybody out here is on alert right now," Dante added. "Nigga Alonzo was like Tony Montana out here. But I'm sure you already knew that, being who your father is."

Their food was pushed through the revolving window slot.

Dante snatched it up. "About fuckin' time!"

As Dante walked back to his car with his arm around Citi, her mind was on the news she had just heard. She wondered why her father would keep such important news from her. She wondered if her brothers knew too. Citi hated being kept in the dark when it came to her father's world. She understood he only wanted to shelter her from any danger, but she wasn't a little girl anymore.

When they made it back to the Maxima, the windows were fogged up, and there was a steady rocking coming from the backseat.

"Look at this shit!" Dante said. He opened the door, and there was

Dana, naked from the waist down, straddling Booboo, riding his dick like a joystick inside of her.

"Damn, nigga, give us like five more minutes," Booboo said.

"I thought y'all were hungry," Dante said.

"Yeah. Shit, y'all were taking too long." Booboo laughed.

"Damn, Dana, you couldn't wait? Get a room," Citi said for a laugh.

"We will."

Citi and Dante jumped into the front seat, while Dana continued fucking Booboo in the backseat. They had no shame getting down in front of company.

"Aaaahhh," Dana moaned.

"Don't be leaving any stains in my backseat." Dante whipped his Maxima out of the parking lot just as a police cruiser turned the corner and stopped in front of the chicken spot.

Citi had become quiet. Her mind was on her father and speculating about Alonzo's murder. Dante had planted a seed of worry in her head. What if the people who were responsible for murdering Alonzo came after her father too? The thought of losing him truly troubled her.

She remained quiet as Dante cruised down Guy R. Brewer, her eyes gazing past the dilapidated bodegas, shabby storefronts, local residents wandering about, and the boulevard traffic. Dana getting fucked like a porn star behind her suddenly became irrelevant to her. She drowned out her friend's moaning by thinking about whether her family was in any danger.

"Why you so quiet?" Dante asked.

"I was just thinkin' about somethin', that's all."

"Thinkin' about what? You okay?"

"Yeah, I'm okay," she replied halfheartedly.

"Yo, Citi, don't worry about that bullshit I told you in the chicken spot earlier."

"I'm not worried about it. I know my father and brothers can handle themselves. If there's any danger, my father is able to handle it."

Dante nodded. "Ya pops is a warrior."

"He never loses," Citi uttered, remembering what her father had once said to her.

CHAPTER 10

The apartment was quiet. Curtis was gone as usual, and Chris and Cane were in the streets handling their business and partying. Citi was left alone in the stillness of home. But the solitude made her relax in the confines of luxury. Clad in her boy shorts and a T-shirt, she rolled up a joint, turned on the large flat-screen, and glued her eyes to music videos. She got high and sat slouched in the leather sofa, sinking into it like she was caught in quicksand. She took a few strong pulls of the burning weed and exhaled. Her eyes drifted into a daze as the R&B from the TV blared throughout the room.

Citi nodded to Mary J. Blige. Her eyes then turned to gaze at her father's bedroom door. Numerous thoughts from possible encroaching trouble to her birthday gifts began spinning around in her head. She wanted to be nosy. She always kept out of her father's room when he wasn't home. He liked his privacy and didn't like anyone snooping into his business.

Citi took another pull from the kush and placed the remnants of her blunt into the ashtray. She stood up, but stumbled slightly, catching her balance against the couch. She walked over to her father's bedroom door and twisted the doorknob. It was locked, as expected. But the locked door was only a minor obstacle.

Knowing how to pick locks since she was nine years old, she went into her room and got a hairpin. She went to the door, crouched down, and pushed the hairpin into the center of the lock. She continued pushing until she felt the lock give.

She pushed the door open and walked inside her father's room. She looked around, scanning how neat and meticulous things were in the room. His king-size bed was always made. His footwear was lined up precisely near the closet door. His jewelry was spread out on the stylish black dresser like a display in Macy's. The blinds were closed. Everything was in place.

Citi opened the closet door first. She moved a few articles of his clothing out the way and searched through his closet. She didn't have an idea what she was looking for. She just wanted to inspect his world. She didn't want to be in the dark. At the bottom of the closet, she found a black duffel bag pushed against the back wall. She squatted down, pulled out the bag, looked at it for a moment, and knew there was something illegal inside. She slowly unzipped it and found over a dozen handguns inside. She removed one—a black 9mm.

She stood up with the gun in her hand. It wasn't an unfamiliar tool to her. Guns were a part of her world. She walked toward the dresser mirror. She aimed the gun at her reflection. She knew how to use it. Her father taught her how to shoot a gun when she was ten years old. She remembered when they used to drive out to the woods in New Jersey and shoot at beer cans and other items. Curtis had taught his daughter how to hold the weapon and aim, using the sights and aiming center mass. She'd learned how to load a clip and cock it back.

Curtis had trained his daughter not to be defenseless. Even though he protected her from the violence of his world, his children needed to know how to defend themselves. They needed to have street smarts.

Citi continued to grip the deadly steel in the soft palms of her hands. The safety was on. It was a loaded gun. She'd already checked the clip. Hollow tips—the most dangerous bullets. Her father only dealt with the deadliest weapons that killed reliably and efficiently. She stared at her image in the mirror and wondered if she were put in the predicament, if she would be able to shoot and kill someone. She'd heard stories about her father—even heard about Cane letting off shots at his enemies—but she had never been tested in the streets herself.

Citi lowered the gun from the mirror and sighed. She turned on her heels and placed the 9mm back into the duffel bag. She zipped it back up and pushed it back against the wall the way she found it. Curtis was very observant. He knew when something in his room was messed with or moved. She had to be careful not to rearrange anything.

Citi shut the closet door. She continued to snoop around the bedroom, but nothing was new or strange in her eyes. She dropped to her knees and peeked under the bed. There she saw a counting machine and two more black duffel bags. The bags caught her interest. She crawled under the bed and reached for one of the bags. It was somewhat heavy. She wondered if it was more guns.

She unzipped the duffel bag, and her eyes lit up like a kid's on Christmas Day. "Ohmygod!" she uttered in disbelief.

Citi reached for the cash wide-eyed. She held up two ten-thousand-dollar stacks—all hundreds, crisp bills. She pulled out more and more cash and placed it on the bed. She had never seen so much money. She estimated that there was over six hundred thousand dollars in cash there. Citi knew it had to be drug money. She knew her father was rich, but she had never seen so much cash all in one room.

She marveled at the sight of so much money. Shopping sprees and beauty spas were all Citi could think about doing with the cash. The spoiled girl couldn't resist. She hesitated for only a moment, and then peeled off $40,000 in cash. She assumed her father wouldn't miss it. He was already swimming in money. So she considered it to be an early birthday gift to herself.

Citi dumped the rest of the money back into the bag and zipped it tight. As she was about to push the bag underneath the bed, she heard the front door open. Nervousness whirled inside of her. She thought it might be her father coming home. He would be highly upset if he caught her creeping around in his bedroom.

She hurried to push the duffel bag underneath the bed and wanted to run out. She clutched the four ten-thousand-dollar stacks, but fumbled with them.

Before she could make her quick exit, Cane appeared. "What the fuck you doin' in Pops' bedroom?" he exclaimed.

Citi stood frozen. She tried to hide the cash behind her back. Cane was blocking the doorway.

"Citi, you picked the lock? You crazy. Pops gonna have your ass when he finds out you was snooping in his room. Yeah, see if you get that car for your birthday now."

"You gonna snitch on me, Cane?"

"You ain't got no right to be in his bedroom. You know how he don't like that shit. What you lookin' for anyway?"

"Nothin'."

"You lying."

"Why don't you mind your business, Cane?"

"You sneaky, Citi."

Citi sighed. She didn't know if Cane was bluffing or not, but she wasn't ready to take that chance. She didn't want to be chastised by her father, and she wanted to keep the money—even if it meant sharing it with her brother.

"Cane," she called out.

Cane turned around. He looked at Citi and waited for her to say something. "What?"

Citi revealed the cash she had hidden behind her back.

"Whoa! Where the fuck you get that from?"

Citi didn't answer him.

"How much?" Cane asked.

"Forty thousand."

"From where?"

Citi nodded toward the bedroom.

"You crazy, Citi!"

"He won't miss it. I found damn near six hundred thousand in a duffel bag. I mean, it's only forty thousand, Cane. Think what we can do wit' the money."

"Where did all that cash come from anyway? I never knew Pops to keep that much cash in the apartment."

"Well, it's here now," Citi said.

Citi had him thinking. He needed the extra cash.

"It'll just be between us. We don't even have to tell Chris about it."

Cane smiled. "Fuck it!"

"So you're driving, right?"

"Driving to where?"

"To the mall."

"You a fuckin' a trip, Citi. But let's go."

Citi smiled. She hurried into her room to get dressed. She couldn't wait to hit the stores to spend some of Daddy's money.

The price tag on the diamond-bezeled Rolex watch was $3,000. Citi and Cane purchased two of them. The diamond earrings cost $1,500, the diamond-encrusted pinky ring, $2,000, and the platinum chain with the TEC-9 pendant, $5,000. In total, the two spent fifteen thousand dollars on jewelry and clothing.

They went into high-end stores in Roosevelt Field and flaunted money like the spoiled teenagers they were. When they stepped into the jewelry store, the employees didn't take the teenagers seriously at first.

Citi asked to see the costly earrings in the glass case, and the Caucasian female employee smirked and wanted to ignore them, waving them off like they were a joke. But when Citi pulled out a wad of hundreds and displayed it across the countertop, the lady had a sudden difference in opinion.

"Do your job, bitch!" Citi barked at her. "We tryin' to shop."

Cane laughed.

The trunk and backseat of Cane's Benz was filled with shopping bags—Gucci, Sean Jean, Prada, Fendi. It was all worth it. Citi was in the passenger seat admiring the bracelet she had just bought. She couldn't wait to show it off to her friends and flaunt it in school. It was one of a kind. The siblings were content with the day's events, and they still had plenty of money left.

Cane drove with a smile on his face. He couldn't help but to glance at the sparkly Rolex around his wrist every passing minute. "Damn! Wait till muthafuckas see me wearing this shit," he said. "And Chris—"

Citi quickly blurted out, "You can't tell Chris, or Daddy."

"Huh?"

"We can't let them see none of this shit we bought today, Cane, especially me. How we gonna explain where we got the money for all this? Yeah, you workin' for Pops, but I'm not. And he ain't payin' you enough to buy fuckin' Rolexes and all this other shit. Daddy already gonna know what's up. And, Chris, he gotta be kept in the dark too."

"Yeah, you right, sis."

"We just gotta keep all this extra stuff hidden until the right time."

Cane nodded.

"Just wear the shit in the streets, but when we get home, everything that we bought gotta come off. If Daddy sees any of it, or Chris, then they gonna start questioning us."

Cane looked at his little sister and smiled. "Let me find out, sis."

"Let you find out what?"

"That you know how to scheme like the best of them."

"My last name is Byrne, right?" She smiled.

"Yeah, it is, yo. This shit? It's in our blood," Cane said. "I love this street shit!"

At first, Citi felt guilty about stealing from her father. He was always good to her. Whatever she wanted, she didn't have to ask twice for it. Curtis gave her everything. But the taste of taking something—even if it was from her own father—excited her. And walking around with forty thousand dollars was an exhilarating feeling.

CHAPTER 11

Maino stopped his truck on the corner of Sutphin and Foch Boulevards. When the local knuckleheads lingering on the corner in front of the bodega saw his Yukon pull up abruptly, they immediately became alert and nervous. He jumped out of his ride with his sagging jeans, swinging chain, and leather coat. He approached the corner with his mean-mug and his pistol concealed in his waistband.

Business had been slow since Alonzo's murder, and that meant money wasn't coming in fast enough. It angered Maino. Profits on the streets had dropped greatly, and knowing that he hadn't found Alonzo's killer or killers yet made him edgy.

He walked up to C.C., a young seventeen-year-old slinging crack cocaine out of his mother's basement. C.C. fixed his posture and looked at Maino nervously. The money in his pocket was for Maino, but it was $1,500 short. He knew Maino didn't accept any excuses when it came to his cash.

"C.C., what you got for me?" Maino asked.

C.C.'s crew diverted their attention from Maino. They all knew how quickly he could snap, and not one of them wanted to be on the receiving end.

C.C. reached into his pocket and pulled out the small wad of cash he had to give up. He passed it to Maino and tried to remain calm. Maino snatched the cash from his hand and at once started to count the profits.

C.C. stood apprehensively near Maino, his frail body no match for Maino's burly frame.

"C.C., what the fuck! You short, nigga," Maino barked. "Really fuckin' short, nigga. This is a fuckin' joke?"

"Maino, shit is dry out here right now."

"I don't give a fuck. You fuckin' wit' my money, C.C.?"

"C'mon, Maino, you think I'm crazy enough to rob you? Nah, it's just been dry out here lately. That package you gave us, it ain't worth shit. These fiends ain't happy wit' it, yo."

Maino glared at C.C. He wanted to punch the teenager in the face, but his cold, black stare already had C.C. ready to piss in his jeans. Maino knew C.C. was right. The ki he had was weak. No matter how many times his peoples stepped on it, it was poor quality. Alonzo's death was hurting his pockets. Emanuel was the new connect, but Emanuel had to go underground for a moment, fleeing the States to lay low from the feds. The murders in Harlem had made his organization hot and put his crew on the feds' radar. Maino needed a new connect, and he needed one fast.

"I'm sayin' though, what's up wit' you and Curtis?" C.C. asked. "Y'all ain't fuckin' wit' each other anymore?"

"What the fuck you talkin' about?"

"Why he movin' the good shit all around Long Island and Jersey, and we gettin' this bogus package?"

"What?"

"Y'all still peoples, Maino? I mean, word is that Curtis is the man to go to with that good shit. You ain't heard?"

Maino stepped closer to C.C., violating his private space. His fiery eyes locked into C.C., and he shouted, "Nigga, fuckin' talk!"

C.C. took a deep breath, holding his gaze down to the floor, and said, "I'm just sayin', I got peoples in Hempstead, and—"

"C.C., if you don't tell me what's up, I swear, muthafucka, I'ma shove my fuckin' pistol down your fuckin' throat and shoot out ya fuckin' heart!"

C.C. sighed heavily. "I heard your boy Curtis hooked Shot up wit' some bricks and they killin' it out there."

Maino was confused. "What the fuck you tryin' to say?"

C.C. was always known to have information, and quality information. He had family everywhere—cousins and uncles in the game in every borough. Somehow, word of other people's business and activity always got back to him, and he would use it to save his own skin every time.

Maino didn't understand it. It was the first time he'd heard this information. How was Curtis moving product when, since Alonzo's death, the streets were somewhat dry? It bewildered him.

"You lying about this, nigga?" Maino asked.

"Yo, Maino, I ain't stupid enough to lie to you. Everybody in these streets knows how you get down."

"You better not be, C.C. If you are, I'll fuckin' kill you."

C.C. swallowed hard.

Maino stuffed the wad of cash into his coat pocket and walked away. He got into his truck with a troubling thought. Had Curtis been stepping out on him, conducting business without him knowing?

The following evening, Maino called Curtis on his cell phone. His first call went straight to voice mail, and so did his second. It took Maino calling for a fifth time to reach Curtis.

When Maino heard his friend's voice, he barked, "Nigga, why the fuck you don't pick up ya phone?"

"I was busy," Curtis replied coolly.

"Busy doin' what? Damn! What if a nigga needed help? Shit, a nigga done been gotten stuck up and already dead by the time you answer ya fuckin' call."

"Nigga, I was wit' a bitch."

"Always in some pussy. You and your bitches, nigga."

"What you want?"

"We need to link up and talk," Maino said.

"When and where?"

"Tonight. It's urgent."

"A'ight. Baisley Park in an hour. I'm not too far from there," Curtis said.

"Cool."

Maino sighed heavily. He wanted to meet with Curtis face to face and talk to him. He wanted to look Curtis in his eyes when he asked about the disloyalty he'd heard from C.C.

▲

Two hours before midnight, Curtis drove his Benz into the empty parking lot of Baisley Park. The streets were sparse with traffic. The winter wind blew steadily, as Curtis stepped out of his ride to smoke a cigarette wearing a stylish pea coat and a wool hat. He took a pull from the Newport and looked around.

He had moved the thirteen kilos with little trouble, and so far, things had been quiet. Emanuel was laying low in Panama until things settled down in the States. The homicides in Harlem were catching worldwide news. Alonzo's murder had stirred up a hornets' nest, and they were stinging hard.

Curtis leaned against his car, wondering what was so important that Maino had to meet with him. He'd left a warm piece of pussy to wait in the cold for his friend.

A short while later, Maino's Yukon slowly turned into the parking lot, rap music blaring from the truck. The Yukon parked two spaces away from Curtis' Benz.

Curtis took one final pull from the Newport and flicked his cigarette into the weeds. He blew smoke from his mouth and turned to greet Maino.

He noticed two silhouettes in the truck, and wondered why Maino didn't come alone.

Maino stepped out his truck and walked up to Curtis.

Curtis didn't see anything threatening about him. He went to greet his childhood friend with a pound and a hug. "What's good, Maino? Everything cool? What you call me out here in the cold so late for?"

"I just needed to talk."

"So talk."

"You got another cigarette?"

Curtis reached into his coat pocket and removed his pack of Newports. He pulled one out and handed it to Maino, who quickly lit it, took a much-needed drag, and exhaled.

"Who in the truck wit' you?" Curtis asked.

"Donny."

"Fuck you doin' riding wit' that nigga?"

"We just riding."

"You know I ain't never trust that nigga, Maino."

"Yeah, trust is a fragile thing right about now," Maino replied matter-of-factly.

"What you mean by that, Maino?" Curtis asked with a raised eyebrow.

Maino took another drag from the Newport. He glanced at his truck and then turned his attention back to Curtis. "I don't know what to think right now. Alonzo's death got a nigga trippin', and it got a nigga thinkin'. I mean, I'm turning this fuckin' city upside down to find these niggas, and it ain't adding up. Whoever hit Alonzo came off good, both with drugs and cash. You know word is, niggas probably came off with over four hundred thousand dollars in cash and damn near thirteen ki's of coke. That ain't shit to sneeze over, yo."

"And what you gettin' at?" Curtis asked.

"Yo, that bitch Juliette, if she did the shit, why she ain't just leave town with whoever? Why the fuck she stuck around?"

"Now you ask these questions—after you put a bullet in her head?"

"I ain't got no regrets killin' that bitch. I ain't never liked her anyway."

"Well, too late for those kind of questions."

"You think? I'm just sayin', shit ain't feeling right. I'm thinkin' this shit is deeper. Yo, we need a new connect right now, Emanuel overseas, and these streets is drying up, but I'm hearing about niggas in Long Island and Jersey getting laced wit' some quality ki's. So I'm thinkin', whoever is hittin' these niggas out there is probably the ones that got Alonzo."

"You got a name?" Curtis asked coolly, keeping his composure.

"Nah, I'm still on the hunt. I mean, what you been hearing out there?"

Curtis shook his head. "Nothing lately."

"Yeah, it's like these niggas just fuckin' vanished. Killed Alonzo and now they in the fuckin' wind. I don't get it. When I hunt for niggas, I find muthafuckas. And I always get to the fuckin' truth, but this shit here? Nah, it's more than meets the eye."

Curtis remained silent. Maino's personal investigation was making him itchy. He felt the walls closing in around him. Maybe the bubble was about to burst, but he was ready to contain the trouble around him for as long as he needed to. He had his family to think about.

Curtis stood tall and said, "Yo, just go home and get some sleep."

"Nigga, fuck sleep. I'm hearin' shit."

"What you hearing?"

"Yo, how long we been friends, Curtis?" Maino asked with a sharp stare at his friend. "I mean, we ain't never hid shit from each other, right?"

"Yo, what the fuck you tryin' to say, Maino?" Curtis exploded with a fierce gaze at Maino. "What the fuck you assuming?"

"Nigga, I ain't tryin' to assume shit. I'm just talkin'."

"Talking? Right now, I don't like the way you talking."

"What you so concerned about, Curtis? You makin' extra money on the streets without me?" Maino boldly asked.

"You think I had something to do with it?"

"Did you?"

"Nigga, who the fuck you think ya talkin' to? Remember who the fuck I am!" Curtis shouted, stepping closer to Maino.

"And remember who the fuck I am!" Maino shouted back. He stood his ground when Curtis closed in on him.

"I loved Alonzo. We were brothers."

"Yeah, we were, but things change. Shit is different."

"Maino, don't go there wit' me. We knew each other for too damn long. Yo, you're the godfather to my daughter. We're supposed to trust each other in these streets. I ain't the one for you to point your fuckin' finger at," Curtis barked through clenched teeth.

"I'm just tryin' to make sense of the situation, Curtis. Yo, if it was you dead, I would be goin' just as hard in these streets to find your killers."

"That's understandable." Curtis took a deep breath. He calmed himself and added, "Look, let's cool our heads. Come by the crib tomorrow so we can really talk, okay?"

Maino took his final drag from the cigarette and tossed it. "A'ight."

Curtis reached for Maino and pulled him into his arms. They hugged each other. It was a brotherly hug. Curtis then said, "I love you, man."

"I love you too."

"We brothers, right?"

"Brothers." Maino pulled himself away from Curtis' brotherly embrace. He turned and walked back to his truck.

Curtis stood near his Benz and watched Maino climb into his ride and drive away. He felt tension building. If push came to shove and Maino tried to leap, then Curtis was ready to put his dog down. It was a hard decision to make, but in his mind, his family's safety came first.

CHAPTER 12

Citi strutted into her high school like she was a ghetto celebrity, her new jewelry gleaming. The earrings, the bracelet, the watch, and the pricey trinkets turned heads as she walked the hallways. She felt picture-ready for the red carpet in a pair of Seven jeans with pink stitching to match her baby pink Benetton shirt with her crème and pink Prada sneakers.

Citi was only in school to show off. She sat in the classrooms playing around with her smartphone and admiring her jewelry for everyone to notice. Some of the girls showed contempt for Citi the way she pranced around the hallways like she was untouchable, but her status in the hood and around the school made the girls think otherwise about robbing or confronting her. With a father like Curtis and a crazy brother like Cane, she had the muscle to do whatever she wanted.

Citi sat in the cafeteria among the popular girls in the school. The girls took hints in fashion from her since she came to school in items that celebrities were seen wearing on TV. The boys steady eyed her, ready to lick her like she was a special flavor of ice cream. She was the queen bee bitch at the lunch table.

"Damn, them joints is nice, Citi," Lola said with vigor, her eyes fixated on Citi's diamond hoop earrings. "I need those in my life."

Citi smiled. "They are right. I paid enough for them."

"Where you get those from? I need to go snatch me a pair."

"I got these from Long Island, over in Roosevelt Field Mall."

"How's security in that mall?" Lola asked.

"I don't know. They be around. Bitch, I know what ya thinkin'. You tryin' to boost you a pair, huh?"

"Shit. How else I'm gonna get them?" Lola replied with a mischievous grin. "My pockets ain't deep like yours."

"You crazy, Lola. They gonna lock your ass up."

"Bitch, they gotta catch me first. And I'm too nice at it, and I've been doin' this for a long time. I know all the tricks, so fuck their security."

Citi had nothing but respect for Lola. They had come up in the same building, but had different backgrounds. Lola was a foster child who never knew her biological parents. She was entrusted to Ms. Terry's care. Ms. Terry had three other kids she'd adopted from the system, and Lola was the eldest foster child. Ms. Terry didn't have the income to provide Lola with the luxuries and designer clothing she craved, so Lola always wore hand-me-downs. Tired of the run-down look, she took to shoplifting and boosting, and over the years, she became better at it. She knew how to bypass certain security systems, what stores were the easiest to steal from, and how to remove the security tags from clothing and not set off the alarm. In time, ninety percent of her clothing, amongst other things, came from stealing. Ms. Terry, an elderly woman, couldn't keep up with or discipline Lola, so she got away with a lot of mischief.

Lola had been drawn to Citi since she was twelve. She loved Citi's style of dress and how she carried herself. She noticed the outfits Citi would be wearing, and a week later, she would boost the same thing.

"Lola, if you steal these earrings and get them for free after I paid like five hundred for them, I'm gonna be pissed," Citi said.

"Bitch, I told you to come to me first. I don't know why you be paying all that money for stuff when all you gotta do is put me on to the store, and I'm in there and back out with them shits. Easy like one, two, three." Lola smiled.

Citi shook her head. "Well, I ain't telling you the store."

"Fine, be like that. I'll find me a pair that's much better than yours, and come to school and have you hating."

"Then do that."

"Whatever, bitch."

Citi continued to sit at the lunch table and eat her lunch, while the other girls marveled at her iced-up wrists, ears, and neck. The young thugs would come over, trying to get the ladies' attention with jokes and stories.

One knucklehead thug Citi hated was Brice. He disgusted Citi like he was a fly buzzing around. Brice was a wannabe and a bully in the school, starting fights and clowning on individuals too scared to hit back. He was a broke nigga, and Citi didn't deal with broke niggas.

"Why you gotta be like that?" Brice spat.

"Be like what?" Citi replied with an attitude, rolling her eyes at him.

"Why you gotta catch an attitude when I come around?"

"'Cuz I can. And you a bum nigga. Look at you."

"What?"

Brice stood up. He wanted to show everyone in the cafeteria that he wasn't afraid of Citi. But just then, Cane walked into the cafeteria with his circle of thugs. Brice at once noticed Cane and changed his demeanor toward Citi.

Citi smirked. "Pussy."

Cane stared over at his sister and then gazed at Brice unkindly.

The girls at the table laughed when Brice walked away like a dog with his tail between his legs. Citi took delight in embarrassing him and pulling his thug card. She knew that, at the drop of a hat, she could get her brothers to fuck him up.

"He's so fuckin' wack!" Citi announced to her girls.

"Ain't he?" Lola cosigned.

After lunch, Citi breezed through her day. The only good thing about going to school was the gossip she would hear from her crew, hanging out with her friends, being able to show off her wealth, and the envious looks she would receive from hating bitches who wanted to be her.

The end of the school day, students poured out the front entrance to the building. Cane's gleaming Benz was parked out in front of the school like it was on display at the auto show. His rims twinkled like mirrors, and the candy paint was flawless and gleaming. Citi lounged in the passenger seat of her brother's car, smoking a cigarette and looking pleased that she was the center of attention. The fleeting looks and hard gazes made her day.

Citi turned up the radio and let Lil Ru's "Nasty Song" blare for the students to hear. She nodded to the catchy beat and danced in her seat.

Lola walked over to the car, all smiles. "Bitch, turn that shit up more," she said. "This my fuckin' song."

"Ah, shit."

Citi hopped out the car and started singing and dancing to the upbeat track. She moved like a stripper on the sidewalk, and Lola soon joined her. The girls turned heads as they flaunted their sexual moves like they were in a club.

Within a minute, all eyes were on them, as they danced with each other like no one was watching. Citi moved her hips with precision, dropping it like it was hot, showing off the round bubble in her jeans and winding against Lola like the two were lovers. It was a free show for the students leaving the school.

"Yo, y'all need to cut that shit out, before y'all start a riot and get niggas arrested out here," Cane said, walking up to his car with a smile.

"You know you like it, Cane," Lola replied.

"Not wit' you freakin' my little sister like this some strip club."

"So how about I give you your own private show then?"

"Yeah, we can talk later."

"You better leave my brother alone."

Cane got behind the wheel of his Benz and started the ignition. "Citi, c'mon, let's go!"

"Damn! Why you rushin' a bitch? Can't you see we having fun?"

"Then I'ma leave ya ass if you don't get in this car."

Citi sucked her teeth. "You need a ride home, Lola?"

"Nah, I'm not goin' home. 'Bout to get on this train and go to Queens Plaza Mall and look for some earrings."

Citi laughed. "You crazy. You ain't gonna find a pair like mines."

"Watch me."

"Just don't get your kleptomaniac ass locked up. I ain't got bail money for you," Citi joked.

"I ain't gonna need it."

After the two friends hugged, Citi jumped back into the passenger seat, and Cane sped off. The students walking to the bus stop glared at the siblings in the passing Benz; some couldn't hide their envy.

Citi rode around Queens with her brother. It was a pleasant winter day. Spring was almost around the corner, and Citi couldn't wait. She was dying to get back into her spring attire—her short skirts and open-toed shoes. She had plans to do it big for her birthday. The only thing on her mind was getting her car.

The siblings drove around Queens smoking Hawaiian skunk weed, which gave them a supreme high.

Citi asked Cane, "Yo, where you get this shit from?"

"My niggas from Far Rock got the illest connect. Shit is like straight off the banana boat."

"You need to get some more of it."

Citi was blasted. The extra potency in the Hawaiian marijuana increased the smell in the car. Citi rested her head against the headrest and closed her eyes. She felt like she was walking on the moon. The weed was making her horny, and the first male she thought about was Dante.

Cane pushed his car down Rockaway Boulevard, his eyes red from smoking. He almost ran every light on the busy boulevard and just missed hitting a parked car. It was a miracle that he didn't get into an accident.

Citi was in her own world. Her pussy tingled from smoking, and she was creaming in her panties. She wanted some dick. As soon as she got home, she was going to call Dante and spend some quality time with him at his crib.

Cane parked his Benz on the street and stumbled out of his car. "Yo, I'm fucked up right now, Citi," he said.

Citi laughed.

As the sun set, the temperature began to drop rapidly. The night was about to cover the sky. The two had had their fun for the day, and now they wanted to rest up and get fresh for the night.

Citi and Cane stepped off the elevator laughing, their high coming down gradually. They both had the munchies and planned on raiding the fridge like savages once they stepped into their apartment. Citi opened the door and was shocked to see her father home when she walked into the living room with Maino seated opposite him. He was never home during the late afternoon hours on weekdays.

The two men turned their heads up at Citi and Cane entering the room.

"Oh shit. What up, Pop?" Cane greeted with a mile-wide smile.

Curtis cut his eyes at his son. He was trying to convince Maino that he had nothing to do with Alonzo's murder, that he wasn't the one selling to Shot in Long Island and other crews in New Jersey.

Maino was ready to believe him, until Cane and Citi walked in. Both men immediately noticed the extra bling on Cane and Citi. Cane's watch stood out like a herpes sore on a celebrity's lip, and Citi's earrings sparkled. The children had forgotten to hide their lavish trinkets.

Curtis kept tabs on everything he'd bought his daughter, and he knew the diamond hoop earrings, the bracelet, and necklace didn't come from him.

Maino never mentioned the jewels. He kept silent but was simmering inside. The heavy jewelry Curtis' children sported was an indication to him that he had been lied to. He strongly felt that Curtis was playing him.

Maino stood up. "Yo, I'ma be out, Curtis," he said calmly. "I got some business to handle."

Curtis stood up also. He said his good-bye to Maino with a hug and a pound. "You good?" Curtis asked him.

"Yeah, I'm good," Maino said, his black eyes locked on Curtis. *You fuckin' bitch-ass nigga*. He left the apartment peacefully.

When the door shut behind Maino, Curtis spun around on his heels and stormed up to Cane and Citi. He marched behind Cane and roughly grabbed him by his shirt and then wrist. "What the fuck is this?" he yelled, holding up Cane's wrist and staring angrily at the Rolex watch.

"Pop, what up?"

Curtis glared at Citi, who stood dumbfounded in the kitchen. She'd realized her mistake too late.

"Where the fuck you get this watch from?" Curtis shouted.

"Yo, Pop—"

Before Cane could finish his sentence, Curtis struck him with a hard blow to his jaw, and Cane dropped to the floor.

Citi was taken aback. She stood rooted in the kitchen with fear.

Curtis marched over to her and stared at the bling around her neck. His disappointment with her was evident across his face.

"Daddy—"

Slap!

Curtis struck his daughter with an open hand, and she stumbled backwards wide-eyed, clutching the side of her face. She started to cry.

Curtis then turned to Cane and with brute force grabbed him by his shirt again and threw him against the kitchen wall. He punched him again. Then he pulled out his pistol and shoved it into Cane's face like they were strangers in the street.

"Cane, where you get the cash to buy all this shit? Huh? You fuckin' stealing from me?"

Cane scowled, shocked that Curtis came at him so violently. He didn't fight back, though. "I ain't take shit from you, Pop."

"Then where you get the money to afford this watch? I don't pay you that much to be blinging like this."

Cane refused to snitch on Citi. He braced himself for the impact. "You gonna shoot me, Pop?"

"How dare you steal from me, Cane? I give you everything!" Curtis shouted. "And you do this!"

"I didn't take shit from you!"

"Then who did?" Curtis yelled.

"I did, Daddy!" Citi yelled out.

Curtis, surprised to hear that Citi was the culprit, turned to glare at her. "You?"

"I'm sorry, Daddy. I didn't mean to get you so angry. I just took it."

Curtis sighed heavily. "How much?" he asked sharply.

"Forty thousand," Citi answered meekly.

"Forty thousand?" Curtis barked. "Forty fuckin' thousand, Citi? Are you out your damn mind?"

Tears flowed down Citi's face. It was hard for her to look her father in the eyes. She knew she'd fucked up, but she didn't think her father would get so abusive. He'd come at Cane like he didn't know him at all.

"Daddy, I'm so sorry. I didn't mean to. I was in your room and I just…"

"You shouldn't have been snooping around in my room, Citi."

"I know."

"Just be quiet, princess. I need to think right now," Curtis said.

Citi remained quiet. She dried her tears and wished she could turn back time. But the damage had already been done.

Curtis didn't tell his kids what they'd just done. He didn't want them to worry about his problems. Curtis knew it was risky having that amount of cash in his home, but Pandora's Box had already been opened, and it would take extreme force to close it, if that was even possible.

"Listen, I need y'all to be careful in these streets. You keep your eyes and ears open, and be alert to everyone and everything around you," Curtis stated. "And mind your sister, Cane."

"Why, Pop? What's goin' on wit' you?" Cane asked.

"Is this about Alonzo's death?" Citi asked.

Curtis shot a look at his daughter that said, *How you know about it?*

"I just heard about it on the streets," Citi told him.

"Look, I just want y'all to be careful out there," Curtis repeated firmly. Then he went into his bedroom and shut the door, leaving Cane and Citi standing there in bewilderment.

CHAPTER
13

The fuse had been lit. Maino was up in arms and fuming. Seeing Citi and Cane with the costly jewelry had sealed his friend's fate. He did some snooping around in the streets and reached out to a few sources—well-known goons in certain hoods —and came up with information that bothered him. He felt Curtis had played him by pushing bricks in Long Island, New Jersey, and Yonkers; places they'd never touched before. The fact that he was left out in the cold while Curtis continued to get rich didn't sit too well with him.

The past two days had Maino tripping out. *How could Curtis shit on me, leave me out of money like I'm some off-brand nigga?* Maino thought. Doing the unthinkable crossed his mind.

Maino sat at the edge of his woman's bed in a solemn mood, naked and hunched over in the dark, his elbows pressed into his knees, exposing the scars and tattoos across his skin. The words *Murder Inc* riddled with bullet holes showed diagonally on his chest in bold, inked letters that dripped blood. He clasped his fingers together, seething. His eyes sank into the darkness of his mind. Everything was changing, and changing fast. Friendship and trust were merely words.

His guns were on the floor next to his bare feet, his clothing scattered all over the bedroom. His sanity was becoming unfamiliar to him. Alonzo's death and Curtis' treachery were pushing him closer and closer to the edge. He was already a violent man, but now nothing but the thought of bloodshed consumed his mind.

"Baby, what's wrong?" Vicky asked, rising up to gaze at her lover hunched over at the edge of her bed.

"Just fuckin' go back to sleep!" he barked.

"Damn! Why the fuck you gotta snap at me like that? I was just concerned."

"Well, don't be. It ain't ya fuckin' business, Vicky. Go back to sleep."

"Fuck you, Maino!" she hissed. "See if I care for ya dumb ass again. You think you just can come over and fuck me then disrespect me in my own fuckin' crib?"

"Vicky, shut the fuck up, 'cuz right now, I'm really not in the fuckin' mood to hear ya shit."

"Whatever, muthafucka!" She sucked her teeth and rolled her eyes. She knew not to push it. "Fine. If you leave, just make sure you lock the fuckin' door behind you."

Maino ignored her. He continued to sit at the edge of her bed with an increasing hatred building inside of him and a scowl on his face. Murder was about to get heavy in Queens. It was the only way he knew how to take care of a problem. The pit bull was ready to break away from its chain and start attacking.

Maino stood up and grabbed his cell phone from off the nightstand. He went into the hallway butt naked to make an important call. He heard Vicky sigh as he walked out. She rolled her eyes at him and pulled the sheets over her head to try to get some sleep.

Donny picked up. "Yo, what's good?" he said, his voice booming through the phone.

"You in town?"

"Like the damn wind blowing, my nigga. What's good?"

"I got a job for us; somethin' major," Maino said.

"I'm listening."

"I ain't tryin' to talk about it right now, but it's some serious bread in it for you."

"That's all I need to hear. Ya talkin' my fuckin' language right now, my nigga. Just let me know who and when."

"The when is ASAP, and the who . . . I'll pull your coat to that when we link up."

"Definitely. One, my nigga."

"One."

Maino walked into the bedroom to find Vicky under the covers and out of his business. He assumed she had fallen back asleep. He stared at her thick frame lying under the sheets serenely and thought about putting in one last fuck before he made his exit. She could be a pain in the ass, but her pussy was always worth coming back for. Maino tricked on her with money and gifts, and in return, her place became a stash house for his drugs, guns, and illegal tender. Not too many people knew where Maino rested his head, and they didn't know Vicky's place of residence. Maino was always on the move. He couldn't relax too long at one place. He couldn't become predictable like Curtis, living in the projects with his family. Maino saw that as a weakness.

Maino stared at Vicky. She had been his ride-or-die bitch for years. Her attitude and mouth was always reckless, but at the end of the day, Maino trusted her to some extent. Twenty-five years old, she was just as gangsta and 'bout it as any OG in the hood. She'd put in much serious work in her hood—shooting guns, selling drugs, robberies, and willing to fight anybody—niggas or bitches. She'd helped him rob rival dealers and aided in stickups with him, setting niggas up with her beauty and sexuality to catch niggas slipping. She'd even helped Maino murder niggas.

Maino decided to make his exit. He'd had enough of Vicky for one night. Curtis had been on his mind, and the stress and anguish he was feeling was almost tearing him apart.

Maino and Donny sat parked in front of the project building smoking, both of them itching for action. Donny was a live wire. He didn't give a fuck who it was or what it was about. If it involved gunplay, murder, and money, he was always down. He was the only person Maino knew who would be bold enough to help make a jack-and-murder move on Curtis. When Maino told him about the setup and attack on Curtis, Donny didn't ask any questions. He just wanted to get it done with and collect what was owed to him. He'd never liked Curtis anyway, and they'd always had their differences in the past.

"Yo, where this nigga at?" Donny shouted impatiently.

"Be easy, nigga. He comin' through. Just do what I told you to do, and we gonna get that payday."

Donny nodded. He took one last pull from the cigarette and extinguished it into the ashtray. He pushed open the passenger door and jumped out, leaving Maino seated behind the wheel of his truck. Donny tucked his Glock 17 snugly into his waistband, his eyes wild with anticipation, and trotted toward the back of the project building, creeping like a ninja in the afternoon light.

The hood was quiet. The warm day was soothing after a cold winter. Maino watched the block carefully. His plan was coming along okay. He was about to shake up the hood and have those loyal to Curtis in fear and overwhelmed with anger. He felt no remorse. It was inevitable. It was time for Curtis to expire. The streets were talking, and the game was watching. His longtime amigo was getting rich on the streets while he was starving for scraps. He had no new drug connect yet, and no friends he could trust. It was either kill or be killed.

Maino knew today was Citi's birthday. She turned sixteen. He picked today to make his move, because he was her godfather. It was an excuse to come by the apartment. It was the perfect cover.

He sat and waited for a half hour. Curtis' car finally turned onto the block and he parked. Maino watched him from a distance. He gazed at Curtis stepping out of his Benz looking fresh from head to toe. He was alone. He carried some balloons, a birthday card, and a small box in his hand. Maino assumed it was more jewelry for Citi.

He surveyed Curtis crossing the street with gifts in hands. He made the call to Donny to let him know things were about to come into play.

When Curtis touched the sidewalk, Maino grabbed his gift for Citi from the backseat and got out his truck. He hurried in the direction of his longtime friend.

"Yo, Curtis," he called out, approaching him quickly.

Curtis turned. "What's up, Maino?"

"Damn, nigga! You lookin' fresh like always," Maino joked.

"It's a special day."

"I know. My goddaughter turns sixteen today," Maino said with a smile.

He held up his gift for Citi. It was draped in candy-printed wrapping paper, and it was the size of a shoebox.

"What you got there?"

"It's for Citi's eyes only."

"We spoiling that girl. You know that, right?" Curtis said.

"She only turns sixteen once."

Curtis chuckled. "Yeah, you right."

"So, what you got planned for the day?"

"I'm gonna spend the day with my princess. Take her shopping in the city, dinner at Sylvia's Restaurant in Harlem and shower her with gifts."

"That's what's up. It's hard to believe she's sixteen now."

"They're growing up fast."

"I know," Curtis responded.

"Yo, you goin' up to the apartment, right?"

"Yeah, what's up?"

"Just wanna talk to you. I need to pull your coat to somethin'."

"Like what?"

"I rather have this conversation wit' you upstairs."

"A'ight." Curtis looked hesitant.

"Yo, Curtis, you don't fuckin' trust me all of a sudden? What you thinkin' about?" Maino said meanly. He rested Citi's birthday gift on the concrete and pulled up his shirt to show Curtis he wasn't carrying a pistol.

"Yo, all that ain't necessary, Maino."

"You makin' a nigga feel really uneasy right now. I just wanna talk to you and give Citi her birthday gift. It ain't that difficult."

"Yeah, you right. It's just a lot has been going on lately."

"Yeah, I understand. A nigga gotta keep on his guard."

Maino followed behind Curtis. They stepped into the lobby and proceeded into the elevator. Both men were quiet. Stepping off onto the floor, Maino said, "How much did the little princes break your pockets for this year?"

"Man, you don't even want to know."

"She's gettin' more expensive every year, huh?"

"Yeah, this year, she wanted a car, a Honda Accord, nothing too flashy. I got it for her though."

"You bought that girl a car, Curtis?"

"After I put my hands on her a few weeks ago, I just felt guilty about it."

"You put your hands on her? For what?"

"It ain't anything."

"You sure?"

"When you have kids—You know what? Don't have kids. It's a fuckin' handful, man," Curtis said in a lighter mood.

Maino chuckled. "Yeah, I hear you."

Curtis stopped at his apartment door. He went through his pockets and removed his keys, exposing the butt of his pistol from underneath his spring jacket. Maino knew his partner would be armed. Curtis went everywhere strapped. Maino glanced at the stairway entrance. They had to move precisely. It was their one chance. One error and Curtis could end up killing them both.

When the key was in the lock and the apartment door was opened, Donny sprung into action. With his Glock 17 gripped tightly in his hand, he rushed out from the stairwell like a bat from hell and charged at the two men with his focus on Curtis.

Before Curtis could react, he was staring down the barrel of the large. He was forced into his apartment and pistol-whipped severely by Donny.

Curtis fell to the floor, blood trickling from his face. The gifts and balloons he carried were scattered across the living room floor. The blow to his head was hard. It had broken his skin and had him a little dazed.

Maino snatched the weapon from Curtis' waistband.

"What the fuck!" Curtis tried to get up but stumbled.

Maino yelled "Stay the fuck down, nigga!"

"Maino, you lost your fuckin' mind?" Curtis yelled.

"Nah, I didn't, but you did."

"You set me up. You do this me? What the fuck is wrong you?"

Donny charged over and cracked Curtis upside his head again with the butt of his pistol, and Curtis flew back against the floor.

"Yo, drag this muthafucka into the bedroom," Maino instructed Donny.

Donny nodded. He stuffed his gun into his waist and snatched Curtis up by his shirt and pulled him into the bedroom.

Maino walked over to the stereo system, turned it on, and raised the volume up a great deal. He didn't want any neighbors to hear the commotion. When Maino walked into the bedroom, Donny had Curtis face down on the bed, his gun placed to the back of his head.

The two men began duct-taping Curtis' wrists and legs and had him hog-tied on the bed.

"I'm gonna fuck you up, Maino!" Curtis screamed.

Maino snatched Curtis up by his shirt. "No. You know who's the one that gonna get fucked? It's you, muthafucka. And then you know what? I'ma fuck Citi next. Yeah, nigga, I'ma stick my monstrous dick into your little fuckin' princess. I'ma twist my dick into her and make her squeal like a pig."

"I'll kill you, muthafucka!" Curtis screamed. "You stay away from her!"

"Oh yeah, I'm gonna take my time in that sweet-sixteen piece of pussy. Fuck my little goddaughter six ways from Sunday."

"You better not fuckin' touch her, you muthafucka! I swear to God, I'm gonna fuckin' kill you for this, Maino."

Donny laughed.

"You're in no position to make threats, nigga. I'm running this show now. So bend the fuck over and take it like a man."

"Bitch-ass nigga!" Donny chimed.

"You know why we got you here tied up and lookin' fucked right now? Huh, nigga? You think I'm stupid? You thought I wasn't gonna put two and two together and find out you was the one responsible for killin' Alonzo? You tried to fuckin' play me, muthafucka! I knew he was fuckin' ya bitch. A little birdie told me that. And you had me goin' around the hood lookin' crazy when, all along, the muthafuckin' truth was staring me right in my fuckin' face."

Donny began trashing the bedroom, searching wildly for his payday. He ransacked the closet and went through the drawers, tossing clothing onto the floor and tearing apart the dresser with his bare hands.

"Where it at?" Donny shouted.

Curtis squirmed and fought, but his restraints were too tight. The more he fought, the more entangled in the web he became. His eyes leaked tears. He suddenly became full of regret. His mistakes and actions finally had caught up to him.

"Please, Maino, just do me, but leave Citi out of this. That's your goddaughter, for Christ sakes."

"Yeah, she is. I watched her grow up too. Watched that little girl come into her own, and now she lookin' right. But you know what? I'ma still fuck her 'cuz that body is lookin' right. And I'ma pop that cherry. Even though I doubt she's a fuckin' virgin. And your sons, I'll keep them niggas breathing, maybe have them come work for me, as long as they don't rise up and come against me. But if those little niggas do, I'ma body them muthafuckas and give you a damn reunion."

"Bingo!" Donny shouted. He pulled two duffel bags from underneath the bed. "We on it, Maino."

"We happy?" Maino asked.

Donny unzipped the bag, and the cash lit up his eyes. "Yeah, we definitely happy," he responded with a smile that stretched across his face.

Maino smiled heavily.

"You ain't gonna get away with this shit, muthafucka!" Curtis shouted.

"Nigga, I already have. Think about that shit when I fuck ya li'l princess in all three fuckin' holes." He pressed the gun to the back of Curtis' head.

"Fuck you, muthafucka! I'ma see you in hell real soon," Curtis screamed, his eyes flooded with tears, and his heart thumping like a drumbeat. The regret of not being able to protect his family became overwhelming for him.

"Tell the devil don't wait up for me," Maino replied.

Curtis braced himself. He closed his eyes and tightened up for the impact.

Guard the Throne

Maino squeezed the trigger without hesitation, and Curtis' brains and flesh splattered across the bed in a gruesome display. Maino stood over the body and smirked. *It needed to be done*, he thought to himself.

"Fuck that nigga!"

Maino closed his eyes for a moment. Over twenty years of friendship had just come to a violent end. The smoking gun in his hand had him feeling frozen for a moment.

"C'mon, nigga. We got what we came for." Donny gripped the duffel bag like it was surgically glued to his hand as he neared the exit.

Maino twisted his face and gazed at the pool of blood forming under the body. He snatched the second duffel bag and began to depart the crime scene. When he stepped into the living room, Citi's birthday gifts spread across the living room caught his attention. Maino arranged Citi's birthday things neatly on the table. It would be the last decent act for the family he once loved like his own. She would smile at the spread before finding the horrors awaiting her in her father's bedroom.

CHAPTER 14

"**C**iti, what the fuck happened? Who the fuck did this to Pop?" Cane screamed madly as the tears streamed down his grief-stricken face. The horror in Curtis' bedroom looked like a scene from a Freddy Krueger movie. His father's body was contorted and lying facedown on the blood-soaked bed.

The pistol in Cane's hand was loaded and cocked back, and he was marching around the bedroom screaming. He shook Citi aggressively and continued to shout at her. His little sister was in a trancelike state, her eyes bloodshot from crying. He had found her curled up in the corner near the body, crying hysterically. Now she was trembling.

Cane didn't know what to do. His instincts told him to immediately call Chris or Maino. He figured they would probably know how to handle things better. Seeing his father dead with two bullet holes in the back of his head sent a dark rage through Cane. He began to turn over furniture and break things in the room. "Muthafuckas!" he screamed. "I'ma murder and butcher whoever did this shit! I swear, it's fuckin' on! It's fuckin' on!"

Cane stormed in the direction of Citi again, screaming like crazy, "Citi, fuckin' talk to me! Who did this shit?"

"I don't fuckin' know!" she shouted back. Her hands and birthday attire were stained with Curtis' blood. She had thrown up numerous times. She couldn't move. Her body felt rooted to the floor, and her feet felt like they were cemented in concrete.

Guard the Throne

The tears continued to fall. The shock and hurt of her father murdered and gone continued to grow inside of her. It wasn't a nightmare. The realization of it all was displayed gruesomely in front of her.

Cane marched out the room, pistol in hand. He was itching to avenge his father's murder. He snatched the cell phone from his jacket pocket. Cane wasn't too fond of police parading in his home and being all up in his family's business, so he hadn't called 9-1-1 yet. He dialed Chris. When Chris answered, Cane became choked up. He didn't know how to break it to his older brother.

"Yo, Cane, what up?" Chris answered. "You calling me, right?"

"Yo, it's Pop," Cane said despondently.

"What about Pop?"

"Yo, you need to come home."

"Cane, you scaring me. What the fuck is goin' on? Talk to me, nigga!"

Cane quickly uttered, "He's dead!"

When Chris heard the news, he sent a piercing scream through the phone that sounded almost inhuman. Chris couldn't believe it. He raced home. It had to be a twisted joke. Their father was supposed to be untouchable. He was Curtis Byrne. He was supposed to live forever. He was too smart to become a murder victim.

Detectives and NYPD officers roamed through the Byrnes' apartment investigating the shocking crime scene, taking statements and pictures of the body. The detectives were very familiar with Curtis' legendary status in the neighborhood, since his rap sheet was an arm's length. The assumption was that the murder was drug-related. The fear with law enforcement was that a drug war might be brewing.

The news of the murder started to spread through the hood like wildfire, some taking the death harder than others.

Cane and the other teens were fuming over the way cops and detectives stampeded through their home and swamped them with question after question. Cane was ready to explode on the NYPD. He hated cops. He hated how they'd ransacked their rooms looking for any kind of evidence. They were the victims, but the cops treated them like suspects.

The drugs, the cash, and the guns were all gone. Chris had made Cane get rid of every gun in the house and dump any drug paraphernalia in a faraway trash bin. When the officers went to the apartment, it was free of any criminal evidence.

The siblings watched the coroners place their father into a body bag and carry him out of the apartment.

Citi started to sob again. Her grief and tears were uncontrollable. "Noooo! They can't take him. Get away from him! Nooo, he can't go!" Citi screamed. She went charging at the coroners.

A few cops dived in to grab her, and there was a scuffle. Citi threw punches and tried biting a few police. She wanted to go with her father.

"Yo, get the fuck off my sister like that!" Cane yelled at the cops trying to restrain her.

"Calm down, son," a detective said.

"Yo, I ain't your fuckin' son."

A serious situation was about to ensue between the children and police. Ms. Eloise decided to intervene. She was able to calm Citi and the storm brewing with Cane. She took hold of the grieving child and held her. Citi cried in Ms. Eloise's arms. She bawled like a baby. She slumped toward the ground while still in Ms. Eloise's embrace, her crying echoing out into the hallway.

"It'll be okay, chile, it'll be okay. Just let it out. Let it all out," Ms. Eloise said calmly in Citi's ear, holding her like a mother.

Cane and Chris stood watching, tears trickling down their faces. The only thing the brothers thought about was revenge. Chris learned that there wasn't any forced entry into the apartment, so he figured his father had to know his assailants. While Cane was ready to shoot at the world, Chris was ready to do his own investigation.

Not only did cops swoop into the children's lives, but Child Services was now a threat to them. With Curtis dead, they no longer had a parental figure around. Everyone was a minor, since Chris wouldn't turn eighteen for a few months. He had to brainstorm. When detectives began asking questions about a parental figure, he told them about their mother in Harlem. He gave the detectives her number, and then Ms. Eloise confirmed their story. Chris knew it would buy some time until he could think of something solid to keep the State from interfering with his family's structure. He wasn't about to let Child Services separate him from his brother and sister.

After the police, detectives, and CSU (Crime Scene Unit) dispersed, Cane and Chris started to clean up the apartment while Citi was next door at Ms. Eloise's. Their father's bedroom door remained shut because they didn't want to see or enter that room.

"Yo, you call Maino?" Cane asked.

"Yeah, he's coming around. He just wants the police gone before he shows up," Chris said. "I don't blame him."

"Yo, I'ma be on the streets every day fuckin' asking questions, fo' real, wit' my gun, and I ain't playing."

"We can't stay here," Chris said.

"Why the fuck not?"

"Look at this shit, man. It's fucked up here, and police gonna be all in our business. And the State, they gonna come snooping around, asking questions about us and our parental guidance. I'm not trying to go through that shit."

"What about Citi?" Cane asked.

"She can stay with Ms. Eloise. I'm sure she ain't gonna have a problem with that."

Chris' cell phone rang. He quickly answered, "Yo."

"It's Maino. Come talk to me outside. I'm in my truck."

"All right." He hung up and looked at Cane. "Maino's outside."

"It's about fuckin' time. Let's go holla at him. See what he knows." Cane marched toward the front door fervently. Chris followed behind him. They exited the lobby and saw Maino's truck parked by the curb.

Maino stepped from behind the steering wheel puffing a cigarette. He was calm and collected. He fixed his attention on Chris and Cane approaching him. His pistol was hidden away in his waistband, and his guard was on high. Maino knew Chris would be the cool one. But Cane was unpredictable.

Maino approached them with open arms and giving his condolences. He hugged Chris and then Cane. "Yo, y'all all right?" he asked, pretending to be sincere.

"We need to find out who did this shit, Maino," Chris said.

"I got my peoples on it right now as we speak. We gonna find these muthafuckas, I promise you that," Maino said with conviction.

Chris wiped the tears away from his eyes again.

"Where's Citi?" Maino asked.

"She's upstairs with Ms. Eloise," Chris replied.

"How she holdin' up?"

"She fucked-up, man. How you think she holdin' up? It's fuckin' wit' all of us," Cane chimed.

"I know this shit is hard . . . Alonzo, now Curtis. Yo, I want y'all to keep alert out there. This shit ain't right, but we gonna make it right," Maino said. He took another pull from his cigarette. He exhaled, looking at the brothers intensely. "How y'all holdin' up wit' expenses?"

"Niggas took it all, cleaned us out," Chris replied.

Maino shook his head. "No disrespect, but your father fucked up."

"What the fuck you talkin' about, Maino?" Cane exclaimed.

"I mean, what the fuck was he thinkin', for one, not setting up some kind of insurance policy for his kids, and keepin' his stash where he lay his head? I know Curtis was smarter than that. He became a stickup man's paradise."

"We ain't tryin' to hear this shit right now," Cane said. "What the fuck is your point?"

"I was just speaking. But, look, I'm gonna step in and help pay for some of his funeral expenses. But y'all little niggas gotta step up now and pull y'all own weight. I'm gonna help out how I can."

"We appreciate that, Maino," Chris said.

Maino took a few more pulls and flicked his cigarette. He warned the brothers to watch their backs in the streets. "Yo, if y'all need anything, don't hesitate to give me a call."

He climbed into his truck and drove away, leaving Chris and Cane standing at the curve like two pups.

CHAPTER 15

Queens started to buzz with the news of Curtis' murder. The brutal murder of a drug kingpin on his daughter's birthday had made the evening news and was the headline on several newspapers. Those loyal to Curtis wanted war, but the enemy was unseen. The Queens hood was becoming uneasy with tension. The streets were on alert, and police doubled their patrol from corner to corner.

Citi took her father's death really hard. She sat for hours alone in Ms. Eloise's apartment. It was hard for her to eat and sleep. She didn't want to do anything and would stare out the window for hours on end. Spring weather brought about the blossoming of the flowers and trees, and warm air, but she was trapped in a brutal winter storm without shelter.

The nightmares were recurring. She couldn't erase the brutal image of her father's murder scene from her mind. Some nights, she would wake up screaming and find herself in a cold sweat. It would take hours for Ms. Eloise to calm her down. The tears were endless, and the pain was eternal.

His funeral was in several days. Citi made no effort to help with the arrangements. Ms. Eloise and Chris handled everything. The only thing she did was mope and cry. Deep inside, she felt at fault. She stole from her father, and it bothered her that the forty grand she took probably played a heavy role in why he was murdered.

Citi hated herself. She wanted to die too. She wanted them to bury her with Curtis. She sulked in the bedroom next door and hid her pain under pillows and sheets. She would wail for hours. Her spoiled life was transformed into an absorbing daze of anguish and tears that pooled against the pillow she cried on.

There was a fast knock at the door. She lay still under the sheets in a fetal position like she was in a cocoon.

The bedroom door opened slowly. Ms. Eloise, clad in her housecoat and house slippers, craned her head inside the room and gazed at the grieving girl. She sighed heavily, entering the bedroom with a mug of hot chocolate in her hand.

She glided toward Citi and sat at the edge of the bed. The raised lump underneath the sheets was the only indication that Citi was in the room.

"Citi, here's a cup of hot chocolate. I know it's your favorite."

No response from Citi.

"I loved him too, chile. He was a good man."

She could hear Citi sobbing underneath the covers. Ms. Eloise placed the mug of hot chocolate on the nightstand. She leaned forward and lightly touched the lump underneath the sheets.

Ms. Eloise felt the pain too. She had known Curtis for years. He was like a son to her.

"I wish I could make the pain go away, chile, but it won't happen overnight. I know the feeling. I remember when I lost Henry fifteen years ago. One day he's in my world, making me smile and laugh, and loving me every single day, and then next, he's gone. I miss him. Oh, you were just born when Henry passed. You would have loved him." Ms. Eloise sighed heavily once more. "One life gone while another life received—it's the way things work. It's the way God wants it. And we can't change it, but we can only accept it and have faith in Him."

"Why him? Why he had to die? God didn't take him away from me; some asshole with a gun took away my daddy," Citi cried.

It was a compelling statement.

"It's the world we live in, unfortunately," Ms. Eloise sadly replied.

"I hate this world! I hate everything about it. I just wanna die wit' him," Cit exclaimed.

"Citi, that's nonsense talking. You be strong and continue to be strong. Curtis wouldn't want to see you like this. You're his princess, and you continue like it."

Citi sobbed. "I miss him already, Ms. Eloise."

"I know you do. I miss him too."

Silence fell upon them in the room. Citi could still be heard sobbing beneath the sheets. She twisted and turned in the bed, still wrapped up in the fetal position and soaking the pillow with her tears.

"I know you want some time alone, but I'm here if you need anything. I'm family and will always be family to you and your brothers. Remember this, chile, time doesn't heal all wounds. It's what you do with that time that will heal you," Ms. Eloise stated. "I have some smothered pork chops and macaroni in the kitchen, along with my famous chocolate cake, if you get hungry."

Citi didn't respond.

Ms. Eloise stood up and looked down at the bed. She said a silent prayer, and then she slowly removed herself from the bedroom, shutting the door behind her. She wanted to give Citi her time alone.

The pews at Mt. Zion Baptist Church on Linden Boulevard was overflowing with mourners from the projects and the streets. The aisles were teeming with people ready to view Curtis' body, which was laid to rest in a Wellington honey walnut casket. He was dressed in a gray three-piece Armani button-down suit with a stylish blue tie, along with his jewelry and wing-tip shoes. Numerous sympathy flowers, framed pictures of Curtis when he was young and of his age, funeral wreaths, and cross tributes adorned the casket.

The funeral was a costly $16,000. The kids didn't have that kind of money lying around to bury their father in the style he would've wanted to go out in, so they were forced into selling off their possessions. The flat-screens in the house were pawned off first, along with a few pieces of jewelry, clothing, and anything else of value to sell. After selling off everything they could, the siblings were still short. The rest of the money came from handouts and favors.

Maino only dropped off five grand to help with the funeral expenses, and he rarely came around. While the children were struggling to bury Curtis, he was getting rich on the streets. He had suggested that they call up a few of Curtis' old flings and have them come up with the rest. Curtis had put enough money in a few bitches' pockets and treated them to shopping sprees and gifts, and it was only fair that they helped put him to rest.

It was a daunting task. Victoria, Lesley, and a busty female named Cindy Mae weren't easy to persuade. They were all hurt over Curtis' death, but simply offered to help when Chris damn near begged them to. But with stipulations. They didn't want any other bitch at Curtis' funeral. It was an impossible demand, but Chris assured each girl that they would be the only ones there, sitting in the front pew with the family and riding in the limo to the burial site with the family.

The electric organ played for the teary-eyed mourners. The gangsters and thugs came out in droves, each one ready to pay respects to the deceased, before he was laid to rest in Bayside Cemetery. The line to view the body stretched out to the foyer, and the crowd continued to grow, inside and outside of the church.

Chris and Cane sat silently in the front pew. The brothers were dressed immaculately in matching black Armani suits and polished shoes. They wanted to represent their father until the end. They had fallen on hard times but refused to show it at their father's funeral. Cane remained stone-faced, cracking his knuckles repeatedly, disguising his pain, while Chris wiped the few tears trickling down his cheeks.

Citi sat next to her brothers wearing a sheath dress and four-inch heels, her eyes saturated with tears. It was hard for Citi to see her father lying there, so close to her and not expecting him to get up and console her.

The mortician did a wonderful job with the body. Curtis looked like himself. He didn't look like a plastic doll and didn't appear to be bloated. It seemed that he was just resting comfortably.

Ms. Eloise sat next to Citi and held her hand throughout the service. She wiped a few tears from her own eyes too. She'd watched him grow up, and then watched his children grow up too. It felt like her son was lying in the casket. It felt like Henry's death all over again. The days that lay ahead for the family—his children—would be difficult.

Maino stood in the back of the church with a few of his goons. He was looking suave and dressed in a dark gray YSL suit and handmade David Chu bespoke Italian wing-tips, jewelry on his wrist and around his neck, and a diamond pinky ring on his finger. His expression was stone cold. He didn't attempt to walk toward the front to view the body. He remained flanked by his two goons and didn't plan on staying long to hear the service. He only came to show respect.

The ladies in the church were all looking marvelous. Some were dressed like they were ready to hit the club afterward, clad in skimpy skirts, skin-tight black jeans, high heels, low-cut blouses, and long hair whisking all over the place.

But the three women who showed up outdoing themselves were Curtis' exes, Victoria, Cindy Mae, and Lesley. They each strutted down the aisles at different intervals clad in revealing black funeral attire, legs showing, heels click-clacking, breasts pushed up, and dresses highlighting their striking curves. And the showstopper—each lady decided to get

Curtis' name tattooed somewhere on their bodies. Lesley had gotten his name tattooed in script on her right arm. Cindy Mae had a tattoo across the back of her neck in red ink outlined with hearts and flowers. And Victoria had a tattoo in bold italic across her left breast: *Love you Curtis, your ride or die bitch forever.*

Folks at the funeral couldn't believe what they were witnessing. Citi glared over at Victoria and Cindy Mae and had the urge to scratch their eyes out, but Ms. Eloise held her down by her hand and continued to console the hurt child.

The eye-rolling, snide remarks, crying, and screaming started to begin once the pastor started to say the eulogy. The funeral was becoming dramatic. The packed house fell silent, with only the occasional sniffling and emotional outbreak from a mourner.

The pastor said to the large gathering, "This is not the end for us. It is only the beginning . . . because there is a special place, a home . . . a wonderful and marvelous home for us that is far away from here when we pass on and depart from here. Curtis, he was loved, and he will continue to be loved and remembered. Some of us might get there sooner and some of us later, but thank God, we will get there!" the pastor shouted. "We will get there!"

"Amen!" a few people from the crowd shouted.

The pastor had uplifted the mourners with his words. Some stood up and hollered.

Citi and her brothers remained unmoved. Citi just sat there with her head lowered and her eyes closed. Cane had revenge on his mind, and Chris was worried about their financial woes. It was the first time in their lives that money was scarce.

The pastor gazed at the sea of faces. "I know some of y'all would like to say a few words today, so I ask, does anyone want to come up and speak their piece?"

Victoria was ready to jump up and proclaim her love for Curtis at the podium, but before she could leap from her seat, a woman from the back shouted, "I would like to say a few words about my husband."

People instantly turned their attention to the voice.

The crowd parted as Ashanti paraded herself down the jammed aisle. She was the center of attention, dressed gloriously in a black ruched top and skirt—sleek, yet undeniably feminine. Her black six-inch heels looked like they were lifting her to the church's ceiling, and her flowing black hair fell around her shoulders like a soft cloud. She was the spitting image of Citi, but only older-looking.

Ashanti cut her eyes at Curtis' whores, who sat nestled amongst the people in the pews. Her eyes rested on Citi and her two sons. She hadn't seen her children in years. Her sons were handsome, and her daughter was so beautiful.

Ashanti smiled at them, but Citi wasn't having it. She glared at her mother with disdain and disgust. Chris and Cane remained nonchalant.

Ashanti stepped up to the podium and stared at the people. She had their undivided attention. The pastor nodded and stepped away. She was quiet for a moment, collecting her thoughts and looking at the ladies who swore they were Curtis' main lady. She wanted to show and prove she was Curtis' wife—the woman he truly loved. She smirked at Victoria, making the woman uncomfortable in her seat. She had a few choice words for them other bitches, but decided to save them for later.

Ashanti started her speech with, "I loved my husband very much, and I still do. We always had something special from the first time we met, until his passing. I loved him dearly, and he loved me just the same. Even though we were separated, Curtis made it his business to come visit me in Harlem on a weekly basis, and we definitely had some special times together." She smiled at the thought of it then she let out a deep sigh. "Nobody could compare to Curtis. He was so handsome, and his style was remarkable. My boo was a trendsetter. When I first laid eyes on him, I fell in love with him. He used to make me smile and laugh. And, I swear, whoever took that away from me, from us, they're gonna pay. The streets talk, and his murderers will get dealt with, I promise you that."

"They sure will!" someone screamed from the pews.

Ashanti wiped away the tears that trickled down her pretty face. She then went on to say, "I loved him. He truly understood me. He did. And he gave me four magnificent things that he never gave another woman— three beautiful children and his last name. I was, and I am still a Byrne."

Ashanti's eyes cut toward Victoria and then to the other two whores, who shifted uncomfortably in their seats as she spoke. She smirked at them again.

Maino couldn't take the eulogy any longer and decided to made a speedy exit with his goons. He didn't bother to say good-byes to anyone or give his condolences to the family. There was business to take care of out in the streets, and he couldn't waste his day around a grieving widow and kids. He felt no remorse for murdering Curtis. Business was business. If Ashanti had the balls to interfere with his business and throw out accusations, then he wouldn't hesitate to lay the bitch down too.

Ashanti stepped from behind the podium and walked off the platform. She stared at her three children with soft eyes. Chris and Cane looked at their mother with a deadpan gaze. It was awkward for them, seeing Ashanti after so many years of her being out of their lives.

Citi's disdain and hatred for her mother was evident. She didn't hide it, not on her face or in her actions. She fought the urge to yell out, *Fuck you, bitch! Why are you here? We don't want you here!*

Ms. Eloise gripped Citi's hand tightly. She understood the child's pain and didn't want an outburst at the funeral.

Ashanti looked at her children, but she didn't make an attempt to say anything to them. She felt she'd said what she had to say when she was on the platform, and now wasn't the time to mend any pain that she had caused her kids. She turned on her heels and walked out the church. She needed a cigarette. She ran into Maino in the foyer, where the two locked eyes for a moment.

Maino gave her a head nod. "You okay?" he asked.

Ashanti carried a scowl. "I could be doing much better, but I'm always gonna be okay," she replied matter-of-factly.

"It's been a long time."

"Yes, it has."

"We should link up and talk."

Ashanti chuckled at his suggestion. "Are you really trying to hit on me at my husband's funeral? Are you serious?"

"I'm just making small talk, Ashanti. We go way back."

"And that don't mean a damn thing to me." Ashanti marched out the foyer.

Maino glared at her, hoping she wasn't going to be a future problem.

Inside the church, Citi continued to cry against Ms. Eloise's shoulder, and the sons sat perfectly still, while half a dozen people stepped up to the podium to say something pleasant about Curtis and share personal memories they had of him.

The following day, the siblings, along with two-dozen mourners, stood under the rapidly graying sky and watched the groundskeepers place Curtis' solid honey-walnut wood casket slowly into the ground. The children's moods matched the overcast sky. Their lives would forever be changed.

CHAPTER 16

Cane drove around aimlessly for hours, rap music blaring inside his Benz and his mind drifting to the problems his family was enduring. With no steady income coming in, their posh lifestyle was quickly fading. The Benz and the watch Cane was wearing were the only valuable assets he had left to flaunt. Everything in their apartment was either pawned or sold off to keep them above water.

Also, Maino wasn't coming around to check on them, and he wasn't providing protection like he'd vowed to do. The streets figured it was a separation from the family. That left the brothers exposed to their enemies, and Citi vulnerable to the perverts who'd been lusting after her for a long time.

Cane made turn after turn on the dark Queens streets, his rage displayed on his face. He gripped the steering wheel tightly with a fist and was leaned back in the seat. The only thing he could think about and wanted to think about was revenge.

He came to a stop at a red light on Merrick and Farmers Boulevards. The traffic was sparse at the midnight hour, and the barren streets looked like a ghost town. A warm breeze blew through his car. Cane took a pull from a Newport and exhaled. He sat reclined in his seat, gangsta-lean style, sitting slung low and tilted toward the passenger seat. His eyes narrowed at the road ahead of him. Just like his future, things looked empty and dark.

His cell phone buzzed in the passenger seat. He glanced at who was calling and decided to ignore the call. It was Chris. Cane wanted to be alone. They had been bickering with each other for the past week over money, drugs, and their future. Cane just needed to escape it all. He'd stayed over a few bitches' cribs, fucking his brains out and getting lifted. There was no need for his family to worry about him. He was a grown thug who knew how to handle himself.

Before the red light changed to green, a dark-colored Charger came to a stop beside his Benz. Two young men in their early twenties were in the car. Cane glanced at them but paid them no attention. The young men nodded to Lil' Wayne blaring from the car speakers, their interest turned away from Cane.

The light changed green, and Cane sped off. He glanced at the fuel gauge and saw he was running low on gas. He pulled into the nearest gas station on Merrick and drove closer to the gas pump. He took one more drag from the cigarette and dowsed it into the ashtray in the center console.

He stepped out of his car and strode toward the attendant, who sat in the gas booth reading a book. "Yo, let me get twenty dollars on pump six," he announced. He slid the twenty-dollar bill underneath the small opening in the partition and walked off.

He began fueling up his Benz. Twenty dollars wasn't much when it came to gassing up the pricy car, but he couldn't afford to fill up the tank. It was the first time the kids had ever been on a budget. Cane gripped the nozzle and watched the illuminated digital numbers rapidly add up on the tiny screen on the gas pump. Just then he heard his cell phone ringing in the passenger seat. It was his sister calling.

Cane's mind drifted into a momentarily stupor. He had just come from Daisy's place, a jump-off he'd met on the avenue a few weeks back. It was where he was resting his head from time to time. They'd met when things with the family were still good, when Cane was able to trick on her every day and shower with money and gifts. In return, she broke him off a piece of that sweet pussy. She was older than him, mid-twenties, and her cunt was like the sunshine. She was Cane's cougar. The soon-to-be seventeen-year-old didn't know what hit him.

When Cane gripped the gas nozzle to remove it from the tank, the same Dodge Charger he'd seen earlier at the light zipped into the gas station. Cane turned on his heels and fixed his eyes on the car, his street sense on attentive. His .38 lay under the driver's seat, far from his reach.

The driver and passenger stepped out the Charger looking intensely at Cane, who quickly placed the nozzle back on the pump. Before he could grip the handle to the driver's door and reach for his gun, both men took off into a full sprint at him.

The driver reached under his shirt and pulled a 9mm from his waistband. "Don't make this shit hard on yourself, nigga! Just give up the watch and keys to the Benz," the driver shouted.

"Y'all niggas know who the fuck I am?"

"A dead nigga, muthafucka!"

Cane poised into a fighting stance and balled his fists. He charged forward recklessly, not caring that the man had a gun. He was ready to die for his. No one was going to punk or disrespect him. The man raised and fired his 9mm, but the gun jammed. Cane took full advantage of the situation. He leaped off his feet and came at the two stickup men like a bull. His fist landed upside the man's head, the one clutching the gun, with a solid thump, staggering him and causing him to drop the gun. Cane continued to punish him with blows.

The second attacker swung at Cane with a baseball bat. Cane moved with blinding speed and ducked then moved sideways from the oncoming attack. He then lunged forward and slammed a brutal combination of blows to the second attacker's body and head, and the man collapsed to the pavement. But Cane showed him no mercy. He kicked the man in his side, crushing his ribs with the tip of his boot and caving in his chest with the heel.

"Y'all niggas tryin' to rob me? Y'all niggas fuckin' crazy? You know who the fuck I am?" he screamed.

Cane suddenly felt a powerful blow to his back that thrust him forward, and a sharp pain rocketed through his body. There was another hit to his back that made him slam against the car. The third hit from the baseball bat dropped him to his knees, and he doubled over on the concrete.

"Yeah, what now, muthafucka? I told you not to make it hard on yourself," the attacker shouted, standing over Cane with the bloody baseball bat.

In a daze from the hit, his face coated with blood, Cane couldn't move.

The second man picked himself up from the ground. He was holding his side and scowling at Cane. He walked over to Cane and started to land brutal kicks on him. "Fuck you, nigga!" he shouted.

The men pistol-whipped him and then snatched the watch off his wrist and removed his car keys from his pocket, while he lay slumped on the ground, barely able to move. Next thing he knew, his Benz was speeding out of the gas station.

The gas station attendant was on the phone dialing 9-1-1, but Cane didn't want to deal with any police. He mustered the strength to pick himself up. He slowly scraped himself off the ground and limped away from the gas station, his face trickling with blood and bumpy with bruises.

He reached the nearest pay phone and dialed home, and Chris picked up the call.

"Chris, come get me," he said faintly into the phone. "I need you, man."

"Cane, where you at? What happened?"

Cane, hurting from the pain, was silent for a moment.

"Nigga, talk to me," Chris shouted.

Cane clutched his side and hunched over. "They fucked me up bad, man. I'm at a pay phone on Merrick, near Farmers."

"Yo, hang tight, nigga. I'm on my way right now." Chris hung up.

Cane dropped on his ass and rested his back against a brick wall and waited for his brother to show up.

Chris arrived twenty minutes later and found Cane sprawled out across the boulevard like he was homeless. He stopped short at the curb and sprang from his car to rush to his brother's aid.

"Cane, get up! What happened? Nigga, who the fuck did this to you?"

"Just get me the fuck outta here and take me home," Cane replied weakly.

Chris gripped his brother by the arm and slowly picked him off the ground. Cane used his brother for support, staggering in Chris' hold toward the car. His legs felt like wet noodles, and his back felt like it was broken.

Chris helped him into the backseat, and Cane lay on his side. Cane's blood-covered face disturbed Chris. He peered at his little brother.

"What the fuck!" Chris muttered.

"J-just get me home," Cane stammered.

Chris raced back to the apartment with Cane squirming from the pain in the backseat. He refused to go to the hospital. He kept chanting, "I'm okay. I'm good."

"Nigga, you need a doctor."

"I just need to get the fuck home."

Chris helped Cane into the apartment, Cane's arm slung over his older brother and barely able to move.

Citi's eyes widened with terror, seeing her brother's condition. "Oh my God! What the fuck happened to you?" she cried out.

"I'm okay, Citi. Just relax." Cane dropped on the couch, relieved to be at home and around family.

"You're not okay. Look at you! Who did this to you?"

"Niggas that will be dead really fuckin' soon," Cane replied cynically.

Citi quickly tended to her brother's wounds. She cleaned the blood from his face and called Ms. Eloise, a retired nurse. Ms. Eloise rushed over after the phone call and aided Cane methodically. Fortunately, he had no broken bones and no serious injures—only some bruises and cuts that she would be able to bandage.

Cane downed a fifth of Hennessy while Ms. Eloise patched him up, telling him he needed some rest.

Citi couldn't hold back the tears. Her brother's battered condition struck her, and she couldn't stand for it any longer. Their family was meant to be impervious to this type of nonsense. These types of things didn't happen to the Byrnes. They were always respected, and their family's reputation always preceded them. Now life for them was becoming a series of bumps and bruises.

Citi spun on her heels and went into her bedroom and slammed the door behind her. She lay across her bed curled into a fetal position and tried to find that happy place in her head, but the darkness surrounding her life was too overwhelming.

▲

Cit sat in her father's bedroom and looked around. It was still. The room was picked clean of any valuables and trinkets. His clothing was either stolen or sold off, his many stylish coats traded away to pay off debts, and his jewelry pawned to keep food in their mouths.

The past two months had been draining and trying for the family. Between the eviction notice placed on their door and lack of income, Citi was embarrassed beyond belief. She was forced to try and take things into her own hands. She felt determined to keep the Byrne name strong on the streets, but she didn't have an solid plan yet.

Guard the Throne

Sitting in Curtis' room brought some comfort to Citi. She could still see his smile and hear his voice booming in her ear. The streets may have snatched him away in the physical world, but spiritually, she could still feel him everywhere.

She stood up from his bed and walked toward the mirror. She gazed at her beauty for a moment and then closed her eyes to capture the good times she had in the room. She was and would always be daddy's little girl. His princess.

Everything had turned into shit the past two months. Cane had recovered quickly from his injuries, but was still lying about the apartment all day looking defeated. Chris seemed to have lost his leadership capabilities. He mostly smoked and got high all day and fucked bitches. They hadn't seen their mother since the funeral. The brothers had gotten into selling weed, moving grams and dime bags on the streets, but it was small money, and didn't come close to what they were used to.

Citi witnessed the deterioration of her family day by day. She'd dropped out of school. She was too ashamed to be seen in the hallways in her troubling condition. Her haters would marvel and snicker at her downfall. Her wardrobe had lessened, and her jewelry became a memory, so she'd decided it was best to not attend school at all.

She continued to gaze in the dresser mirror. She clenched her fists and saw a pretty girl transforming into her worst nightmare—a broke bitch. She was one step away from the Salvation Army and being homeless. The longer she stared at her defeated image, the angrier she became.

Citi was ashamed to see their father's legacy go down the drain. Curtis had raised them to be hustlers and live a certain lifestyle. She was used to nice things, and Chris was supposed to become the new man of the house. He was supposed to step up in the game and help maintain their lifestyle. The only thing her brothers did was mope around all day, get high, and sell weed.

Citi stormed out of her father's bedroom and went into the living room to find Cane lounging on the couch with a couple of local hoods, T-Black and Mellow. Cane had a joint between his lips. Empty liquor bottles, dirty laundry, food wrappings, and ashtrays filled with blunt guts and extinguished cigarettes were scattered throughout the living room. The place was a pigpen.

"What the fuck is this? What's y'all's problem?" Citi screamed, startling everyone in the room. "It ain't supposed to be like this!"

"Citi, why you buggin'?" Cane asked.

"'Cuz shit is fucked up around here!"

The sudden commotion caused Chris to come out his bedroom. He was shirtless and seemed to have been busy in his room with someone of the opposite sex.

"What the fuck is your problem, Citi? Why you screaming for?" Cane spat.

Citi knocked the bottles off the table, causing a scene among the guests in her home. "This is my fuckin' problem. Look around—We have nothing anymore."

"Citi, you trippin' right now," Chris told her. "Why don't you go cool off in your room?"

"Don't tell me to cool off!"

"You're embarrassing yourself right now in front of company."

"I don't give a fuck who in here. Fuck company!"

Chris stepped into the living room. Barefoot and shirtless, he gazed at his baby sister and said, "You need to really calm down and chill."

Citi glared at her brother. "We need to talk. Everyone, get the fuck out my house!"

No one attempted to budge. They didn't take Citi seriously.

"Yo, y'all niggas ain't gotta go nowhere," Cane said.

"Oh, it's like that?"

"Yeah, it's like that. You don't run things around here, Citi," Cane returned sharply.

Chris stood there as the two bickered.

"I got company, Citi, so you need to keep quiet in here," Chris said.

Citi was taken aback when Dana emerged from Chris' bedroom in her panties and bra. Ever since Curtis' funeral, Dana had distanced herself from Citi. She stopped coming around and calling. When Citi needed her most, Dana wasn't there, telling Citi that she was a fake bitch. Citi didn't have the funds or the means any longer, so Dana jumped on someone else's bandwagon. She'd heard that Dana and Meeka were close now. Citi couldn't stand Meeka. But seeing Dana fuck her brother made her want to puke.

"You fuckin' that bitch, Chris?" Citi was ready to scratch her eyes out.

Dana smirked.

"She my business now, Citi," Chris replied.

"Shit is goin' to hell around here, and you have the audacity to bring that fake bitch into our crib after she done dissed me?"

"Who you callin' a fake bitch?"

"You, bitch! I thought you were my friend."

"Fuck you, Citi! You always thought you were better than everyone else!"

"What, bitch!" Citi rushed forward, ready for a confrontation.

Cane and his two goons became excited over the fight. They were all high and tipsy.

Chris stepped in between the two girls, pushing them back.

"I just wanna talk to you and Cane, Chris, and I can't even get that right now, 'cuz you choose to put that bitch and these lame-ass niggas first, before your baby sister," Citi said loudly. "You chose some pussy over your sister. Fuck that bitch!"

Chris didn't respond. He only matched Citi's hard stare at him.

"Fuck it. Fine then. I'ma get my fuckin' respect," Citi said, marching into her father's room.

Everyone thought the beef was over, but the fuse had just been lit. Citi pulled open the top drawer in her father's room and grabbed a .45 that was hidden inside. She checked the clip, cocked it back, and marched right back into the living room with the gun in her hand, her eyes red with anger and rage.

Seeing the gun, everyone went into panic.

"Yo, Citi, what the fuck!" Cane shouted.

"Yo, shorty, chill," Mellow shouted, leaping from the couch in a panic.

Citi, her arm outstretched, aimed it at everyone, darting it around the room wildly. "If you ain't fuckin' family in here, then get the fuck out my crib!" she shouted.

"Yo, what is your fuckin' problem?" Chris spat.

"I wanna talk to my fuckin' brothers without anyone around in our business."

T-Black and Mellow rushed from the apartment, sobering quickly from their high.

Dana, still in her underwear, hurried toward Chris' bedroom to retrieve her clothing, but Citi told her, "Nah, bitch, you leave just like that. Show the building the ho that you are."

"Citi, is you serious?" Dana asked.

Citi aimed the gun at her head. "I'll fuckin' drop your triflin' ass right now, bitch! I ain't got shit else to lose."

Dana took the threat seriously and ran out the apartment in her underwear.

"Citi, you done lost your fuckin' mind," Chris barked.

"I lost my mind? Are you serious? Look at us—look at this place. What's wrong wit' y'all?" she screamed. "You think Daddy would want to see us living like this? Huh? He would be so fuckin' ashamed to see what has happened to us. This ain't right!" Tears streamed down her face.

"We tryin', sis," Chris chimed. "Shit is dead out here in these streets. Niggas ain't tryin' to get up wit' us like that. When Pop was alive, it was different."

"Then we go out there and do our own shit."

Chris said, "You tryin' to start a war wit' rival crews. We ain't got the muscles or paper for that."

"I'm ready to live again," Citi said. "I'm ready to do whatever."

CHAPTER 17

Lola laid a few outfits across Citi's bed: skinny jeans, some summer tops, and a few blouses. She had just come from doing a successful boost with her girls at the mall. Knowing about Citi's sudden hardship, Lola, the true friend she was, decided to share some of the clothing she'd stolen with Citi. The jeans were Citi's size, as were the blouses.

"Girl, you know I got you," Lola said.

Citi smiled, something she hadn't been doing lately. "Thank you."

The girls' friendship had strengthened during the past weeks. Being parentless brought them closer together.

"You're a true friend."

"I'm always gonna have your back, Citi. Fuck that fake bitch Dana. When I see her in the streets, I'ma cut that fake bitch in her face."

"Don't worry about that bitch. She gonna get hers."

Lola came to Citi's place with a few shopping bags of stolen merchandise. She had Fendi, Gucci, Prada, Seven, and Levi jeans, dresses, hats, and a few shoes.

Citi stared at everything and was impressed. "You ain't no joke, Lola."

"Yeah, but shit is gettin' really hectic out there. Security and the employees in the stores are starting to know my face. It's becoming more difficult to steal shit from these muthafuckas. I had to shake this undercover detective that was on my ass. Fat fuck couldn't catch me, though. I was too fast and smart for his dumb ass."

Citi chuckled.

"Shit. I need help, though."

"Help doin' what?"

"Stealing."

"You serious? I ain't no fuckin' booster, Lola. That ain't my thing."

"Me and your brother Chris was talking."

"Talking?" Citi said with a raised voice, looking befuddled. "What the fuck y'all talking about?"

"I'm just sayin', hear us out, Citi, before you start to judge shit. You got a fresh face, and I know you. You got skills. Ya smart and you can easily get over on muthafuckas," Lola said. "You and me doin' us in these stores. Niggas ain't gonna know what fuckin' hit 'em."

"Did Chris put you up to this?"

"I got a plan that I know will work."

"I ain't no fuckin' booster, Lola."

"I'm just tryin' to help you out wit' your situation."

"Just don't!"

Lola sucked her teeth. "You stubborn, Citi."

"You know what?" Citi walked out her bedroom and charged across the hall to bang on Chris' door. She knew he was home. She banged on his door like it was the police knocking.

The door swung opened, and Chris appeared. "What the fuck is wrong wit' you, Citi? Why you knocking on my door like that?"

"We need to talk," Citi said gruffly.

Chris shot a steely glare at his sister. He then noticed Lola coming out her bedroom. "What? You ain't down wit' it?"

"I ain't a fuckin' booster, Chris."

"Then what you gonna do? I stepped up, tryin' to pull my weight around here now, and you need to do the same. We need some extra cash comin' in."

"Not this."

"Then what the fuck else, Citi? Huh? You wanna go out on the corners and hustle with the thugs? That's you. Or, better yet, let me put you out on the track and have you sell some pussy, or go strip in the fuckin' club. You're cute enough to get those tips."

Chris had stepped up his hustle with the help of Citi. Chris had gotten three grand pawning the gold and diamond locket of her mother's picture, a birthday gift from her father. It was enough cash to buy a package. Within the week, he was on the streets selling hand to hand. Within two weeks, Cane was right beside him, helping him hustle. They were determined to build their status back up. Slowly, they were beginning to replace what was sold off in the household.

"You gotta do this, Citi. You always talk that talk; now you gotta walk that walk. So, you gonna be real wit' your words, or become a fuckin' hypocrite?"

Lola and Chris stared at her intently and waited for her reply.

Citi sighed. "Fuck it, I'm down," she said matter-of-factly.

"Now that's a Byrne talking," Chris said.

▲

The plan was simple. Lola would walk into the place first and browse around. She was already known for shoplifting from the same store numerous times. When she stepped into the store, security was already alerted, and the uniformed guard and the employees began watching her like a hawk. She smirked at the chubby security officer that played her closely. Every move she made, he was on her. He didn't say a thing. He only followed her around the clothing store. Lola moved slowly and carefully. She wanted his eyes on her.

Citi entered the store ten minutes after Lola. Her look had changed dramatically. She had gained weight. She appeared to be pregnant, but the look was a complete fraud. Citi wasn't pregnant, but was wearing a pregnant suit underneath her clothing, giving everyone the impression she was pregnant. The suit was discreetly lined with deep pouches to stash any dresses, tops, jeans, and trinkets.

Citi played her role to perfection. She was a little nervous but moved throughout the clothing store like she was interested in purchasing a few items. She'd concealed a security tag remover on her person, and while Lola had everyone's attention, she started to remove the security tags off the dresses and a few blouses. She had to be swift at it and watch out for the eyes in the sky—the security cameras.

When Citi was sure no one was watching, she quickly swiped a two-hundred-dollar Fendi blouse and stuffed it into the pouch. She dumped the security tag in the trash. She continued to walk through the store, while Lola distracted security. She picked up a pair of jeans and held them in her hands. Then she went for a couple of shirts on the rack.

Within fifteen minutes, Citi had over eight hundred dollars worth of items concealed in the hollow belly of the suit. She carried a pair of fifty-dollar jeans slung over her arm to the cash register.

"Excuse me miss, I need to search your bag," the security said to Lola when she attempted to head for the exit.

Lola smirked. "Why y'all harassin' me?"

"I'm just doing my job," he responded with a stern look.

Lola sucked her teeth and caught an attitude with the security guard. While she was being hassled at the entrance, Citi was at the cashier paying for her fifty-dollar jeans. She grabbed her bag and strutted past Lola, and they both acted like they didn't know each other.

The guard was disappointed that he didn't catch Lola with any stolen merchandise in her bag.

"You happy?" Lola barked. "Always gotta be prejudice against a black woman. I can't come into a store without being accused of a fuckin' crime. Fuck y'all!" She purposely tried to cause a scene to embarrass the security guard.

Other shoppers turned to look at the spectacle.

"I'm sorry," he apologized.

"Fuck you, bitch-ass nigga!"

Lola stormed out of the store looking like she was hurt and embarrassed. She laughed silently to herself and hurried to meet with Citi in the ladies' bathroom.

Lola looked around and found Citi in the last stall. "Yo, that shit was crazy," she said.

"I know. I know," Citi replied, smiling.

"What you got?" Lola asked excitedly. She stepped all the way in the handicap stall and locked the door.

When Citi started to remove items from the pouch, Lola's eyes lit up.

"Damn, Citi! You went in and you got some nice things."

"I was so fuckin' nervous."

"But you did your thang, though. Shit, I taught you well."

Citi laughed.

"A'ight, let's get the fuck outta here before security decides to be nosy and shit."

Citi walked out the restroom first, still masquerading as a young pregnant female, and Lola walked out the restroom five minutes later. The girls met up outside the mall at the bus stop. They were relieved by what they'd accomplished. They couldn't wait to hit the hood and start fencing what they had stolen.

▲

A few days later, the two girls hit Green Acres Mall, implementing the same system. Lola and a friend walked into the pricey fashion boutique and started to browse around, catching the workers' attention. Ten minutes later, Citi strolled into the store disguised as a pregnant woman. While Lola and her ghetto friend caught everyone's attention, Citi was busy stuffing costly items into the pouches of the suit. The group exited at different times. Citi made it a habit to always purchase something at the cashier for fifty dollars or less, to throw off any suspicion.

The scheme was becoming very profitable. Citi and Lola were making good money from fencing the clothing and other items to the locals. Word had gotten around, and Citi's apartment became the hangout spot for her clique. If someone needed something, they came to the apartment, where she had all kinds of merchandise displayed in her bedroom—jewelry, shoes, sneakers, hats—even electronics. She was hooked on stealing.

Within weeks, Lola and Citi had created an intricate system of stealing. They'd linked up with two thugs, Midtown and Flash, known for hijacking trucks on the highway and doing smash-and-grabs in stores out of state. Citi was running her own crew of girls, and she and Lola were teaching them the tricks of the shoplifting trade.

They implemented numerous schemes in various locations, creating a web of thievery from borough to borough. The stores in Brooklyn, Queens, Long Island, and Manhattan didn't know what hit them. Sometimes it would be the pregnant suit, or one of the girls would cause a commotion in the store, picking a fight with an employee or shopper to create a diversion for their accomplice to steal a few things. Other times, it was simply a smash-and-grab, or an inside connection with a corrupt store employee helping them with their theft for a nice price.

▲

It was a hot August day, and Citi lounged around in her bedroom, which was now overflowing with stolen clothing, shoes, and cell phones that Midtown had boosted from Best Buy. She fanned herself lightheartedly with the wad of twenty-dollar bills she had in her hand. The money was good. Her opulent lifestyle was gradually returning to her.

She had learned the ropes very quickly from Lola about the art of stealing, and she refused to be used any longer. She had a string of young girls working for her. They were daring enough to enter any store and steal for the crew. She grew tired of taking all the risk. Raised and groomed to be a boss bitch, she wanted to be like her daddy. She was meant to be running things, not taking unnecessary risks with her freedom.

The girls she had working for her ranged in ages from twelve to nineteen, and they all looked up to Citi and Lola as queen bee bitches. Her young crew of rebellious girls was lounging around in the living room smoking weed, drinking Grey Goose, and talking shit; mostly about dick and money.

Citi had locked herself in her room for a moment and was thinking. She just could not be poor. It wasn't in her blood. She peered out the bedroom window and watched the traffic in the courtyard. It was a beautiful summer day. She had a fistful of cash and a priceless wardrobe in her closet. Her come-up was surely happening. She strutted around her apartment in a short miniskirt, exposing her meaty thighs and fresh tattoo, and a tight metallic plunging neckline that showed cleavage, making the room feel almost x-rated.

Knocking at her bedroom door made her turn around from the window and shout, "Who is it?"

"Cane."

"What you want, Cane?"

"I just need to holla at you for a minute."

Citi sighed. She wasn't in the mood to see her brother. "Come in."

Cane opened the door and stepped into the bedroom, clad in a wifebeater, sagging denim jeans, and Timberlands. A large bulky gold chain hung around his neck with a 9mm pendant, and the butt of a .45 could be seen in his waistband. Ever since the night he was robbed and beaten, Cane had become more aggressive and temperamental. His name was ringing fiercely out in the streets. He'd become a violent soldier for Chris. Where Citi and Chris had leadership abilities, Cane was the opposite. He was indecisive at times, impulsive in the streets, and bitter. Detectives had picked him up for questioning on a few shootings, but he was never charged.

"You got a cigarette, sis?"

"You always beggin' for somethin'. Why don't you go out and buy your own pack sometimes?"

"'Cuz I'm asking you for one." Cane moved a pair of items to the side and sat on her bed.

Citi sighed and handed him a cigarette.

Cane lit up, took a few pulls and exhaled. He looked at his sister and said, "You tryin' to do it big, huh, sis?"

"I'm doin' me," she replied quietly.

"I know. I see that," Cane said, looking around her room at the abundance of merchandise spread out.

Citi had to watch Cane and make sure he didn't leave her room with sticky fingers. He was known for swiping something and then selling it on the streets to make a profit. Cane was family, but he was also conniving.

Cane continued to remain seated on the bed and smoke. With an impish smile, he gazed at his little sister and asked, "Yo, what's up wit' ya girl, Misty?"

"She's only fifteen."

"So? That little bitch is bad, and she cute. You think I can fuck her?"

"Don't be fuckin' wit' any of my girls, Cane. I know you. You a whore."

"Yeah, and? I'm just tryin' to get some pussy, and that bitch Misty, I'm feelin' that bitch," Cane said.

"She's one of my best boosters. I don't want you fuckin' wit' her head."

"I ain't tryin' to fuck wit' her head, just what's between her legs."

Citi shook her head at her brother. "You is so stupid, nigga."

"Whatever, Citi. I'm still gonna try and get at that, wit' or without your approval. I'm feelin' that bitch." Cane took one last pull from the cigarette and put it out in the ashtray on the dresser. He stood up with a creepy smile and looked at Citi.

"You an asshole."

"Yeah, I know. But my dick is hard, and Misty, she can get it. Watch me work, sis, watch me work," Cane said, grabbing his crotch while he made his exit from the bedroom.

Citi followed behind him. Her eyes stayed on Cane as he walked into the living room and went over to Misty, who sat on the sofa in her coochie-cutting shorts and tight top that highlighted her balloon tits. Cane stood over her, and Misty looked up at him with a sparkle in her eyes.

Citi scrutinized the conversation between Cane and Misty. Misty's body language spoke loud and clear. She was ready to fuck Cane. Citi cringed at the thought of Cane getting involved with one of her boosters. She had a good thing going and was afraid that Cane's affair with Misty would fuck up her flow and cause unneeded drama within her business.

Frowning, she watched her brother work his magic on Misty, who was eating his words up like cake. Cane took a seat next to her and threw his arm around Misty, and it appeared that she was ready to lay her head into his chest. Citi had to respect her brother's game, but she was hoping he didn't have to spread it so thick on one of her boosters. But she wasn't a hater and didn't plan to cock-block.

CHAPTER 18

The September breeze was cool and comforting, and the sun was at its peak in the sky when Citi climbed out of Chris' truck. Together they trekked across the cemetery lawn and walked somberly to their father's gravesite. Citi held onto his arm tightly, for confidence. She hadn't been to the grave since the day Curtis was buried. She'd brought a batch of fresh flowers to place on her father's grave.

Five months later, their father's murder still lingered fresh in their hearts. His killer or killers were still out there. The family hated that those responsible for killing Curtis were still breathing. Maino had promised to be on the hunt for them, but he was now the shot-caller on the streets of Queens. Avenging Curtis' death was no longer a priority for him, so the family was left on their own. It was becoming a cold case.

The siblings came to a stop at the laser-etched black granite tombstone that indicated Curtis Byrne's final resting place. The grave was covered with flowers; some dying, others freshly placed there. The tombstone read: *Curtis Byrne, beloved father, you will truly be missed. Gone, but never forgotten.* It also showed the years of his birth and death.

The minute Citi rested her eyes on the grave, tears began to fall against her cheeks. She clutched Chris' arm tighter as they stepped closer. She sighed heavily as she stood over her daddy's final resting place. Her eyes were now in full-blown tears. She couldn't help but to break out into a profound cry.

Chris consoled his baby sister, whispering to her, "It'll be okay, Citi."

The two stared at the grave. It was hard to believe it—their abrupt loss. Today would have been Curtis' birthday. He would have turned thirty-seven.

Cane had refused to come with them to the grave. He didn't want to be reminded of his loss. He was still bitter and angry. He also felt he'd disappointed his father by not finding his killers. He opted to stay home. He'd rather be in some warm pussy than face such harsh reality.

Citi leaned forward and placed the batch of flowers onto her father's grave. She tossed away the dead ones and made sure his place of rest looked presentable. Chris hugged her and had a few tears streaming down his face. The two lingered at their father's grave for a long while.

"I miss him so much," Citi cried out.

"I do too, sis. I do too," Chris said quietly.

Their tears of grief simultaneously fell to the ground, their heartbreak evident under the bright afternoon sun. The memory of their father would never fade from their minds and hearts. What he'd taught them would always stay with them. He was the epitome of a genuine hustler. Curtis would now live through them.

After Chris and Citi paid their respects to Curtis, they slowly walked back to the truck parked outside the gates of the cemetery.

"I'll promise you, we gonna get the muthafuckas that did this to him. I ain't giving up on it, Citi. They ain't gettin' away wit' this shit."

Citi wiped the tears with the back of her hand and turned to glance back at her father's grave. She knew her brother's words were legit. She climbed into the truck and Chris drove off, and they rode silently for a moment. Both of them had a lot on their minds. They had come a long way, but there was still a treacherous journey ahead of them.

When Chris came to a stop at a red light, he turned to look at his sister and said, "I'm proud of you, Citi."

Citi looked at him. "Proud of me about what?"

"You stepped it up. You came through for the family. Yo, what you and Lola got going on with that crew of girls? It's crazy."

"You're the one that encouraged me to get involved with the idea."

"I know, but you elevated that shit. I know Pops would have been proud of you . . . proud of us. Yo, being a boss is in our blood. But I can't say the same thing for Cane."

"Cane is always gonna be Cane."

"And that's what worries me," Chris said.

Citi fell quiet in the passenger seat and stared aimlessly out the window as Chris continued to drive. He glanced at her and thought about their future. He had to set an example for his brother and sister. He knew he had to be the one to pull his family through the fire without them getting burned. He had to stand tall and step into his father's shoes. He wished he had help, but it didn't seem to be coming soon; especially not from his brother. Chris realized that Cane was only reliable as a soldier—not a chief— and that had him worried. If something happened to him, there was a strong possibility that Citi and Cane might be doomed.

CHAPTER 19

Citi got the phone call from Lola late on a September evening. By the frantic sound in Lola's voice, she knew something had happened. She walked into her bedroom and shut the door to have some privacy. "What's up, Lola? Talk to me."

"Some shit went down yesterday evening, Citi. Misty got locked up."

"Locked up? How the fuck she got locked up?"

"For shoplifting and attempted murder."

"What the fuck are you talkin' about, Lola? We ain't had shit goin' down yesterday. I told the girls to chill out. What the fuck was she thinkin'?"

"Your fuckin' brother, Citi."

"My brother? What the hell you talkin' about?"

"Cane had Misty stealing for him on the low, and the bitch got caught up in Macy's at Green Acres Mall. When the guard tried to stop her, she pulled out a knife and stabbed him three times in the stomach."

Citi was boiling over with rage and anger. "What the fuck is his problem?" she screamed. "Where's Cane?"

"He wasn't around. He had the bitch go down alone. I heard he took off from the scene."

"I'ma kill that nigga! I told him not to get Misty into any shit. Now he fuckin' wit' my money."

"I know."

"Where's Misty now?"

"They got her detained down at Central Booking. She's in a fucked-up predicament."

"Fuck!"

Citi pranced around her bedroom, her mind running wild with thoughts. *What if Misty decides to snitch? What if she takes a plea?* She knew there was a strong possibility that the investigation wouldn't just end with Misty being arrested. Her young protégé decided to go out and shoplift under her own free will. She wasn't forced. But she was a minor. However, the attempted murder charge was the bulk of her problem. If Misty decided to talk about the operation to get any charges reduced against her, then Citi and Lola had a serious problem.

Citi stormed out her bedroom and was ready to confront Cane, but he wasn't home. Chris wasn't home either. She was fuming. Citi couldn't calm down all evening. She smoked cigarette after cigarette, waiting for Cane to come home or Lola to call her back with more news about the situation. The only thing on her mind was how Cane had fucked up the one good thing she had going, because he couldn't keep his dick in his jeans.

She called his cell phone repeatedly, but he wasn't picking up. Unable to free her mind from the looming problem, she got dressed and stepped outside for some fresh air. October was right around the corner, and along with the fall season came the holidays. Citi knew with Black Friday approaching in a few weeks and Christmas right after, it would have been a huge moneymaking opportunity. The more she thought about the loss of income she could have generated, the more she wanted to kill Cane.

She loitered around her building for an hour on the nice, balmy evening. The streets were buzzing with people, hustlers, and residents. She sat on the bench in front of her building and watched the people and cars drive by on Guy R. Brewer. In her tight jeans and top, looking like a hoochie, she generated a lot of attention. Citi was that get-money bitch, by any means necessary. Everyone knew her reputation—sharp with the tongue and wicked in the streets.

As she sat on the bench, her cell phone rang. It was Lola. "Yo, tell me somethin' good."

"It ain't good, Citi. I'm gettin' word that Misty is scared and she ready to talk. Police pressuring her to give up everyone."

"Yo, that bitch can't talk. She knows too much."

"I know."

Citi was scared. It was her first real situation. If Misty truly cooperated with the authorities, then everyone would be going down, being part of a criminal organization. She was only sixteen, and too cute and too young to be in jail. Citi didn't know what to do. She had no lawyer to run to for counseling. Her only option was to seek advice from Chris or Maino.

The midnight hour came, and Cane came strolling into the apartment. Citi was in the living room waiting for him. The place was dark and quiet. The dim glow from Cane's cigarette could be seen in the dark.

When Cane flipped on the lights, Citi hit him with a hard right-hand punch. The cigarette flew out his mouth, and he staggered and fell back against the wall.

Cane glared at his sister and shouted, "Citi, what the fuck is your problem?"

"You is so fuckin' stupid, Cane!" she screamed. "I swear, you are so fuckin' retarded!"

Cane massaged his jaw gently and shot a harsh look at his sister.

Citi was in his face. She attacked him again, swinging wildly, but Cane blocked a few of her punches and moved from the attack.

"I told you, nigga, don't get Misty caught up in ya shit."

"Yo, fuck that bitch," Cane shot back.

"No, nigga. Fuck *you*!" Citi punched him again.

"Yo, Citi, you gonna stop puttin' ya hands on me like that?"

"Or what?"

"Don't fuck wit' me, sis."

"You put me and Lola into some serious shit. Misty's locked up 'cuz of ya dumb ass."

Cane sucked his teeth. "And what that gotta do wit' me?"

"If she snitches—"

"That bitch ain't gonna snitch on nobody."

"You don't know that."

"Yo, that bitch is stupid. I thought she was ya best booster. I ain't tell that bitch to stab the fuckin' guard. Fuckin' bitch is crazy."

"Look who's talking."

Cane marched away from Citi and headed toward the kitchen. He swung open the fridge door and searched for a snack.

Citi followed behind him, and they continued the heated argument. Cane tried to ignore her, but she kept getting in his face. Venomous words spewed from her mouth, and Cane tried to resist punching his little sister in the face.

Before things got out of hand, Chris walked into the apartment. He could hear the argument from the hallway. When he walked in, Citi was screaming her head off, and Cane had his fists clenched, towering over Citi with a nasty scowl.

Chris intervened, shouting, "What the fuck is wrong wit' y'all?"

Citi was so angry and busy bickering with Cane, she didn't even hear Chris come in. "I'ma fuck him up, Chris! He's a fuckin' fool!" she shouted.

"Bitch, what ya mouth," Cane responded furiously.

"Yo, y'all need to really fuckin' chill right now," Chris yelled. "What the fuck y'all fighting over?"

"This idiot done put me and Lola into a serious situation."

"What you talkin' about, Citi?"

Citi went on to explain the situation to Chris. Chris listened intently while Cane sat on the couch and rolled up a joint.

When Citi finished explaining the story to Chris, he turned to Cane and exclaimed, "Nigga, you don't think this shit is serious?"

Cane sighed heavily and wanted to forget about it, but with Chris getting into the mix of things, he had no choice but to sit up and listen.

"What the fuck is wrong with you, yo?"

"Nigga, I was tryin' to get some money. That bitch fucked up! Why we gotta worry about it?"

"That was stupid, nigga!" Chris shouted. "Do you understand the severity of this shit? If that bitch talks and snitches on Citi and Lola, that brings heat closer to us, and that means they might be all over our shit and shut our shit down. Nigga, I'm tryin' to get paid, and you out there fuckin' minors and got them stabbing security guards."

Cane slumped into the couch and remained quiet.

"I've been tryin' to tell this nigga."

Chris glared at his brother. He couldn't believe Cane's stupidity. They couldn't afford to have police investigating into their operation. It had taken time for Chris to rebuild trust and respect on the streets and network with key players in the game. He wanted to build an empire— continue where their father had left off. Chris understood that if police came at them with warrants and arrests, then everything would surely crumble, brick by brick. They didn't have the cash for an upscale attorney just in case the detectives came knocking with charges, and they didn't have the muscle to forcibly make sure Misty would keep her mouth shut.

Chris paced around the room. He had to come up with a plan. He knew Misty would snitch to have her charges reduced. She was only fifteen—still a scared little girl. She was looking at an attempted murder charge. The security guard was in critical condition at Jamaica Hospital.

"I gotta call Maino," Chris said.

"We don't need that nigga. Fuck him!" Cane shouted.

"Yes, we do," Chris returned. "For now, this shit is over our heads." Chris disappeared into his bedroom, leaving Citi and Cane alone in the living room.

Citi continued to throw sour looks at Cane. Cane shook his head and took a few strong pulls from the joint. Citi could no longer stand to look at her brother. She hurried into her bedroom and slammed the door.

The meeting with Maino was brief. He showed up to the apartment the next day, flanked by goons, and heavily bejeweled in platinum and diamonds. The last five months had been really good to him. He had a strong drug connect and a powerful hold on the streets. It was clear to everyone that he had taken control where Curtis left off.

When Chris informed Maino of their situation, Maino made the solution clear as day to them. "Y'all just gotta kill that bitch," he said

Citi was shocked to hear his response. Misty was a friend.

Maino noticed the stunned expression on Citi's face. He looked at the teenage girl with a deadpan gaze and said to her, "Citi, this is your freedom at stake. That bitch talk, and it's lights out for you. Y'all gonna have so much police up y'all asses, none of you gonna be able to take a shit without wiping your ass on brass. When it comes to the streets and friendship, them two don't coexist. You do what you gotta do to survive and stay on top."

Citi remained quiet.

"We ain't got the muscles or paper to make them kind of moves," Chris said.

"I figured y'all don't." Maino smirked.

Maino stared deeply at Chris. He had been watching the young teen come into his own lately. Chris reminded him of Curtis. His talk, his swag, and his looks were like his father's.

"I'll look into this shit and see what I can do for y'all," Maino said. "But this ain't for free. Y'all gonna owe me."

Chris heaved a sigh. "I know."

"I'll get my peoples on it."

Before Maino left, his eyes fell upon Citi once again. He marveled at her beauty. She was growing up to become a very beautiful young woman.

Maino's graceless gaze at her made Citi somewhat uncomfortable. He was her godfather. He made his exit, leaving Citi befuddled by his strange stare at her. She didn't know what to think of it.

A week later, Citi and Chris got the news that Misty was dead. She'd been stabbed repeatedly in the neck while incarcerated in Rikers Island and had died instantly. They didn't know who or how Maino had gotten someone to commit her murder in the jail, but the job was executed. Citi and Lola felt they could breathe a little easier. It was a bittersweet achievement. The violent world that Curtis wanted to protect his daughter from was staring her in the face.

The crowded A train that zipped underneath the pitch-black tunnel for Harlem wasn't Citi's cup of tea. It was late evening, and the masses of people pushing up against her in the train car made her want to shout and become hostile. She had been chauffeured all her life, via her family or a cab. The A train was a whole new world for her, but she decided to tag along with Lola to meet up with two young men in Harlem. She needed a change—needed to get out of Queens—so she was willing to chill with them for the day.

Misty's arrest and death came with a backlash. They didn't want to risk going into stores anymore to shoplift, so the money had stopped. Citi had some remaining merchandise that she could fence for a profit, but the gravy train was about to stop flowing. Chris warned them to keep a low profile.

The murder of a fifteen-year-old girl on Rikers Island made the headlines and even caught the mayor's attention. An investigation was brewing. All ties to Citi and Lola had been cut off, but that part of the business was done for them.

The way Maino had stepped in and handled everything so coolly made her see him in a whole new light. She loved the authority figure and felt drawn to Maino's power.

The train roared into the 42nd Street, and hordes of people got off. Citi and Lola were able to relax a little more. The two stunning young ladies drew plenty of in tight-fitting jeans that emphasized their womanly curves, their long, stylish hair, and matching light brown leather jackets.

▲

The girls were on their way to meet with Big Kev and Lloyd—L for short. They had met the two guys in a Brooklyn nightclub the previous night. L had invited the girls to join him in the VIP section, and Citi and Lola didn't hesitate to take him up on his generous offer. For the remainder of the night, the girls danced and popped bottles with him, Big Kev, and the rest of their crew.

L was a slender, caramel cutie with cornrows and tattoos and rocking bling like he was a rap star. Big Kev was a little heavier, massive-looking, and darker, with a bald head and a stoic personality. He had money to burn in the club, and a lust for women and living the fast life. It was clear that Big Kev was the top dog—the alpha male of the crew. He sat like a king in the VIP booth, flanked by his crew with a bottle in one hand and a fist full of twenties in the other.

Lola quickly pushed up on Big Kev, while Citi was left to socialize with L, who was more talkative and affable than his friend and business partner. Citi found him to be cute, but Big Kev was the boss. He was more her style. As L chatted in Citi's ear, she couldn't help but to watch Lola flirt with and nestle against Big Kev.

They'd just met, and Lola was acting like he was her boyfriend. Big Kev ate the attention up, fondling Lola underneath the table. He caressed her thighs and neared his touch closer to her pussy and fingered her. Lola didn't stop him. She didn't mind it. Big Kev was looking for a quick fuck, but Lola was looking for a king to hold her down.

After the club, the four went to get something to eat at a local diner. L made it clear that he was interested in Citi, but Citi seemed aloof at times, showing just enough interest to keep him chasing. After the diner, both parties exchanged information and went their separate ways.

Guard the Throne

L had invited them to come hang out in Harlem the next day. Besides needing a a break from Queens, Citi wanted to find out more about Big Kev. Citi was always looking for the next come-up. She needed to make her money, and with their shoplifting organization going down, she needed to find another way to generate income. Big Kev appeared to be seriously paid, and she was ready to infiltrate his world, though Lola already had her hooks into him.

▲

Citi and Lola exited the train station at 125th Street, which was bustling with activity, as the sun faded behind the horizon. People were everywhere, retail stores lined the city block from corner to corner, and vendors flooded the sidewalks with an abundant variety of merchandise.

Lola and Citi looked around for their dates, who'd promised to meet them the minute they exited the train station.

"You see them?" Lola asked.

"Nah," Citi said, looking in every direction. "These niggas better not have stood us up. I ain't come all the way out here for nothing."

"Word."

Less than five minutes later, a black Range Rover rounded the corner onto 125th Street, its chromed-out rims and dark tinted windows attracting attention on the streets.

"There they go right there," Citi said, pointing.

Lola smiled. She couldn't wait to see Big Kev again.

The Range Rover came to a stop at the corner near the train station, and Lola and Citi walked over. The passenger door swung open, and L climbed out, smiling, dressed in a throwback Lakers jersey, a fitted ball cap, and a gold chain and bracelets.

"What's up, beautiful?" L said with a smile and an open invitation for Citi to give him a hug, which she did.

Big Kev didn't attempt to move from behind the steering wheel to greet Lola so eagerly. He remained stoic when the girls climbed into the backseat of the Range. The truck drove off, merging into the Harlem traffic, and they headed north on Eighth Avenue.

Big Kev turned up the music, "Light Up" by Jay-Z and Drake. He took a few pulls from the burning joint held between his fingers before passing it to L, who took a few pulls. He turned behind him to hand Citi the joint for her and Lola to hit.

The men hustled and lived together in a tenement building on 137th Street. The stream of cars on the tree-lined block made it difficult for Big Kev to find a parking space. Once he found one, the foursome climbed out of the Range Rover and headed toward the building.

Big Kev walked into the dark apartment first and switched on the light, followed by Lola, Citi, and L. Citi looked around and was impressed.

The level was comprised of a spacious living room, a main dining area, and a luxurious TV area. The décor, with its stylish sofa, high-end stereo equipment, large LCD TV, and fully equipped kitchen made Citi think about her own home when Curtis was still alive and before their apartment became the hangout spot for everyone in the PJs.

"Y'all are living nice," Lola uttered, her eyes big as marbles.

"Yeah, we do us," Big Kev replied dryly.

L made the girls feel more at home than his friend, offering them a drink, some snacks, and showing them a couple of features in the room. Despite his rough image, L was a true gentleman.

Citi knew everything in the room came from drug money. Everything about Big Kev and L screamed out "uptown hustlers." Citi assumed, by the pricy Range Rover and the tricked-out pad in the tenement building, they were probably ki-a-week niggas.

Citi sat on the couch, and L came over to give her some company. He placed his arm around her and snuggled close. Citi didn't mind it. He smelled fresh. His cologne opened up her nostrils and triggered her memory. He was wearing Nautica Ocean, the same cologne Curtis used to put on. It was rare to find a young thug like L smelling so good. It was a turn-on for Citi.

Big Kev turned on the 60-inch TV. Lola was seated on the couch. Big Kev decided to roll up another joint. He lost himself in the kitchen, while the others watched music videos and sipped on Hennessy Black.

"So, ladies, y'all staying the night?" L asked.

Lola was ready to say yes, but Citi interrupted her. "Nah, we can't stay too long. We got business to handle in Queens."

"Business? What business y'all bitches got goin' on in Queens?" Big Kev asked harshly. He was a thorough thug and didn't give a fuck about watching his mouth or impressing his female company.

Citi cut her eyes at him. "Nigga, you ain't the only one gettin' paid out there," Citi replied sharply. "I get my ends too."

Big Kev chuckled. "What y'all do? Strip? Oh, my bad—let me be politically correct—Y'all dance?"

"No, nigga, we don't dance. We get fuckin' money, like y'all do."

"Oh, word? So y'all some baller bitches, huh?"

"Nigga, do I look like I'm a broke bitch?" Citi stood up so Big Kev could take a better look at her attire. Everything was name brand and expensive.

Big Kev fixed his eyes on Citi's lustrous style. He then uttered, "You sure ya man ain't buy you that?"

"Nigga, I ain't got no man. And I don't need a nigga to make me look nice and buy me things."

"Yo, Big Kev, just chill," L chimed.

"L, I'm just asking questions. Ain't nothin' wrong wit' asking our company some questions, right?" Big Kev wetted the joint with his lips.

"Nah, ain't nothin' wrong wit' asking questions," Citi said. "Just watch how you ask 'em."

Kev chuckled again. He had Citi's attention. For some reason, she loved his frankness. Big Kev was bombarding her with questions. It made her want to smack him and fuck him at the same time.

It didn't take long for Lola to disappear with Big Kev into the main bedroom. While Lola got down on her knees and gladly took Big Kev into her mouth, sucking his dick like a porn star in the five-star bedroom, L kept Citi company on the couch.

As the night progressed, L wanted to know more about Citi. He wanted to get closer to her. He wasn't in a rush to fuck her, like every other nigga she had been with. His conversation was intriguing. When L opened his mouth to speak, Citi immediately knew he was intelligent. The words he used and the shit he was talking to her about made her sit up and listen.

In a strange way, she saw a piece of Curtis in him. He knew how to play chess, he watched programs on CNN, MSNBC, and the Fox Network, he read *The Times*, he knew history, and he read books. L was impressive. While other thugs were only into getting high, getting money, and fucking bitches, he seemed to want more than that.

Despite her attraction to L and being captivated by him, Citi just couldn't bypass the fact that he was second string under Big Kev's wings, and she didn't do second string. Citi only fucked with first-string niggas in the game. If the man wasn't a boss—the alpha male of his crew—then Citi didn't want to deal with him.

In a way, it burned her up that Lola had Big Kev trapped in his bedroom and was probably sucking and fucking the shit out of him. Citi knew she could have thrown it on Big Kev so much better. Her pussy would have turned that massive 235-pound hustler into a cream pop.

Citi had an agenda. She needed to make money. She needed a nigga like Big Kev in her mix. Lola was her friend, but Lola was used to fucking with second-string niggas. Citi thought the couples should have been reversed, she with Big Kev, and Lola seated on the couch with L, since her friend wouldn't know how to keep her hooks into a nigga like Big Kev.

Citi and L ended up falling asleep on the couch together. They looked like a loving couple, with her nestled in his arms. L held her lovingly. Citi wasn't used to that kind of affection from a nigga, but she was comfortable.

▲

Citi felt herself being nudged by someone. She stirred softly in L's arms. The nudging continued. "Citi, wake up," she heard Lola say.

Citi slowly opened her eyes to find Lola standing over her. Lola was fully dressed, but her hair was in disarray, and her clothing was a bit wrinkled. She'd definitely had a good time with Big Kev in the bedroom.

Lola smiled at them. "Y'all look so cute together."

Citi was still fully clothed and lying against L, his arms wrapped around her like he was securing her from something. Her pants weren't unbuttoned, and her top was still on. From the faint glow of the television she saw the empty fifth of Hennessy, weed remnants, and uneaten snacks on the cluttered coffee table. It was the first time Citi had ever slept with a nigga into the early morning without having sex. Most niggas would have probably tried to take advantage of her and look for a cheap feel or a blowjob, but surprisingly, L was a gentleman to her all night.

"Fuckin' Romeo and Juliet," Big Kev said.

Big Kev was shirtless, exposing his tattoos, hairy chest, and gut, and wearing a pair of beige shorts and flip-flops, looking completely satisfied. He didn't have a smile, but Citi knew the look of a nigga content over some pussy when she saw one. He and Lola had spent hours in the bedroom, and there were times when L and Citi could hear the moans, especially Lola's. He must have been pounding that pussy something serious.

"C'mon, Cit, we out," Lola said.

Citi raised herself free from L's gentle hold.

When L woke up himself, Big Kev began to clown him. "What? You in love, nigga?"

L flipped him the bird and then looked at Citi. "You good?"

Citi nodded. She collected her sneakers and jacket.

L wanted her to stay, but Big Kev thought otherwise. The girls gathered up their belongings in the apartment.

"How y'all gettin' home?" L asked.

"Same way they got here."

"Yo, that's some fucked-up shit, Kev."

Big Kev didn't really care for either girl. His preference was Hispanic ladies. He loved their style, their language, and felt they were better bitches in the bedroom and better girlfriends to hold him down. Lola was just something to keep his dick entertained.

"Yo, I'ma put y'all in a cab," L said.

"Thank you," Citi replied.

L walked them outside while Big Kev went into his bedroom scratching his nuts. Big Kev didn't give Lola a second thought. Citi was the cuter one in his eyes, and he wanted to fuck her too.

The black four-door Lincoln, a gypsy cab with the Haitian driver behind the wheel, sat idling outside the tenement building. The early-morning hours were quiet, and Harlem seemed still for a moment—no traffic, no people.

Lola climbed into the backseat, but Citi hesitated.

L stood close to her, anticipating a kiss or something. "I had a good time wit' you," he said.

"I did too."

"So when I'm gonna see you again?"

"Call me."

"You know I will."

Citi smiled as she leaned into his hug. L hugged her with so much passion, it seemed like he didn't want to let her go.

Unbeknownst to L, Citi was only out for her come-up, and she had Big Kev in her sights. Her way of thinking didn't allow her to fall for L's generous manners, never mind his thuggish appearance. Being second string blocked any chance of her being serious with him.

Big Kev appeared to be the one with the connect and the resources. He was the one she needed to get alone and have a talk with—and if need be, fuck the shit out of—to capture his undivided interest.

Citi released herself from L's mellow hold and climbed into the backseat of the cab. She smiled at him.

L leaned into the front passenger window and handed the driver forty dollars. "Yo, you make sure to get these ladies home safely, a'ight?" he said with firmness in his voice.

The driver took the money and nodded.

L looked back at Citi smiling. "Yo, hit me when you hit ya pad, to make sure that y'all got home safe, okay?"

Citi nodded.

L backed away from the cab, and the driver slowly drove off. L kept his vision on the cab until it turned the corner.

"Damn, he's cute. You ain't fuck him?"

"No. But you fucked Big Kev. I heard y'all."

Lola grinned. "Damn. You heard us?"

"Well, I heard you."

"Hey, he got a big dick, and that shit was good."

"Ho."

"Hey, wit' dick that good inside of me, I'll be any ho that nigga wants me to be."

Citi and Lola laughed.

The cabdriver remained indifferent at the girls' vulgar conversation in the backseat of his Lincoln. They didn't give a fuck who was listening. Lola went on to give details about her freaky rendezvous with Big Kev like they were in the privacy of their bedroom.

The girls made it home to Queens thirty minutes later. When Citi walked into her apartment, it was dark and empty. There was no loud music or a mess of hood niggas lingering around in the living room. It was obvious that Cane wasn't home.

She went straight into her bedroom and started undressing. She dived into her bed, forgetting to hit L back to let him know she had reached home. Her mind was on sleep and the next day. L wasn't a primary. He was cute, but not her cup of tea. But she planned on using him to get closer to Big Kev. L was the pawn in her chess game.

CHAPTER 21

The winter months were brutal once again. It seemed like spring and summer had passed by in one big blur. It was a gusty February day and a cold twenty-two degrees with snow in the forecast. Citi hated the winter. She stood in the plush bedroom near the window gazing at the cold she had to endure in a few hours. She didn't want to leave his place. The ice and cold frosting up the windows made her want to get underneath the covers with him and become wrapped in his arms once more.

"I need to move to fuckin' Miami, fo' real," she muttered to herself.

Citi turned to see that he was out like a light and naked under the covers. Dressed in her panties and bra, her pussy was still throbbing from the way he'd fucked her earlier. They had fucked like porn stars. She was ready for round two with him, but decided to let him sleep a little longer. She had put it on him, rode his thick dick like a jockey on a horse, and when they both came, the bedroom walls seemed to shake.

Citi's dealings with L had been up and down during the previous months. L had treated her like the queen she was. He would take her out to eat at some of the best restaurants in Manhattan, telling her at times to order whatever she wanted. He was willing to take her out of town with him, put her up in high-end suites luxurious hotels, and take her out to tour the city. He was in love with her, and since their first meeting in the club, his way of thinking toward her had never changed. He wanted to wife her up, but Citi was never into him like that.

Citi had never met this kind of thug before. He was street-smart and book-smart, and he had that thug loving that many women craved. She had fucked him a few times, and the sex was good, but Citi couldn't shake the fact that he wasn't the boss of his own shit. She felt that he was just too sweet for her tea, and she was only using him to get closer to Big Kev.

L steadily chased her, but he wasn't stupid. He always had been cautious. He'd noticed Citi's attraction to Big Kev. He would catch her staring at his friend, and sometimes catch them having private conversations when they thought no one was watching. It angered him, but he decided not to trip over it. He wasn't one to get upset over some petty shit. His mamma raised him better than that. He understood that there were plenty more fish in the sea. So sometimes when Citi called, he wouldn't answer. And when she and Lola took that time-consuming trip by train or cab into Harlem, he'd suddenly make himself unavailable.

Citi didn't give a fuck. She had a new interest in her life— a nigga who held down blocks and had a street reputation. He was the king on the chessboard, not the pawn. He had started pushing up on her recently.

Meanwhile, Lola was still fucking and sucking Big Kev. She had become his personal whore. Big Kev never made one trip to Queens to see Lola or come to pick her up, and he never took her anywhere except to his bedroom, the backseat of his truck, or some public area in Harlem to get a quick blowjob. Occasionally, he would trick on her, take her to McDonald's or a movie theater to get his dick sucked in the dark, or order her some Chinese food so they could stay in his bedroom to watch movies and fuck.

▲

Citi was smoking a cigarette as she gazed at Maino asleep in his king-sized bed. It felt unbelievable for a moment. She was fucking her father's best friend, and her godfather.

Guard the Throne

Maino had low-key been pushing up on her. He didn't care about her age. She would be almost seventeen, and statutory rape was the farthest thing from his mind. He had been coming around the family more often, pretending to be concerned with the kids. He started talking to Chris, advising him and the family here and there, stating he would always be there for them, and that he was still actively searching for Curtis' killers.

Maino was always in Citi's ear, praising her beauty, telling her things she liked to hear, and buying her things she liked to wear. Then he started to buy her little trinkets—watches, earrings, bracelets, the things she loved to have and parade around in. The gold had her eyes, and the wealth and status had her heart, and her body language around him made it clear she was interested. They soon hooked up, unbeknownst to her brothers.

Citi would leave the apartment in her sexiest attire, eager to meet with Maino discreetly at a location he'd chosen, to be safe from any eyes in the hood. She would quickly get into his truck, and he would whisk her away to his crib in Brooklyn. Sometimes during the ride, she would suck his dick in the truck, giving him a sneak preview of what was to come.

When Citi first fucked him, it almost felt unreal. They were in the backseat of his tinted truck, parked in a dark alleyway. Maino had the gun in the front seat. Citi had come to meet him in her tight jeans and jacket. She climbed over the backseat, and Maino got a good look at her perfect ass. Maino climbed in the backseat after her. His husky presence excited Citi. She couldn't wait to fuck him. His thick beard screamed at her and his beady eyes locked onto her angelic beauty.

"Ya fuckin' beautiful, Citi."

Citi smiled.

Maino pushed Citi on her back, and Citi gazed up at him, ready for the beast to ravage her body. It was his to take. She'd blocked the memory of him and her father being best friends. She didn't want to spoil the mood.

Maino had Citi out of her top and was working on her jeans. With one smooth motion, he removed her jeans. When she was in her panties and bra, he gazed at her for a moment. It felt like he was searching for something, but he was truly admiring her young body.

He quickly undid his jeans and pulled out his large manhood. With an erection, he was nine inches long and thick, almost looking artificial. He started to kiss her navel and then went down on his pretty young prize.

She squirmed, feeling his powerful tongue digging inside of her. "Ooooh shit!" she moaned.

Citi was ready for some dick. "I want it doggie-style," she cried out.

Maino had no problem obliging. The curves on Citi were amazing. Her skin was smooth like cocoa butter. Her sexily trimmed pussy hair and her Hershey chocolate nipples made his mouth water.

He flipped her around in the backseat, having Citi grip the headrest and push her hand against the glass, her knees pressed down into the soft leather of the seat. Then he mounted her from behind and rammed himself into her cream, pounding in and out of her.

Citi cried out, but took pleasure in how he took it aggressively. She loved how he fucked her. It was a quick and pleasing fuck for the both of them. Citi got her nut a few times, and when Maino came, he grunted behind Citi, clutching her waist tightly.

The first time Citi stepped foot into Maino's Brooklyn place, she saw extravagant wealth. He lived in Dyker Heights, a high-class residential neighborhood sandwiched between Bay Ridge, Bensonhurst, and Gravesend Bay, a place far away from Jamaica, Queens. It was the first time she had ever been in the area.

She walked into the two-level brick home with freshly cut grass, and the apple cinnamon fragrance immediately welcomed her. There were two big mirrors on each wall, and the golden living room set sat on soft tan carpet. Down the hallway to her right was an office with everything in polished cherry wood. Upstairs, there were three bedrooms, and the master bedroom with walk-in closet and double-sink bathroom, a large oval tub, and three showerheads. The basement was mainly one large playroom with a home theater, complete with projector and large screen, a pool table, and a pinball machine.

Citi was in awe the first time she saw how Maino lived. He had done very well for himself since he'd taken over the streets after Curtis' demise.

Maino made Citi get comfortable. He would turn on the large TV or his state-of-the-art stereo system with surround sound, and during sessions at his crib, they would watch movies, listen to music, drink, get high, and fuck their brains out. Citi would suck his dick on the couch while Maino looked at music videos and smoked a joint.

Maino's place became her escape from the hood. She was going to ride or die with him, so she could step her game up and get hers.

CHAPTER 22

C hris sat in his truck under the corner streetlight deep in thought about the game he was in. The block was quiet, but the drug game wasn't. It was hard in the streets. Problem after problem kept arising for the young hustler. With his father's murder still lingering in his mind, he couldn't help but feel angry at times, reminding himself that someone in the streets—a friend, a business associate, or a worker—was probably untruthful to him and his family. Everyone was a suspect in his father's death. He fought with himself every day to keep his sanity and the business growing.

He sat listening to rap music, the pistol close by his side. He stared out into the darkness of the early hours in the morning. The digital numbers embedded into the dashboard said it was three a.m. The cold outside was unbearable.

Chris felt he had not other choice but to go hard in the streets or go home. He continually had to prove he was built to last without his father being around to hold his hand in the streets. He refused to become a failure and be embarrassed. Some people had chosen to come at him, knowing Curtis or Maino wasn't out there to protect him and his business. The wolves were at his front door, and they were vicious and hungry. Chris had to bite back much harder and more maliciously. He had to be ready for anything that came at him.

He sat in the truck watching the dilapidated row house on the rundown block. He waited patiently, staring at the porch. He smoked his cigarette and remained cool. The row house was a known drug spot with a steady traffic of fiends and hustlers in and out on a daily basis. The stickup kids frequented the area, and the police and undercover officers always did drive-bys at the location.

Chris kept an eye out for Tiko. The man had stolen from him and violated him. He'd snatched the drugs from one of Chris' workers easily and acted like there wasn't going to be retaliation against him. Three ounces of cocaine stolen from his stash house was nothing for Chris to take lightly. Some folks in the streets thought Chris was soft— that he wasn't built like Curtis or Cane.

Tiko should have known better, but his daily drug habit made his thinking become irrational. Now Chris had to come at the thirty-nine-year-old veteran in the streets with vengeance or give up his hustling card.

Chris didn't tell Cane what Tiko had done. Cane wouldn't have hesitated to attack Tiko, beat him, or shoot him down. Ever since the robbery and attack a year earlier, Cane had become a completely different person. He refused to be caught slipping in the streets again. He stayed strapped, sometimes having one or more guns on his person. And everyone in the hood knew he wouldn't hesitate to use either one.

Chris understood he had to become more violent himself. He had been the brain, and Cane was the brawn, but he had to step up and get his hands dirty to prove to the doubters in the game that he was built for the hustle on both ends.

Tiko staggered out of the well-known drug spot with a high smile. He stood over six-three and weighed 225 pounds. He was wearing a torn winter coat and no hat, exposing his nappy Afro to the cold. He concealed a 9mm in his waistband. His age showed significantly in his face. The gray hair on his head, the sunken pupils, and the wrinkles around his eyes made him look older than he was.

Tiko had lived a hard life. The drug use, violence, being in and out of prison since he was twelve years old, and seeing everything from murder, kidnapping, to rape made him a hardened soul. A young punk like Chris was too easy to get over on. The ounces of cocaine he stolen had either been sold or used to feed his addiction.

Chris watched Tiko leave the shady premises alone. He picked up the Glock 17 from the passenger seat and cocked it back.

When Tiko stepped onto the street, Chris swung open the driver's door and made his move, clad in a dark hoodie and winter hat. His boots hit the pavement with a sense of urgency. He gripped the gun tightly behind his back and out of view from his victim. He just wanted his respect, and his drugs or the money back.

Guys like Tiko, the veterans in his hood, looked at Chris as an underling, a young'un who still couldn't pee straight. Tiko felt it was easy to take from juniors like Chris. While Chris was still sucking on his mother's tits, he was running blocks. When Chris was playing in the sandbox, he had a stable of bitches and was taking frequent trips to Vegas. But the game done changed, and the young hustlers were taking over in swarms. It angered Tiko that the young heads were changing the rules of the game.

Tiko continued to stagger toward his car, a dark blue Chevy Impala, a small remnant from his glory days. As he walked, he reached into his coat and pulled out a pack of cigarettes. He hesitated to get into the Impala. The cold didn't seem to bother him. He lit up.

"Yo, Tiko."

Tiko turned to see who was calling him. The cold streets were barren and still. To his right, he saw no one, but when he turned to his left, he saw the hooded stranger approaching. It didn't occur to him that he was in immediate danger.

He narrowed his eyes at the young kid approaching quickly. "What the fuck you want, young'un'?" he hissed. He suddenly noticed the outstretched hand and then the barrel of a large gun pointed at him. His narrowed eyes popped open in shock, and the cigarette fell from his lips.

Bam!

The straight shot ripped through Tiko's upper thigh and crippled him at once. He howled and stumbled against his car.

The second shot went through his other leg and dropped him to the pavement in pain.

He stared up at his attacker approaching silently. He was defenseless. The gun in his waistband had fallen underneath the car.

"What the fuck!" Tiko cried out.

"You took something from me, muthafucka! And I want it back. You owe me," Chris screamed at him.

"I ain't take shit from you, nigga!"

Chris towered over him. He removed his hood to reveal his identity.

"Chris, what the fuck!" Tiko shouted.

"You steal from me, muthafucka!" Chris screamed madly. The palm of his hand pressed against the butt of the gun, he started to pistol-whip Tiko savagely, splitting his head open with the butt of the gun, and knocking out a tooth. Hit after hit with the butt of the gun brought Tiko closer to unconsciousness.

"Stop! Fuckin' stop!" he shouted, barely able to move.

"I want what's mine, nigga."

"Okay, okay," Tiko uttered faintly.

Chris went rummaging through his pockets and removed three hundred dollars. He was furious. "This is fuckin' it!" A swift kick into Tiko's side crushed his ribs and made him wail out in pain.

"You think I'm weak, Tiko? That's why you steal from me?" Chris screamed.

Tiko lay rooted to the cold concrete, helpless, blood oozing from his wounds and saturating his jeans and his hands coated in it.

Chris glared at him and aimed the gun at his head. He was tempted to shoot and put Tiko out of his misery. He had never killed a man.

Tiko gazed up at Chris, his eyes pleading to live. "Don't do this! I'll get you back what I stole," he pleaded weakly.

"Fuck you!" Chris screamed.

Chris had his finger on the trigger. It was too easy. But he thought, *Dead men can't pay their debts*, and Chris needed his money.

"I'm giving you a fuckin' week to give back what you stole from me, nigga, and if I don't get it back, then we gonna continue this conversation, and it's gonna be the last one you'll ever have on this fuckin' earth. I'll personally make sure I'll be the last face you'll fuckin' see."

Chris pivoted on his heels and hurried back to his truck, leaving Tiko squirming near his car, bleeding heavily. He climbed into his ride and sped away from the crime scene to the sound of sirens blaring in the distance. Chris had to make a point. The wolves were heavy at his door, and he had to show his foes that his bite was much louder than his bark.

▲

The streets were talking about Tiko's assault. Chris had beaten him down badly and crippled him with the gunshots. In the drug game—a world filled with killers, stickup kids, and hustlers—there was only one way to get any full respect from everyone: violence and bloodshed. You had to be a vicious muthafucka for the darkest soul not to fuck with you. Chris understood it. He knew what respect looked like from being under his father's wing for so long. He saw how men of all ages, killers and hustlers alike, respected his father, and how many feared him. With the status his father had in the hood, the wicked thought twice about doing something stupid and crazy to him, his family, and his organization. Curtis and Maino were a strong team; a powerhouse in two boroughs.

Chris sat reclined in his car, his mind spinning with problem after problem. His drug connect was on the lam, and he needed a new supplier.

Then, he had to worry about Tiko. He wondered if his foe had the balls to retaliate. Tiko was an aging, washed-up veteran in the game, but he was still a danger. Something Chris had learned from his father was to never underestimate the slightest threat. No matter how big or small the threat came, when it came, Chris was taught to take care of it right away. Curtis had warned him to never sleep on any man. From a friend to a fiend, it was dangerous to trust anyone when you were in the game.

Chris became skilled at carrying and concealing guns on him at all times. His vehicle was equipped with stash boxes. In his mind, it was best to be tried by twelve than be carried by six.

He took a pull from the cigarette between his lips and exhaled. He kept his gun close. He sat parked outside his building like his father used to do and analyzed his situation. There was a lot going on. The streets were watching, and the game was listening. Cane would sometimes go MIA, making him undependable at times, and Citi had found a new love he was unaware about. Chris just hoped that his little sister wasn't out there whoring herself and leaving a stigma on the family's name.

The tapping at the driver's side window caused Chris to reach for the Glock in his lap. He twisted quickly with the gun ready for action and saw it was Donny at the window, one of Maino's goons.

"Easy, playboy. I just came to talk to you," Donny said. "Ain't no need for you to become trigger-happy."

Chris lowered the gun and rolled the window down halfway, his grip still around the gun, his nerves edgy. "What you want, Donny?"

"Maino wants to see you. Looked for you upstairs, but find you down here."

"What he want?"

"Hell if I know. He just sent me out to come find you, and I come find you," Donny replied in a chilling tone.

Chris sighed. "A'ight. I'll come through."

"He wants to see you now, Chris. Says it's important. You can ride wit' me," Donny suggested. "You got another cigarette?"

Chris handed him a Newport and a light. As Donny lit up, Chris thought about meeting with Maino. Donny didn't budge from the window. He took a few drags and waited for Chris' reply. Chris wasn't in the position to say no. Maino was the man in charge on the streets. If he asked for you, then you didn't ask questions. You just went to see him.

"Give me a few minutes."

"How about one minute?"

"This better be important," Chris said, removing himself from the vehicle.

Chris followed Donny to his Lexus and climbed into the passenger seat. Donny started the ignition and sped off into the traffic.

They arrived at Maino's warehouse-turned-underground strip club in East New York, Brooklyn. The cars lining the street were an indication of the heavy activity inside.

Chris and Donny bypassed the security at the front entrance and moved into the dim, crowded club, naked strippers scattered everywhere, weed and cigarette smoke circulating in the stale atmosphere. The makeshift stage was decorated with voluptuous nude females pussy-popping and booty-bouncing to Tyga's "Rack City" blaring throughout the club.

Donny led Chris toward the office located at the back of the club. It was isolated down the narrowed hallway, and under protection from a few goons. Chris stepped into the spacious office with cameras watching everyone everywhere. Two flat-screens hung on the wall, and two abstract oil paintings decorated the wall behind Maino's desk. With concrete flooring, and leather sofas, everything was ultramodern in the windowless office.

Chris walked into the office and saw Maino seated behind his desk, pulling from a cigar, a big-booty topless stripper on his lap.

Maino spun his attention over to Chris and greeted him with a smile. "Chris, welcome to paradise."

Chris didn't respond. He wasn't in the mood to joke around.

Maino slapped the bitch on the ass and then said to her, "Babe, give us a minute. I got some important business to take care of."

"Sure, daddy," the topless stripper replied pleasantly. She jumped off Maino's lap and strutted by Chris in her thong and six-inch stilettos.

The other goons cleared the room, so Maino and Chris could have their privacy.

Chris stood a good distance from where Maino was seated, and Donny was situated behind him.

Maino wore a wifebeater and a long platinum chain with diamond-encrusted boxing gloves for a pendant. He was tatted up and his thick facial hair was shaped up. He took another drag from his cigar and gestured for Chris to have a seat near his desk.

Chris took a seat in one of the two chairs by the desk.

"You a natural-born hustler, Chris," Maino spoke out.

"What?"

"I mean, I see you out there doin' ya thang, making moves and shit. I like that. Shit, I look at you and see Curtis written all over you. You look and move just like your father. Y'all got that ambition, that unstoppable drive, and you're smart too."

"I'm just tryin' to survive, Maino. It ain't been easy for us this past year."

"I know. It's ugly out there. If muthafuckas can't run wit' the wolves, then they get devoured. And you still running wit' the wolves, I see." Maino chuckled, sizing Chris up. He then continued with, "I heard about that incident wit' you and Tiko. You really beat that nigga down. Didn't know you had it in you."

"It needed to be done. He stole from me," Chris replied coolly.

"Shit. Ain't no judging on this end. You already know my reputation. Question though, why you let that fool live?"

"A dead man can't pay his debt."

Maino took a pull from the cigar, his eyes on Chris. "Damn, you ain't lying about that. You did what you had to do to let these muthafuckas out here know you ain't nothin' nice to fuckin' play wit'. But sometimes you gotta set a stronger example and you kill a muthafucka for fuckin' wit' ya ends. It gives the next nigga doubt about coming up short wit' ya money or stealing from you . . . raise the ante. But what you did to Tiko, yeah, that was some thorough shit."

Chris didn't care for Maino's compliment. He'd watched for over a year as Maino continued to get rich right after his father's death and barely came through to help out him and his siblings. Maino wasn't as supportive to them as he'd promised, and it made Chris question things. He remained seated and listened to Maino talk about the game and how it should be played. Maino had been around for a long time. He was a concrete dude. Nobody fucked with him. If he didn't kill you himself, then he got one of his soldiers to do it. But Maino wasn't the type of dude to ask one of his goons to do something that he wasn't willing to do himself.

"You know what you need, Chris?"

"Nah. What I need?"

"You need to be under an umbrella. So when that storm comes raining down, you ain't gonna be caught up in it and washed up."

"What you getting at, Maino?"

"Come work for me."

"What?"

"I know ya in a bad situation. Your connect went MIA on you, and these streets are out there still testing you. You buy your weight from me, and I'll put you under my umbrella, so no one won't fuck wit' you or your family. I like you, Chris. You a natural-born hustler. You still will be the boss of ya own shit, but buy your work from me, at a reasonable price of course. I need niggas like you around."

"How much we talkin' about?"

"Sixty-forty split."

Chris remained silent for a moment. The offer was reasonable. Maino had a solid point. Once word got out that Chris was under Maino's protection, the risk of the wolves coming to take a bite out of what was his would greatly diminish. He would be a fool to turn the proposal down. He looked at Maino and nodded silently.

"My nigga. I knew you were fuckin' smart," Maino said excitedly.

Chris and Maino hugged each other. For Chris, it felt like he had a father figure around him once more. It was a good feeling.

Donny stood on the sidelines watching everything. He smoked and smirked at Chris. The fool was getting in bed with the man who'd murdered his father. Donny had to respect Maino's intelligence, though. It was a ballsy move.

"Anything you need, you come to me. Remember that."

Chris nodded. He turned from Maino and walked out the office.

Donny watched him leave and shook his head. When the door shut, Donny asked Maino, "Yo, you sure it was smart to bring that little nigga onboard like that?"

"Yeah, it was. Keeping my friends close and my enemies closer."

Donny took a drag from the cigarette, nodding. "Right, right."

"Anyway, he's smart, and he knows me and trusts me. It's gonna be good to have a nigga of his intelligence and motivation on the team. He knows how to make money, and I'm in this shit to get rich," Maino said. "He ever leaps, then we just knock his ass back down."

Donny smiled.

Maino now had Chris in his pocket, moving weight for him, and he was fuckin' Citi and had her open like a good book.

CHAPTER 23

Citi stepped out of the Hummer H2 at Penn Station in Midtown Manhattan dressed like a young college student. She carried a small backpack, wore glasses, and moved toward the busy station like she wasn't concealing five kilos of cocaine on her person. It was early afternoon, and the traffic was like a parking lot. The summer months were approaching gradually, and the warm spring air was comforting to Citi. The warm sun on her face and the gentle spring breeze against her skin was like a high for her.

She was ready to get on the Amtrak to meet with ruthless drug dealers out of state. Her trip today was to Maryland. The butterflies in her stomach came in droves. Security at Penn Station was high, with cops and the National Guard everywhere keeping a sharp eye out for terrorism and anything out of place.

It was crazy for anyone to try attempting any illegal activity with so many law enforcement officers about, but Maino had the gift of gab and had talked Citi into becoming a drug mule for him, carrying ki's from state to state. The out-of-town dealers were paying an extra five grand for the door-to-door service.

Citi was in love with him, and she was willing to do anything for her man. The sex was amazing, and spending time with him in his plush, Brooklyn home made her yearn to have her own someday—the stylish home, the trendy décor, and money longer than a Hail Mary pass.

Maino had made her plenty of promises. Despite her young age, he gave off the impression that he was ready to make her his ride-or-die bitch. They would get money together and become the dominant couple in the hood, but they had to keep their relationship on the low for the moment. It was too risky to reveal their feelings for each other, so Citi spent numerous nights at his Dyker Heights home. They were rarely seen together in Queens or anywhere else.

Most evenings at his home were spent with Citi fucking or sucking him off for hours. Maino would bust her pussy wide open, fucking her from the back in a fervent manner, grabbing her neck from behind, pulling her hair and smacking her ass. It was the way Citi liked it—rough and crazy.

As the weeks turned into months, Citi saw less and less of her brothers, her hood, neighbors, and friends. She had forgotten about Lola, Big Kev, and L completely. Maino had captured her time and undivided attention. She was wearing the finest clothes and driving his drop-top Benz through the New York streets.

Before long, Maino became abusive and controlling towards Citi. No matter how hard she tried to please him, he still treated her like a little girl at times, berating her whenever she failed to please him and talking down to her.

"You a young dumb bitch, Citi, fo' real," he would say to her.

Citi put up with the abuse, verbally and physically, hoping to prove that she really loved him. She wanted to prove that she was built for the game and didn't want to look dainty in Maino's eyes. Citi figured that if she kept close to a man like Maino, then the world would be hers.

Citi walked into Penn Station coolly, with nerves of steel. With several kilos of cocaine in her backpack, she couldn't look nervous. She carried a deadpan expression, moving with the crowd, walking by several police officers and making her way toward the Amtrak station. She also carried a few hundred dollars on her and a 9mm. She walked up to the window clerk and paid for a roundtrip ticket to Baltimore. With the train ticket in her hand, Citi had an hour before her train departed. She carried her junior's license for ID and directions for her to meet with Silo, the man Maino was doing business with in B-more.

Citi couldn't drive without restrictions, and a young girl traveling alone on I-95 would raise red flags for the state troopers. So the train was the best option to move any weight for her man. It was crowded and fast, and she was able to blend in with other passengers of all ages. She just had to keep her cool and play her cards right to avoid any suspicion. She didn't want any employees to alert the drug dogs

Maino was already on the highway back to Brooklyn by the time Citi sat in the food court munching on a turkey sandwich, her backpack close. Penn Station was known for pickpockets, so she watched everything and stayed on high alert for police and thieves. By three p.m., she was on the Amtrak to Baltimore, her backpack close to her like it was her own heartbeat.

▲

The train pulled into the Baltimore's Penn Station on North Charles Street before six p.m. Citi exited the station behind the thick crowd of passengers and emerged onto the city street. Baltimore was a strange city to her. She didn't know a soul there, but Maino assured her that no dealer would harm her because they feared his reputation, and it would be bad for business if any harm came to her. In any case, Citi had her own insurance concealed in her backpack. The 9mm was loaded, and she knew how to use it.

Citi walked around with the backpack slung over her shoulder. She tried to remain sharp, keeping her eyes on everyone and everything. Numerous cabs were lined up outside the station, and everyone was in a rush to get to their destination. The only thing she knew about Silo was that he was a black man with cornrows and in his late twenties. He would be the one to pick her up in a black Escalade at the train station.

It was supposed to be a simple transaction. They would meet, exchange product for money, and Citi would stay the night in a motel and leave for New York in the morning.

Citi waited outside the station for fifteen minutes, becoming more impatient by the minute. If caught with that many kilos, she would be looking at a twenty-year sentence at best. She paced outside of the train station with a scowl, her temper flaring up.

Twenty minutes after her arrival, a black Escalade slowly turned into the train station. With the dark tints and 22-inch chrome rims, it screamed drug dealer loud and clear like church bells on Sunday morning. Citi sighed. She thought, if Silo was the one driving, he was a fool to show up in such a showy vehicle. The SUV came to a stop not too far from where she stood, the tinted windows started to roll down, and the passenger door opened up.

Silo climbed out in all his glory—jewelry gleaming, cornrows freshly braided, dark shades over his eyes, and clad in name-brand attire. "What up, baby?" he called out to Citi like they'd known each other for a long time.

Citi went along with the program. She smiled at him. "It took you long enough to come get me," she exclaimed with attitude.

"Traffic was a muthafucka." He walked over to Citi and gave her a passionate hug. He scooped Citi into his arms with strength, and they fabricated the role of boyfriend and girlfriend. They even kissed for a moment to throw off anyone watching them.

Silo was a handsome thug. He stood six-one and was well built.

They shared a few words, and Citi trailed behind him and climbed into the backseat of the truck. She greeted the driver, a heavyset thug with a small fro and a hard gaze. Silo got into the passenger seat, and the truck fused itself into the city traffic coming from the train station.

The driver got onto the expressway, and the ride to the motel was mostly silent. Citi just wanted to get the transaction over with, get some sleep, and get back on the afternoon train to New York. Being alone in Baltimore with two strangers was a risk. She could easily be raped, robbed, or murdered. The five kilos in her bag was enough to lure anyone to beat her down and snatch it from her. The only protection she had on her side was the 9mm in her backpack, but it didn't feel like it was enough. If they were to suddenly attack her, she knew there wasn't enough time to reach for the weapon.

The radio was on 92Q, and a Nicki Minaj song was playing. Citi stared out the window, taking in all of Baltimore and mostly paying attention to the roads and where they were taking her. They went to the 695, the Baltimore Beltway, and headed south into Randallstown. Twenty-five minutes later, the Escalade was pulling into the parking lot of a cheap motel off Liberty Road, the sun slowly drifting behind the horizon and night creeping onto the city.

Silo already had a room reserved. He and his partner jumped out the truck, and Citi was the last to make her exit. She followed the two men in the direction of the Motel 6, a two-level structure with outdoor rooms. She entered behind Silo, walking into the basic room design with twin beds, a TV, a shaky table, and two chairs.

Silo closed the curtains, blocking out the view to the parking lot. This was the moment she had been waiting for. Silo stood by the twin bed, and his driver carried the bag filled with cash. Citi played the door close and kept a sharp eye on both men.

"You ain't gotta be nervous, shorty. We ain't settin' you up. I known Maino for too long now. He good peoples," Silo said.

He nodded at his driver, and the man moved closer to the bed, unzipped the bag, and dumped bundles of money onto the made bed.

"We showed your ours. Now show us yours," Silo said calmly.

Citi walked toward the bed and bit-by-bit removed each kilo from her backpack. She placed it on the bed next to the money.

Silo nodded. "That's so fuckin' sexy right there," he said, smiling.

He picked up a ki and inspected it. Five ki's at twenty thousand a ki, and Silo paid for five birds. He began stuffing the birds into the bag he carried, and Citi started to collect the money in her hands.

"You gonna count that?" Silo asked.

Citi nodded.

"Smart girl." He smiled.

Citi made sure to count every dime of the cash. If she came back short, it would upset Maino, and he would take it out of her small cut. Maino was paying her five thousand for each trip she made out of town.

Silo tossed her the room key. "It's your room for the night. Enjoy." He and his driver made their exit.

Once the truck left the parking lot, Citi collected her things and went to the front desk office to get a different room. She didn't trust anyone. What was to stop Silo or one of his men from coming back, kicking in the room door, then robbing and assaulting her? She asked for a room far away from the old one. She couldn't wait to get back into New York.

The following afternoon, Citi was back in New York with a hundred thousand dollars in her backpack. She moved through the bustling Penn Station beaming inwardly at the accomplishment. Maino would be so proud of her. When she saw his gleaming Hummer H2 idling outside amongst the city traffic, a large smile appeared on her face.

She quickly climbed into the front seat of the truck and kissed her man. "Hey, baby!" She handed him the backpack.

Maino smiled. "You did good, baby. Real damn good. I'm proud of you."

Citi lit up. It was a good feeling to hear the compliment coming from him.

After Maino pulled into the driveway of his Brooklyn home, he handed Citi an envelope containing five thousand dollars and rushed inside to handle his business. Citi went behind him. It was a trying day for her. She wanted to shower, eat, and roll up a joint and smoke in the yard.

Citi peeled away her clothing in the bathroom and stepped into the warm, running shower. The soothing lukewarm water cascaded off her soft brown skin. She lowered her head underneath the wall-mounted showerhead, closed her eyes, and relished the feeling of all the dirt and grime being washed from her body. As she cleansed herself in the shower, tears started to fall from her eyes. Memories of her father began to bombard her thoughts. It had been over a year since his murder, and the killers still roamed free. Citi didn't know why she started to think about her father's killers, but she couldn't escape the thought. She lingered underneath the showerhead, head lowered and eyes closed.

She was in the shower for a moment when the glass shower door was pulled open and Maino stepped into the steamy mist. She turned to see her man naked and swinging like a vine.

"You need some company?"

Citi didn't respond to him. Her eyes stayed fixed on his stocky frame. The tattoos and battle scars exhibited across his skin were a clear indication of his gangster way of life. He reminded her of Ving Rhames; sexy and rough all wrapped into one package.

Maino took Citi by her wrist and pulled her into his arms. "You my number one bitch. You know that, right?" he said into her ear, his lips touching her lobe.

Citi smiled.

His hands began to wander across her body. His touch went from the small of her back to her juicy backside. He squeezed her ass and then lifted her off her feet, suspending her in the air. His strength was exhilarating to Citi. Even though she didn't weigh much, it still excited her how easily he could scoop her off her feet and swing her in the air like she was some doll.

Citi laughed. She was back on her feet and sandwiched between his beefy arms. She wanted to fuck.

Maino twisted her around, her back against his scarred chest and his arms still wrapped around her curvaceous body. He caressed her stomach and then the top of her pussy.

Each caress kept Citi aroused, but the arms and body behind her kept her supported as she felt like her legs could barely hold her up. Maino kissed the side of her neck and slid his fingers into her creamy hole, making her moan under the streaming showerhead.

"I want you to make another run for me," he whispered in her ear, his fingers dipping in and out of her.

"Where to, baby?" she faintly replied.

Her hardened nipples were like small points. Her eyes closed and her body became limp beside him. Her legs trembled from being finger-fucked.

"Philly. I got peoples down there. Same thing like before."

Citi nodded.

"That's my bitch."

"Fuck me, daddy!"

Maino curved Citi over, her hands pressed flat against the walls of the shower. He spread her legs into an upside-down *V*, parted her succulent ass cheeks, and sank his growing erection deep between her wet, pink lips. They fucked vigorously under the shower waterfall.

Maino enjoyed Citi's glorious inner walls stimulating every inch of him. His dick sank deeper into her, and she started humming another tune, her moans bouncing off the shower walls. His breath escaped from him in a small cry and whimper that indicated Citi had some good pussy.

Soon Maino's orgasm rushed from his balls and escaped into her. His dick remained hard and deep inside her warm, pulsating center.

▲

Two weeks later, Citi was on the Amtrak to Philadelphia. She had four bricks in her backpack and instructions on where to meet with Mills, a local hood who had North Philly locked down with his violent crew. It was another smooth transaction for her.

After Philadelphia, it was D.C., then Albany, then Delaware. Maino had set up a pipeline for narcotics, and he had a string of mules to transport the drugs for him. Dozens and dozens of kilos were being trafficked from city to city, either on I-95 or the railroads. Maino's name was heavy from north to south on I-95, and his organization was expanding. Citi felt proud to be part of such growth.

CHAPTER 24

The sun was bright, and the summer day was hot. Chris cruised down Merrick Boulevard in his new drop-top BMW listening to R&B and enjoying the fruits of his hard labor. The gleaming black Beamer was fresh off the car lot of a Hillside Avenue dealership. He'd walked into the high-end dealership with a book bag filled with cash, his sights set on the 650i coupe. The dealer took one look at him in his stylish hip-hop attire, jewelry, and the book bag he carried, and knew he was a drug dealer. On numerous occasions, the middle-aged dealer had to deal with drug dealers looking to buy a flashy car. He knew how to maneuver around the cash transaction. He greeted Chris with a smile, and the two quickly went into negotiations for the coupe.

Getting into business with Maino was paying off for Chris. He had become a three-ki-a-week player in the game, and the money was flowing. Chris was also earning a fierce reputation of his own, breaking away from being known as "Curtis' son." He no longer looked weak and dried up. The way he hustled and ran his crew was boss-like, and his drugs were being sold to people he never saw and who never saw him.

Chris made his way home to Baisley projects. When he turned the corner onto Guy R. Brewer Boulevard, the blaring police lights caught his attention and made him come to a stop on the block. The entire street had been closed off with crime scene tape, and hordes of uniformed officers and detectives were everywhere. There was a crowd gathered behind the crime scene observing the heavy police activity and the blue-and-white bird was in the sky, hovering over the projects.

He parked his BMW and jumped out. He left his pistol underneath the seat and hurried to where the onlookers were gathered on the sidewalk and in the streets. His heart started to beat like drums in a go-go song. He didn't know whether it was something he had to worry about or if it was just a random act of violence on the block.

He couldn't get close enough to the crime scene to get a better look, but from where he stood, he could see two bodies sprawled out across the asphalt and another body slumped behind the wheel of a Cadillac.

Chris instantly thought about his brother. "Shit!" he muttered. He had to find out what happened. *Was Cane involved?* He couldn't see the identity of the dead men. Chris needed confirmation on what had gone down. The murders were too close to his home.

The police were in and out of buildings asking questions, and reporters were around questioning potential witnesses and looking for an inside scoop. The talk on the streets was that it was a shootout with rival drug crews. The three dead goons had been ambushed, and a fourth thug had been rushed to Jamaica Hospital with several gunshot wounds.

Chris walked away from the heavy activity and got on his cell phone. He dialed Cane, but the call went to voice mail. That worried Chris. As he hurried toward his ride, he called Cane again, and that call went straight to voice mail too.

"Fuck!" Chris shouted. He got behind the wheel of his Beamer and slammed the door shut. His peaceful day was turning into a nightmare.

He remained behind the wheel for a moment. The only thing going through his mind was the violence that had been spiraling out of control since the beginning of spring. The shootings were becoming bad for his business. His projects were becoming the Wild Wild West. It was the fourth shooting within the month. A week prior, two drug dealers were shot and killed in the stairwell of his building. Too many bodies were piling up in Queens, especially around his home and business. It wasn't safe to stay there any longer, so he had made up his mind to move.

Chris made a sudden U-turn and drove off in the opposite direction. He tried to call Cane again but got the same results. He tossed his phone into the passenger seat and cursed while driving south on the boulevard. He was becoming worried about his little brother.

He decided to call Citi, and she picked up. "You heard from Cane?"

"No, not in a few days," Citi replied.

"Fuck!"

"What's wrong?" Citi asked, beginning to worry.

"Another shooting happened by our building, three down. Pigs are all over the area. Where are you?"

"I'm uptown with Lola," she lied.

"All right, you stay where you're at for now. Shit is too hot around here for the moment."

"Okay."

"I'll call you later."

Soon after Chris hung up, he received a call from Cane. He answered right away, "Cane, where the fuck are you?"

"Calm down, Chris. I'm at my bitch's crib. My phone was on the charger. What's good?"

"You know what went down by our building today?"

"Nah. You tell me."

"We need to meet up. We need to talk."

"Now?"

"Yeah, now."

"A'ight, in an hour. Where at?"

"The cemetery," Chris suggested.

"Where Pop is buried?"

"Where the fuck else, Cane? It's the only place I know safe enough to talk right now."

"A'ight," Cane replied reluctantly.

"Nigga, don't keep me waiting."

"Chris, relax. I won't."

Chris hung up and headed for the cemetery right away. He wanted to beat the traffic there.

Since his come-up, Chris had tried to stay one or two steps ahead of law enforcement and his foes. He was becoming more like his daddy every day. If he had to meet with certain individuals about important business, it was mostly done in an open area. Curtis' grave was one of the most secure locations Chris could think of. When he conducted business there, it felt like his father was there watching him, and almost counseling him.

As Chris turned onto the narrow road that led to the sprawling cemetery, he had an awkward feeling about the murders he had seen on the street. His gut screamed at him that Cane had to be involved somehow. He guided his BMW toward the end of the roadway, stepped out, and looked around. The area was empty, and the dead didn't speak, so Chris felt secure about meeting with Cane. He made a few phone calls from his cell while he waited for Cane to show up.

Forty-five minutes later, Cane arrived alone in his burgundy Acura Legend. Clad in a wifebeater and a long, bulky chain swinging on his neck, Cane stepped out his ride with a menacing gaze.

"Why the fuck you wanted to meet me here, Chris?"

"Did you do it?"

"What the fuck you talkin' about?"

"Don't play stupid with me. I asked you a question. I know you, little brother, and I got this strong feeling you was involved in that gangland shooting in front of our building earlier." Chris locked into his brother's eyes, looking for the truth from him.

"You called me out here to Pop's grave to ask me that dumb shit? Why the fuck you care about three dead niggas? You act like you kin to them."

"I never said how many were dead, and I didn't tell you about any murders. You just gave yourself away, little brother."

Cane smirked. "Fuck it! Yeah, I got those muthafuckas, Chris! I don't forget shit!"

"What? Got who? And why?"

"Those niggas that carjacked me last year, I finally caught up wit' them and took care of shit. We lit that muthafuckin' car up like daylight."

"Nigga, are you stupid? You do that in public, with countless witnesses around? You tryin' to get locked up? Think, Cane."

"I *am* thinkin'!" Cane retorted. "We a fuckin' powerhouse again, big bro. Pops would be fuckin' proud of us. 'Cuz of me, niggas know not to fuck wit' us. Yo, you think niggas just gonna rob me, steal what's mine, and I'm supposed to let that shit slide? Nah, fuck that! I don't care how much time's passed. I don't forget shit."

"It brings police around, slows up business, Cane. You need to think before you act so fuckin' impulsive."

"Fuck you, Chris! This shit ain't about you. It's about me, and how niggas fuckin' embarrassed me that night. You fuckin' hear me? I ain't out there playin' wit' these muthafuckas. I'm lettin' niggas know not to fuck wit' the kid. Plain and simple. I speak wit' my gun, and these clown-ass niggas is definitely listening."

Chris sighed. "You can be so fuckin' hardheaded, Cane."

"I'm just taking the bull by its horns."

"I'm gonna have to change things up and move shop because of you."

"You handle things on your end, and I'll handle things on my end."

Cane turned and stared at his father's grave. The brothers fell silent for a moment. The tranquility in the cemetery brought about different thoughts with them.

"I'm just telling you, be careful out there, little brother. Shit is good right now, and we don't need the headaches. It's just not you out there, Cane. Think about me and Citi too."

"I am, and because of me, and what we struggled to rebuild, it's gonna have niggas out there stopping and thinking twice about fuckin' wit' our family," Cane returned. "I'm the bogeyman out there, yo; the nightmare other killers worry about."

Chris sighed heavily. It was hard to get any logic into his brother's thick head.

"We done here?"

"Yeah, we done," Chris replied matter-of-factly.

"I love you, bro, but my business is my business." Cane pivoted on his heels and walked toward his car.

Chris' eyes stayed on Cane until he got into his car and sped off. He decided to linger by his father's grave and seek advice from the dead. His gaze didn't divert from the tombstone for several minutes. Maybe Curtis would speak to him from the ground; give him some insight or a solution to his problem. Amongst the dead, tucked away in the cemetery, Chris, for some reason, felt comfortable and protected. There was no one around him watching, no threats looming, no snitches, no cops. Just him standing over his father's grave and the rest of the dead.

CHAPTER 25

"**C**hris, why you fuckin' buggin'?" Citi shouted. "I ain't goin' anywhere. Baisley is our home."

"It ain't my home anymore."

"You ready to turn your back on what Daddy built and what you rebuilt?"

"I'm not turning my back on shit. It's a smart move." Chris stormed to the window and roughly pulled opened the blinds. "Look out there. It's crazy right now . . . a fuckin' war zone."

"But Rochdale isn't any better. It's still Queens."

Chris had made the executive decision to move his family out of Baisley projects and into the Rochdale Apartments, a sprawling complex for middle-class America. The body count surrounding his area was high, and the police had stepped up patrol from corner to corner. The killings brought about too much attention to his illicit business, and he wanted to be away from the drama escalating in the hood.

"It's a start," Chris replied.

"It ain't a fuckin' house or mansion. Daddy would have moved us into a mansion, not fuckin' Rochdale."

"Is he here anymore? No. I'm the one in charge of this family," Chris exclaimed heatedly, becoming agitated by Citi's whining.

"Fuck you, Chris!"

"You need to calm down, Citi. Now is not the time to be catching an attitude, and it's not the time for us to be moving into anything expensive. We need to keep things low-key, like Pop used to do. You don't think Pop could have moved us out the hood a long time ago? But he didn't. He always said that drug money wasn't guaranteed money. And a mortgage gotta have that guaranteed money coming in. All of our paperwork and income gotta be correct. We gotta be able to show proof of income for purchases like that."

"But you're the one driving around in a 650i BMW."

"A straw purchase. Look, until I can show proof of income to keep off the feds' and IRS' radar, I ain't jumping out the window like that. Pops didn't do it, and I'm not."

"You'll never be like Daddy," Citi replied.

"You can be a straight bitch sometimes." Chris scowled at her. "Why would you care, though? You're never here anyway. Who you out there fuckin'?"

Chris stared at his sister in her gaudy attire, gleaming jewelry, and makeup, looking much older than she was. He'd been hearing gossip in the streets about his sister being chauffeured through the streets of Brooklyn in a luxury truck or drop-top Benz.

"It ain't ya business. I'm fuckin' grown, Chris. You don't control me, not you or Cane. But this place is our memory of our father, and you wanna take it all away to move to Rochdale, and not some mansion in Long Island. We got the money, but ya too scared to spend it on anything but yourself. You is stupid! I'm gone. Don't fuckin' come lookin' for me." Citi hurried out the apartment.

Chris refused to chase her. The only thing on his mind was going to see Maino at his Brooklyn home. He watched her leave. He knew she was hiding something from him, but he couldn't dwell on it. He was making the move with or without her approval. He didn't understand why she was so attached to the apartment. Yes, they had special memories growing up there, but Chris wanted to escape from the painful memory of finding their father murdered in his bedroom.

The sister of one of his former jump-offs was moving to Virginia with her fiancé, and she didn't want to give up her apartment in Rochdale, in case the relationship didn't work out. Chris saw his golden opportunity. He offered the sister seven thousand dollars in cash to send her on her way, helping her with moving expenses. He would take over her rent and any other expenses. That kept his name off any paperwork and under the radar. It was a tenth-floor two-bedroom apartment with a terrace. Chris would still be close to the streets, and near his money on the block, but residing away from the drama in his hood.

Citi sat on the park bench under the bright moonlight and street lamps, trying to keep herself from exploding. Chris telling her about moving into Rochdale and losing the apartment she had grown up in, having to hide her relationship with Maino from her brothers and the streets, and not being able to reach Maino when she really needed him had her troubled.

Every time she called and Maino's phone went directly to voice mail, it caused speculation on her end. She'd heard rumors about Maino being with other women, other young bitches her age or slightly older. When he was around, things were somewhat good, but when he wasn't, it made her worry.

She loved him and would do anything for her man. Citi became his number one mule, trafficking drugs to D.C., Virginia, Maryland, Delaware, and other states via the railroads, and always bringing back all his money and guns. Her cut of the profits was good, but she had been yearning for a little more. She was doing all the work and taking all the chances with her freedom and life. It was only reasonable she got more cash in return.

Citi needed to find Maino. She decided to call Lola.

After a few rings, Lola picked up. "What's up?"

"Girl, where you at?"

"Home. Why?"

"I'm surprised you ain't on some dick tonight. What? Big Kev got you on a timeout tonight?" Citi joked.

Lola sucked her teeth. "Fuck him!"

"You know I'm just playin' wit' you. But I need a favor."

"What you need, Citi?"

"I need a ride somewhere."

"Where to?" Lola asked.

"To find my man."

Lola was one of few who knew about Citi's secret relationship with Maino. Citi confided in Lola when things got rough with her and Maino, just as Lola did when she and Big Kev were having problems. But it was clear that Big Kev was only using Lola, and he didn't care anything about the girl. There had been days that Citi preached to Lola to leave him alone, but Lola wasn't listening.

Citi thought, *What good is a relationship with a baller nigga like Big Kev if she isn't getting any money out of him, just good dick and upset afterwards?*

▲

The two drove to Maino's Brooklyn home, but he wasn't there, so they decided to check his strip club in East New York. Lola whipped her Honda Civic through the Brooklyn streets under the cover of night and arrived at his strip club, Dollars and Shakes, before the midnight hour.

Citi strutted toward the club entrance in her short miniskirt that revealed her meaty thighs and long legs, a pair of stilettos, and a tight top that highlighted her breasts. She was easily mistaken for one of the dancers as she walked by security and entered the packed club, where a Rick Ross track was blaring. The dancers were moving about, some butt naked, others scantily clad, giving out lap dances or wall dances, and the fellows were tossing money freely to the booty-shaking ladies.

Lola followed behind Citi, who made a beeline for Maino's back office. When she reached the narrow corridor, she saw a beefy thug posted there. He noticed Citi approaching quickly and stepped in her way to prevent her from charging forward. He figured the young girl would become intimidated by his size and turn away.

But Citi did exactly the opposite. She went straight for the husky goon, shouting, "Get the fuck out my way! I need to see Maino. Is he back there?"

Towering over the young teen, he glared down at Citi and sternly said, "Maino's busy."

"What? He's too busy to see his woman? I'm Citi, so move, nigga."

"He busy, I told you. Step off, shorty."

Citi wasn't taking no for an answer. She tried to rush by him, but the man grabbed her by her arm roughly and almost lifted her off her feet. But Citi had a few tricks of her own. She spun into him, thrusting herself forward with her knee raised, and connected with his groin.

The husky thug folded over and winced. He immediately let go of Citi and dropped to his knees. "You bitch!"

"I told you to move out my fuckin' way!"

Citi stormed toward the back office with Lola right behind her. She reached Maino's office door and burst into the room. There was Maino with his pants down, fucking a high-yellow ho he had bent over his desk.

"Aaaahhh! Fuck me, Maino."

Citi's eyes lit up with rage.

Maino pulled out the pussy and glared at Citi. "Citi, what the fuck you doin' here? Who let you through?"

"Oh, so it's like that? This how you get down? That's why you're not answering my fuckin' phone calls!" Citi screamed.

"Yo, Citi, you don't come barging into my office like you some crazy bitch."

"Why? 'Cuz you were in the middle of something? Fuck that bitch!"

The stripper became panicky and hurried to collect her clothing.

Citi wasn't having it. She rushed for the naked girl and attacked her, throwing blows at the girl's head like she was Iron Mike Tyson. She knocked the petite stripper across her pale face and made her stumble into the wall.

The stripper tried to fight back, but she was no match for Citi.

Maino rushed over to the fight and pulled Citi off the girl, and in one rapid movement, he backhanded Citi and sent her flying across the room. "What the fuck is wrong wit' you, bitch?" he yelled.

"Why you hit her like that, Maino?" Lola yelled.

"You shut the fuck up, bitch!" Maino screamed.

Citi regained her composure and went charging at Maino. "You fuckin' bastard!" she screamed.

She leaped at him, but Maino quickly overpowered her and punched her like she was a man, and she went crashing to the floor. The stripper seized the opportunity and ran out the office in tears.

"Chill the fuck out, Citi!" Maino exclaimed. "Relax, you silly bitch!"

By this time, a crowd had gathered inside the office to witness the altercation.

"I love you, baby," Citi cried out. "Why you doin' this to me?"

Maino sighed. He noticed the people in his office. "Everybody, get the fuck out my office! Get the fuck back to work!"

The onlookers rushed out of Maino's office like it was on fire, leaving Citi and Maino alone. Maino slammed the door shut.

The people outside the office could hear the argument from the hallway. Their hush-hush relationship was now exposed.

CHAPTER 26

"Yo, I'ma kill that nigga, Maino!" Cane shouted.

It didn't take long for the brothers to find out that Maino was fucking their little sister. Citi tried to deny the affair, but the word was out in the streets. News of the altercation at the strip club spread throughout Queens like a virus. Everyone was talking, and they had all had their two cents to add to the story.

"This shit ain't happening right now," Chris said.

"What you talkin' about, Chris?" Cane replied.

"This shit here, this thing with Citi and Maino."

"Look, when I see that nigga, I'ma pop him."

"You ain't gonna do shit, Cane. Relax, and stop being so fuckin' impulsive."

"What? That nigga Maino is fuckin' our little sister, and you standing there tryin' to tell me to relax. Nigga, you must be out ya damn fuckin' mind! This is family, nigga!"

"I know that," Chris said, "but I'm in business with him. I need you to chill out while I think this shit through."

"What is there to fuckin' think through, Chris?" Cane screamed. "He disrespected our family, put his dick and hands on our sister, and you sayin' he don't deserve to get got? Fuck outta here! You must be thinkin' crazy."

Chris knew Cane was right, but Maino had power and muscle behind him.

Cane didn't want to do any more talking. He didn't want to hear any excuses from Chris. He walked out the Rochdale apartment, the thought of Maino, a grown-ass man, fuckin' his little sister sending him into a sadistic frenzy. Citi had been disrespected, and their family's name had been violated. He got into his Acura and sped away.

Chris stood out on the terrace that had a picturesque view of a sprawling Queens from ten stories up smoking a cigarette. The incident put him between a rock and a hard place. He thought, *How would Pop handle his?* But no suggestions came to him. He felt like he was being thrust into a civil war. Maino was like family to him and had become a father figure to him after Curtis' murder. He felt conflicted. Maino was his backbone and connect on the streets, but that was his little sister.

He flicked the cigarette over the terrace and walked into the apartment. When he neared the wall, the rage bubbling inside of him surfaced. He put his fist through the wall. "Fuck me!" he screamed.

▲

Cane drove around aimlessly, feeling like the Terminator, a .380 with hollow tips underneath his seat and a sawed-off shotgun in the trunk of his car. His mind was on Citi and Maino. It was embarrassing to have his little sister sneaking around with Maino. Everyone was talking, and he was ready to shut them up.

The sun was slowly setting, and night was about to cover the city. The Queens streets were bustling with traffic, people, and activity.

Cane slowly cruised down Merrick Boulevard with his window down, puffing on a joint, and the radio off. His irritation was his sole entertainment. He drove by the popular barbershop, Smitty's Cuts, on Merrick Boulevard, and his eyes lit up when he noticed Maino's truck parked outside. "Muthafucka!"

Cane quickly doubled around and parked a few cars down the block, from where he watched the front entrance of the almost empty barbershop like a hawk. He removed his pistol from beneath his seat and checked the clip to ensure it was fully loaded.

When Maino and Donny emerged from the barbershop, Cane quickly exited his ride and proceeded toward the two men, who were walking toward the SUV. Both men could've been armed, but Cane didn't care about that. He wanted to confront Maino and really put him down.

Just as Donny reached for the driver's side door handle to usher Maino inside like he was the don thug, Cane sprung up on the two men like a flash with the .380 in his hand, his sights on Maino. He fired twice.

Bam! Bam!

The two shots slammed into Donny's side, pushing him back with force and dropping him to the pavement.

Maino spun around to see Cane glaring at him. The gun was mere inches from his face. "Cane, what the fuck!" Maino yelled.

"Shut the fuck up!"

The gunfire sent everyone running for cover.

Maino locked eyes with Cane. He had been caught slipping. He knew his life could be over. "You on a death wish, Cane? You do this shit, and your life is over," Maino said through clenched teeth.

"Fuck you, Maino!" Cane screamed. He was clutching the pistol so tight, it cut into his hand. "I loved you, nigga, and you fuck and hit my sister."

"Cane, let's talk. It ain't what you think it is," Maino said calmly. "I love her."

"Shut up!"

Maino took a deep breath. "Don't do this, Cane. We're still family. You hear me, nigga?"

Tears trickled from Cane's eyes. When he looked at Maino, it was like staring at his father. He had grown up loving and knowing the man since he was in diapers. The hesitation in Cane made Maino realize that he could walk away from death.

Meanwhile, Donny lay on the pavement bleeding like a gutted pig but was still alive.

"Stay away from her, Maino. I'm fuckin' warning you." Cane let off a shot that shattered the window of the SUV, sending shards of glass flying into Maino's face, and he took off running.

▲

"What the fuck is wrong with you, Cane? Are you stupid or retarded?" Chris yelled.

"I had to step to him, Chris, let him know not to fuck with the family."

"You step to him, pull a gun, and don't shoot it? You know what you just started?"

"Fuck Maino! Now the nigga knows not to fuck wit' us."

Chris glared at his little brother and felt like strangling him. He paced around the apartment shirtless and stressed. "I told you to let me handle it!" Chris screamed.

"Well, I stepped up."

"How, Cane? What did you do? Huh, nigga? You pissed the nigga off. Now I gotta go out there and clean up your mess."

Cane twisted his face at Chris. "You ain't gotta do shit, Chris. We the niggas that are up and coming. Maino's about to be washed up."

"You just don't get it, Cane, and unfortunately, you never will."

"Whatever! I'm out. I ain't the one lookin' like the bitch with his tail between his legs. Niggas bleed just like everyone else. I don't fear no fuckin' body."

"And that's your problem—You don't think before you react."

CHAPTER 27

The pussy was like heaven to Cane. He was fucking one of his jump-offs like a jackrabbit, hitting it from the back, pulling her hair, and smacking her ass. Tonya liked it rough, and Cane gave it to her like a beast. Being inside of Tonya was a stress-reliever for him.

Several days had passed since he'd pulled that gun out on Maino. The streets were buzzing about Maino almost being gunned down by Cane. Donny had survived the shots and was in critical condition at Jamaica Hospital.

Chris had warned his brother to remain low-key for a few days. He'd planned to go see Maino and have a serious talk with him, but he never got the chance because Maino had been out of sight, and no one knew where he was. That worried Chris.

Cane was enjoying a few hours of paradise with Tonya in her two-bedroom home in St. Albans. She was a voluptuous, caramel cutie with a big booty and a freakish appetite for sex. In her early twenties, she was mesmerized by Cane's thuggish ways and his cash flow. Tonya loved her bad boys. She gave him a place to stay when he needed to escape from the streets, gave him pussy when he showed up to her place horny and frustrated, and she cooked for him. But Cane, trapped in his street ways, sometimes took Tonya for granted. Tonya was ready to hold him down. All he had to do was give the word, and take her seriously.

Tonya rolled off the dick after Cane nutted inside of her. Once again,

Cane had fucked the shit out of her, leaving her winded. They had just finished round three of straight fornication, and they couldn't get enough of each other.

Cane rose up off his back and reached for his pack of cigarettes next to his .45 on the nightstand. He removed two cigarettes, passed one to Tonya, and lit up. The two enjoyed a smoke and some small talk.

After a moment of talking, Cane started to get dressed. Tonya tried to convince him to stay, but he reminded her that he had business to tend to in the streets. He collected his things and stuffed the .45 into his waistband, smiling at Tonya and headed for the front door.

Tonya followed him. "Be careful, baby," she said to him.

Cane stood on her front porch taking in the early evening. The block was quiet, and there was still about an hour of daylight left. He hit the alarm to his Acura parked across the street.

He took one look at Tonya watching him from the doorway. "I'ma holla at you later, love," he said and started to descend from the porch.

Before he could take his foot off the porch step to approach his car, two hooded gunmen jumped out from the thick shrubbery in front of the porch, both gripping 9mm handguns.

"Baby, look out!" Tonya screamed.

Cane didn't have enough time to react. Before he could pull his pistol from his waistband, gunfire exploded on the block.

Bak! Bak! Bak! Bak! Bak!

Five bullets struck Cane, tearing into his flesh and spinning him around violently, and he fell back against the porch stairs, fighting to survive. It felt like a sledgehammer had knocked him down. Cane made it to the doorway and collapsed on the porch, his .45 held weakly in his hand, and the gunmen fled on foot just as quickly as they'd appeared.

Tonya was screaming her head off, gazing at Cane sprawled out by her feet in a pool of blood, his eyes flickering.

"Baby, get up, get up!" she screamed. She dropped to her knees and scooped him into her arms, and his blood stained her clothing.

▲

The doctors told Chris and Citi that Cane was in a coma, in critical condition. He was shot in the chest, abdomen, and back. He had a collapsed lung, a few broken ribs, and one bullet had almost pierced his heart. He had pulled through after being in surgery for hours. Now he was in ICU hooked up to several machines with tubes in and out of him like he was some robot.

Citi cried out and shouted, "Not again! I can't go through this shit again, Chris. What the fuck!" She slammed her head into her brother's chest and sobbed heavily.

Chris held her closely, shedding tears of his own. He didn't know if his brother would live or die. "I'm gonna handle it, Citi. You got my fuckin' word. I'm gonna take care of this shit. Cane's a tough muthafucka. He's gonna be all right. You hear me, Citi?"

Chris tried to keep a positive attitude. His goons were with him in the hospital to show support. Cane's shooting circulated through the hood like a fast wind. His crew quickly loaded up and was ready to hit the streets on a killing spree, but Cane had so many enemies, it was hard to pinpoint the culprit or culprits behind the shooting.

Jamaica Hospital was active with medical staff, nurses, and doctors running around in every direction. Chris hated hospitals. It reminded him of death. It was a place for the weak, where victims came to die, not to heal. He had one arm around Citi and the other behind the chair next to him. They lay slumped together amid the chaos, waiting for an update on Cane's condition.

The doctors had told Chris that the difficult part was over with: the surgery. They were able to remove three out of the five slugs from his body. The other two bullets were lodged in crucial places, and they couldn't attempt to remove those shells until the swelling went down.

Chris sighed. His family had been through the ringer. The haters were out there. The Byrnes family had red bull's-eyes on their backs, and Chris knew he had to be extra careful.

As the siblings sat together, hoping and praying for their brother to pull through, Chris looked up and noticed Maino walking toward them. Chris didn't know what to think of it. He suspected Maino could have been responsible for the hit on his brother, but Cane had so many foes. Could it have been a coincidence that he'd been shot down a few days after he pulled his gun on Maino and shot Donny?

Maino walked toward them politely, a concerned expression on his face.

After Chris rose up, Citi removed her head from her brother's chest and saw Maino coming her way. She kept a deadpan look. She was unaware of her brother's bold move on Maino. When she saw him, her insides lit up. She forgave him and wanted to continue with their relationship.

"Chris, how is he?" Maino asked with concern.

"He's in a coma, in critical condition."

"Good. Good," Maino said, nodding his head. He looked at Citi seated in the chair and asked her, "You okay?"

Citi nodded. She wanted to jump into Maino's arm and be with him, but her brother was around. Even though their relationship was an open secret, Citi remained content with just seeing Maino come to show support.

Maino had only come to the hospital to feel Chris out. He wanted to see what Chris knew, and to also get closer to the family in their time of need. It was a chess move. The shooters were still in the wind, and no one knew who had hired them, but Maino was certainly among the suspects.

"Chris, you know, you family, and if you and Citi need anything, I mean anything from me, y'all don't hesitate to ask. Y'all feel me?"

Citi attempted a smile, but Chris remained nonchalant, nodding slightly. Maino couldn't read him.

"I'ma put the word out," Maino said, "put peoples in the streets and find out who did this shit. They gonna pay. You have my word on that, Chris. We gonna kill 'em all."

Chris thought, *Like how you promised to find my father's killers?*

Maino gave Citi a hug and Chris too. He started to leave, but motioned for Chris to walk with him toward the exit. He had a few more words to say to him.

When they were out of earshot, Maino said to Chris casually, "Look, I want you to come by the club tonight so we can talk. I wanna politick wit' you."

Chris didn't trust the meeting, especially at Maino's club. It was too out-the-way, and too suspicious all of a sudden. His gut feeling told him it was a setup. He looked at Maino and replied, "Tonight's no good. I gotta stay close by Citi's side, make sure she's okay with this, and then I got other shit to take care of. Maybe next time."

"A'ight. Next time."

After a moment of awkward silence, Maino turned on his heels and walked away, knowing Chris suspected him.

Chris felt he was being pulled into a bottomless pit. He knew when Maino invited him to the club to have words, his chances of walking out alive were slim. Maino had made his move; now it was time for Chris to make his. He had to step up even more and take control of the madness. With Cane down, his right-hand man and top enforcer, it was time for Chris to blaze his guns with a crew of young thugs once loyal to his father and now loyal to him.

▲

The next day, at his Rochdale apartment, Chris began making an attempt to keep what was left of his family safe. With Cane stabilized and in a coma at Jamaica Hospital, he had to be watchful over Citi. He went into his bedroom, pulled open the dresser drawer, and removed a loaded Ruger pistol.

He went into the living room, where Citi sat silently, and shoved the gun into her hand. "You keep this on you at all times," he said to her. "It's for protection."

She looked at the gun and gripped it firmly. "What's goin' on, Chris?"

"We at war, sis."

"With Maino?"

"Who you think? He's been playing us."

Citi didn't want to believe it. She loved Maino and believed he had genuine love for her and her family, despite their ups and downs and their differences. She watched Chris prepare for war.

A few gun-toting thugs lingered in the living room, ready to go to war. They smoked a joint, sipped on a bottle, and talked recklessly about killings and guns. Chris was the one leading the charge. He'd had enough. With Cane down, he'd suddenly become the pit bull in the streets.

Citi jumped up from the couch. "I'm leaving, Chris," she spat.

Chris stopped her. "You ain't leaving by yourself," he said. He nodded to one of his goons on the couch.

A rough, muscular kid named Kadar stood up, his jeans sagging, his cornrows freshly done. He was tall, dark-skinned, and intimidating, with a scar across his cheek and eyes like fire.

"Kadar leaving with you," Chris told her.

"I can take care of myself."

"I'm not taking any chances, and I ain't playing around, Citi. He goes where you go."

Citi reluctantly agreed, sucking her teeth, and Kadar followed her out the door. With Kadar protecting her, and the gun he'd given her, Chris was able to breathe a little easier.

CHAPTER
28

Chris sat slumped in the passenger seat of the tinted burgundy minivan that moved through the Queens street slowly this balmy night. Romo was the driver, and two thugs sat hidden in the back of the van, each man hungry for some action. Both young thugs had a semi-automatic weapon gripped in their hands as they cruised in search of Maino. They wanted to kill him before he got at them.

With Cane recovering in the hospital, Chris felt he had to avenge his brother's shooting and keep the Byrne name intact. Taking on Maino would be difficult and challenging, but he was ready for the backlash. He understood it took risk and heart to rise to the top, so he knew he had to become a full-blown gangster, nothing less.

He also knew it was time to get from under Maino's wing and branch out on his own. He put his networking skills to good use and linked up with a strong Dominican crew out of Washington Heights for his coke connect, made through one of the girls he was fucking. She was able to vouch for Chris to her cousin. Then, being Curtis' son helped to close the deal with them; the Dominicans respected his father and Alonzo. They gave Chris some work on consignment, and he was flipping them birds like pancakes.

The men smoked haze, passing time. They were itching to find Maino, but it proved to be harder than they thought. Maino had gone MIA. His strip club in East New York was closed, and he was nowhere to be found at the spots where he was usually seen.

"Damn! Where the fuck is this nigga at?" Dark shouted from the backseat.

Chris remained quiet. He was so deep in thought, thinking about his next move, he'd tuned out the complaints coming from his goons.

As the hours passed, they were growing edgy and frustrated. Everyone clearly understood the situation when they went hunting for Maino—He would also be hunting for them. But it didn't deter Chris' young crew. They were all headhunters with a vicious appetite for violence and hearty criminal records.

Romo pulled into Rochdale Circle, a vast structure consisting of twenty buildings in five groups. Each thirteen-story building had three sections.

Chris said a few words to his crew, and they nodded in agreement. He then made his exit from the minivan with his pistol concealed in his waistband and his guard on high. It was a smart move to leave his old home in Baisley, but he still felt that he was vulnerable for an attack. He had the urge to go underground more, get out of Queens to a place where he could be invisible.

The building was quiet. He made his way inside the lobby, his hand close to the pistol tucked in his jeans as he walked to the elevator. The gun was already cocked, and the safety was off. The only thing he had to do was pull the gun and shoot.

▲

Chris entered his apartment and found Citi standing out on the terrace. She was in her bathrobe and smoking a cigarette.

"Citi, you okay?" he asked.

She turned to see him. "Copasetic, big brother," she said matter-of-factly.

There was no smile or warm welcome, just heartache and worry.

Chris removed the gun from his jeans and placed it on the counter. He walked into the kitchen, leaving Citi to be alone with her thoughts.

Citi had gone to see Cane in the hospital every day, making sure he was being treated fairly. It was a risk, but Chris made sure she had Kadar with her at all times. The detectives were always around, waiting for Cane to awake. They had a ton of questions for him, but it would only be a waste of time. Cane was rock, no snitch. He despised police.

Citi took a few more pulls from the Newport and sighed. She was stressed. She had tried to call Maino numerous times in the past two weeks, but got no answer. She went by his home on a few occasions, but the place always looked abandoned. The club was shut down, and Maino had seemingly vanished. Chris and Maino's fighting was hard on Citi. The two men she loved now hated each other. It was a nightmare for her.

She remained standing on the terrace for a while. It was a nice night. The stars were out, and from her apartment ten stories up, with Queens beneath her, she was in a whole new world.

With Cane in the hospital, Chris and Citi became much closer. They talked more, and he started confiding in her about everything. She had proven herself. With his new Dominican connect, he needed to reach out. Citi had confirmed that she had resources of her own. Working with Maino and becoming his drug mule for months, she had made her own connections south on I-95, creating trust with the out-of-town hustlers. Some loved her swag, but many yearned to fuck her. She flirted with them and had gotten to know them better. She understood the game better than most men, having grown up around it all her life. She started to move her own pieces on the chessboard and was moving like a skilled player.

"What's up with your peoples in Maryland?" Chris asked as he came out the kitchen.

Citi walked into the living room. "I talked to Silo today, and at the price ya offering him, he's wit' it."

Chris smiled. "I love you, sis."

"We a team, big brother," she said halfheartedly.

"Yes, we are. Fuck Maino!" Chris spat. "His time is up." Chris went into his bedroom, leaving Citi alone in the room.

Hearing her brother curse Maino out like that sent a chill through her heart. Chris was hunting for her man real hard, but she didn't even know what their situation was any longer. She went back out on the terrace and continued staring at the city.

The following night, Citi wanted to break out and get her mind right. She was tired of being alone. She had been cooped up in the apartment for several days, shedding tears and worrying about her brother and Maino. With Cane shot up, Chris at war, and her man vanishing, she'd had enough. It was time for her to escape the madness and have some fun.

She got on the phone and dialed Lola.

"What, bitch?" Lola replied dryly.

"What you doin' tonight?"

"I'm goin' out."

"Where you going?" Citi asked.

"Big Kev got this new spot in Harlem."

"I'm comin' wit' you," Citi said quickly.

Lola fell silent.

"Bitch, you forgot how to speak?" Citi joked.

"Nah, it's cool. What time you want me to come get you?"

"I'll be ready by ten tonight. That's cool wit' you?"

"Cool. Don't have me waiting, bitch," Lola replied.

"Bitch, I need to get out. So much has been goin' on, but we'll talk."

Citi exhaled as she hung up. She was ready to hit the town tonight. Business would be on hold for a few hours, and her shadow, Kadar, would have to take a break from her night out. She didn't want anyone fucking up her groove for the night.

Citi emerged from the lobby in her tight black freak-me dress that stopped mid-thigh and highlighted every curve on her body. She strutted toward Lola's Civic parked in the circle in a pair of stilettos, her shoulder-length hair bouncing as she walked.

She got into the car and quickly hugged Lola. She noticed Lola seemed distant lately. She couldn't pinpoint the reason why, but she was ready to have a good time with her friend. Lola drove off, and Citi was ready to do her.

The small one-level Harlem club on Broadway was abuzz with revelers. The place was up to date with flat-screens, a lounge area, a high-end sound system, and a fully stocked bar. Citi and Lola entered the lively establishment like two divas. Dressed to kill, they were catching all the attention from the boys they strutted by. Citi was impressed. Big Kev seemed to have stepped up his hustle. The club was a moneymaker.

Citi played the bar in her five-thousand-dollar dress, and her jewelry was outshining everyone else's in the place. She made it unmistakably known with her demeanor and stylish attire that she was a boss bitch and getting money.

Lola had disappeared somewhere with Big Kev, leaving Citi alone. When she saw Kev, he was friendlier to her than previous times. She figured word was getting around about her and her brother running things in Queens and making moves out of town, and he probably wanted to get put on. But Citi shunned Big Kev. She was only at his club to get her groove and drink on. Besides, she didn't like the way he was playing her girl. He had her brainwashed on the dick. Citi didn't want to harp on any ill feelings. She was out on the town, making money and looking fabulous. She was turning down drink offers and advances from the men surrounding her and keeping to herself. The men who came on to her didn't meet her standards.

The bartender handed Citi the mixed drink she ordered as Chris Brown's and Fat Joe's "Another Round," boomed throughout the club.

"Damn! You get more beautiful every time I see you," she heard a man say from behind her, as she swayed to the music.

Citi was ready to turn around and tell him to piss off. She wasn't in the mood for lame pickup lines and horny niggas trying to get between her legs. She spun around with a scowl, but when she saw who it was, her entire attitude changed.

"L," she called out.

"In the flesh, beautiful," L replied with a smile. "It's good to see you again, Citi."

"You too." Citi beamed. "Oh, my God. You look good."

"Thanks."

Citi hugged him tight. Feeling L's masculine arms wrapped around her put her somewhere special for a moment. She sized him up immediately. He was looking remarkable, almost good enough to eat. He was dressed in a classy button-down, black slacks, and gators, and his cornrows were looking fresh. His smile lit up the dim club, and his sexy voice sank into Citi.

"You look amazing, Citi. I'm glad to see you finally come out."

"It's good to be out." Her attention stayed fixed on him, and she couldn't stop smiling.

"What you drinking?"

"Sex on the beach."

"You need a bottle. And why you chillin' by the bar, beautiful? You belong in VIP wit' us, or me," L said gently.

"Are you inviting me?"

"Can I ever turn you down?"

Citi smiled. She lit up inside like a Times Square billboard. L had every reason to hate her and disrespect her, but he came to her like a gentleman, and that chemistry between them started to rebuild. It was good to see that L didn't hold any grudges. Citi really needed a friend right now because Lola was probably fucking Big Kev, leaving her standing alone, surrounded by strangers.

L took Citi by her hand and led her toward the VIP area. They had all the attention aimed at them. The goons and male partygoers were bowled over, seeing Citi's thick, defined legs in that tight dress, her cheeky backside formed perfectly.

Citi sat in the VIP area with L, and they quickly reconnected. He made her feel special. They drank and laughed, and instantly, L made her forget about her troubles with Maino, the war her brother was involved in, and everything else. Once again, he treated Citi like a lady, and she seemed to be more appreciative this time.

"You busy, Citi?" L asked suddenly.

"What you mean?"

"Let's get out of here."

"And go where?"

"Somewhere nice, more quiet."

"But isn't this your spot?"

"I help run it, but this is Big Kev's shit. I got other ambitions elsewhere."

Citi smiled. She left the club with L in his Benz, and they headed toward the West Side and parked on Riverside Drive. It was a nice fall night. Peaceful and warm. L and Citi got out the Benz and walked along the pavement. The view of New Jersey across the Hudson River and the illuminated George Washington Bridge from a distance was so tranquil and breathtaking.

As they talked and took in the beauty the West Side had to offer, L stopped in his tracks and pulled Citi into his arms. The way he touched her certified his love for her. They stared across the river in silence for a moment. Citi loved the way he embraced her. She felt secure and safe. His arms were like a blanket of protection.

"One day, I'ma run all this shit," he said. "I know too much, been on the streets and in this game for too long, and right now, Kev is fuckin' up. A few niggas ain't happy the way he's running things."

L's ambition was music to Citi's ears. To hear him talk about becoming a boss made her panties wet. She knew he had the potential. He just needed a push. "So why don't you, baby?" she asked.

"I gotta wait till the time is right."

"And when will that be?"

"I don't know yet, but it's gonna come."

"What if I can make the time right for you?"

"What you mean?"

"I need to introduce you to my brother Chris."

The two started talking, and L was feeling what Citi had to say. He was the one who had held Big Kev down for so many years, the one who'd busted his gun and made his reputation, yet Big Kev somehow snaked his way to the top, mostly off bullshit and lies. But since they were boys, L kept quiet and stayed in the shadows to let Big Kev ride the wave. Now he was thirsty for more, and Citi was right on time to give him that extra push. She would become his muse.

Citi spent the night at his place, and they had passionate sex. After their sex session, L held her in his arms for the entire night. Citi needed the comfort. She fell asleep against him, feeling a little bit of peace in her life.

CHAPTER 29

Citi couldn't help but beam with joy as she watched the heavyset nurse in her blue scrubs wheel Cane out of the hospital lobby and toward the minivan parked outside. Chris, Kadar, and Citi stood proudly by the van on the cool fall day. Cane had spent weeks in the hospital, most of the time in a coma, and then come the rehabilitation. Citi was there to help her brother pull through from day one, so this was a proud moment for her.

Citi watched Cane slumped in the chair. She couldn't stop staring at him. Physically, Cane looked himself, but he was weak. He'd lost a lot of weight. But the worst part was that he had to wear a colostomy bag.

She hugged him. "We missed you."

Cane got a hug from Chris, and Kadar gave him a nod of the head. Everyone was so happy to see him coming home, but there wouldn't be a welcome home/recovery party. It was too risky to have any gathering with Maino still out there.

Citi knew the repercussions of becoming a boss bitch. She and Chris were taking over, and with money and power came hate, jealousy, and betrayal. She and L had a strong bond, and the chemistry between them was rock-solid. She fell in love with L, and this time she was appreciative of his treatment of her. He was a thug and gentleman. She saw the difference between his love and Maino's. Maino was a piece of shit—a coward.

Citi and L were becoming the urban Bonnie and Clyde, but their love also came with consequences. There was a falling-out with Big Kev, who didn't like that she was filling L's head with ambition. L had started to buy his work from Chris, and was becoming the Nino Brown of Harlem. A few harsh words were exchanged, and Big Kev made it clearly known he would take action. A fistfight ensued, and L was the victor.

Citi's friendship with Lola became very rocky. Things had changed between them drastically, and she didn't have a clue why. Was it jealousy? Was it Big Kev? Lola was allowing dick to come between them. Citi felt Lola was the stupid bitch, standing by a man like Big Kev, who treated her like a dog.

▲

Several days had gone by since Cane had come home. He was weak and confined to a bed. Chris had to hire a home health aide to tend to him twenty-four/seven. She was a young pleasant woman who loved her job and made it her duty to help Cane with his continuing recovery. It was costly, but worth the money. Chris felt comfortable leaving his brother in her hands. He had a business to run, and didn't have the time to always look after him.

Chris had to make a run to Washington Heights and meet with his Dominican connect. It was a monthly run, which he usually made with one of his soldiers, but this time he had to go alone because Paso wanted to have a sit-down with him. Their business relationship was strong, and over the months, Chris had built up trust with the Dominicans.

Citi lingered in the apartment, keeping Cane's company, while Chris went to meet with the Dominicans. She was hoping he didn't go alone, but she knew he could take care of himself. As she relaxed in the apartment, she thought about L. His growth on the streets had been fast. He was locking down corners and finally realizing his potential. No longer under Big Kev's wing, he was becoming the main muthafucka in Harlem. Citi saw her father in L—the way he treated her like a princess, the way he moved, almost stealth-like, his cool reaction to certain things, and the fact that he could become dangerous when necessary. Citi was thankful that she had gotten a second chance to be with him.

Finally, things were looking up. Cane was home and healing, she'd found true love with L, and Chris had a solid cocaine connection that brought in tons of cash.

▲

Citi woke up to the phone ringing early in the morning. She had fallen asleep on the couch watching videos on MTV. Cane was asleep in the main bedroom. The home health aide was scheduled to show up in a half hour.

She reached over and grabbed the cordless off the table and answered it. When she heard, "You have a collect call from, Chris Byrne. If you accept this call, press one, if not—"

Citi instantly pressed one. She was befuddled. Why was Chris calling her from jail? Her heart started to race. She gripped the phone tightly and waited for him to speak.

"Citi," Chris said into the phone.

"Chris, what the fuck is goin' on? Why are you callin' me collect from some correctional facility?"

"I'm locked up. I got knocked last night," he said somberly.

"What? How? No, this can't be happening. What they arrested you for?"

Chris sighed heavily. He didn't want to answer the question, but Citi was adamant.

"Two bricks and a burner. Might be a snitch in the camp."

Citi's heart sank into her stomach. The tears started to fall from her eyes. Her legs felt shaky. She felt like passing out. This wasn't happening. It had to be a nightmare. But the shit was real. Chris' words into her ear put her fairytale on serious hold.

"They gonna arraign me tomorrow morning. I don't know about bail. I got fuckin' priors, and the work they caught me with fucks me up."

"What the fuck we gonna do, Chris?"

"I don't know right now, Citi. I might need a lawyer."

Within the blink of an eye, Chris' incarceration had fractured the family, and their business. Citi didn't know what to do, with the brains locked down and the muscle incapacitated. The problems just did not end.

The call suddenly ended, leaving Citi to worry about her big brother. She stepped out onto the terrace, gripped the railing tightly and gazed down, sadness overcoming her. She then looked up at the sky and screamed, "AAAAHHHH! THIS IS NOT HAPPENING!"

Her screaming woke up a few neighbors.

When the home health aide arrived to care for Cane, Citi quickly got dressed and shot out the door. She rushed uptown to see L. She needed to be with him. He was the only man around capable of comforting her in her time of need. She jumped into a cab and hurried uptown to his place.

L comforted Citi and held her close. They talked for hours and made arrangements to hire an attorney for Chris. Citi had spent the entire day in L's apartment. She poured her heart out to him, and he constantly dried her tears. It was therapeutic.

"I can't lose him, L," she cried out while being held in his arms.

"You're not gonna lose him, Citi. He's gonna be okay. I promise you."

Citi wanted to believe L. Being with him, there was a glint of hope. The way he talked to her reminded her of the way Curtis spoke to her. Both men had that assurance in their tone.

"Go home and be with Cane," L advised her. "He's gonna need you too."

Citi shook her head, agreeing with him. "I love you."

"I love you too," he replied.

She exited the Harlem building with L by her side. The Thanksgiving holiday was approaching, and she was hoping to spend the holidays with all of her family intact. She followed L onto the sidewalk. His Yukon was parked across the two-way street. The traffic had slowed as dusk had come over the town, and the evening was calm.

Citi and L got into the money-green Yukon, and he sat for a moment watching the block. Something had caught his attention. He started the ignition, but he felt something wasn't right.

L removed his Glock 19 from under his seat and cocked it back, his attention focused on the maroon Lexus with tinted windows parked a few cars down from them. He had seen that car before on previous occasions, and he swore it had been following him around Harlem for the past two weeks.

"Baby, what's wrong?"

"You know that car?" L asked, pointing to the maroon Lexus.

Citi shook her head. "What's goin' on?"

"I don't know."

Instantly, gunfire exploded, shattering the back windows, causing Citi to scream and duck down in her seat.

Bak! Bak! Bak! Bak! Bak! Bak! Bak!

L screamed for Citi to stay down and rose up to return rapid gunfire at the assailants. His Glock exploded at them like fireworks. "Y'all fuckin' come at me?" he screamed. He hit one of the assailants in his chest, dropping him to the pavement dead.

The second shooter was suddenly shaken up by his fallen comrade, and he decided to flee the scene.

L jumped from the truck and sprang into action like a trained soldier. He gave chase, shooting at the fleeing goon, but was unable to hit his target. The maroon Lexus took off suddenly, an indication that the car was part of a setup.

L's Yukon looked like Swiss cheese, and his windows were shot out. He snatched open the passenger door to make sure Citi was okay. "I got you, baby, I got you."

L peered at the dead goon sprawled out on the street. He had no idea who'd sent the shooters, but he was determined to find out. He sent Citi away in a cab, knowing she already had a lot on her plate to deal with, and he stayed to sort out the confusion and deal with the aftermath.

A week later, they found out that the dead guy on the pavement with the hole in his chest was one of Alonzo's lieutenants. It puzzled L and Citi. L had heard about Alonzo. He was a legend on the streets and was getting money for over a decade in Harlem. However, he had been dead for almost two years, so L couldn't understand why one of his men was trying to kill them.

▲

It took two months for Citi to see Chris on Rikers Island. The assistant district attorney had persuaded the judge to deny Chris bail, labeling him a kingpin and remanding him. They wanted to hit Chris with a conspiracy indictment and a slew of charges—including the Kingpin Act. The ADA was aware that he had taken over his father's drug empire after his demise, so they were coming at him with everything they had. They wanted both brothers badly, but Cane, so far, had been able to elude indictments.

Citi walked into the stench of the visitation room trying to keep her head up and wear a smile, but the conditions she had to see her brother in made her feel hopeless. The place was loud and crowded with mostly women and kids visiting their fathers, sons, brothers, husbands, and boyfriends, and COs stood about everywhere, watching for anything suspicious.

Earlier, Citi had to deal with the long line of women and children outside Rikers Island, with mothers corralling children and shouting over the roar of jets. The correction officers were unsympathetic and cranky.

Guard the Throne

Moving through the metal detectors and having to remove garments was an agonizing process for her, but she put up with it to finally see her brother.

Citi was assigned to a seat by the guard. As she moved through the visitation area, fleeting looks and lasting stares were directed toward her. The inmates already knew who she was. They dared not say anything to her. Chris already had "made his bones" in the jail.

She sat down at the small table and chair and waited for Chris to be brought into the room. A short while later, Chris was escorted into the visitation room, clad in an orange jumpsuit with "D.O.C." printed in large black letters across the back. He wore beige sandals and tube socks. He seemed to have aged rapidly. His eyes were cold and his look blank, but when he noticed Citi across the room, he smiled instantly.

He slowly walked over, and Citi stood up and hugged him passionately.

"Hey, Citi," he greeted softly.

"I miss you."

"I miss you too," he replied.

They took a seat opposite each other.

"How you holding up?" he asked her.

"I'm good. I'm keeping this business going, with the help of L."

"How thorough is that nigga?"

"He saved my life, Chris. You know that."

Chris nodded.

"Why you asking this?" she inquired.

Chris didn't hesitate to tell her that she was in danger.

"What you mean?" Citi responded quickly. "What's goin' on, Chris? Does this got somethin' to do wit' that hit on me and L two months back? We took precautions. I got security wit' me twenty-four/seven, and I'm tryin' to keep a low profile. And L has been on top of things."

"Shit is ugly out there, Citi. I think the same people that killed Alonzo killed our father too."

"What? Why? But why would one of Alonzo's lieutenants come gunning at us then? It doesn't make sense."

"I know. But word is, Emanuel Martinez is back in town, and he's on some vicious shit."

Citi didn't know the name. She seemed puzzled, so Chris had to enlighten her.

"He's Alonzo's brother. Pops used to talk about him. He's a dangerous man, and for some reason, he's got a vendetta against our family."

"I don't understand, Chris. What is goin' on?"

"Look, Citi, chances are he's gonna come at you, so you gotta come at him hard and fast when the opportunity arises. You hit that nigga, and his whole crew will fold."

"But how?"

"I don't fuckin' know, but I'm gonna put this in your ear—Watch your back; trust no one. I mean, no fuckin' one. And, most likely, the one individual that comes to you with this information I'm giving to you now is the nigga you definitely can't trust."

"Why, Chris?"

"If he knows something behind our father's death, or shit to do with Alonzo, giving you personal details, then most likely, he the nigga also responsible for it all."

Citi sighed.

"Also, I want you to get Cane out of the city."

"To where?"

"Miami. I got a beach house down there. Send Cane down there to recuperate."

The beach house in Miami was something she didn't know about. She looked her brother square in his eyes. "Alone?"

"I got peoples down there."

"And when were you goin' to tell me about the beach house?"

"There are a lot of things I kept secret from you for a reason."

Citi sighed.

"Also, tomorrow, I need you to go into the city, go into the Wells Fargo bank in downtown Manhattan. I have three safety deposit boxes set up in there. The information you gonna need to access the boxes is in my room. I learned from Pops' mistakes, not to keep money and drugs in the house."

Citi nodded.

"But you gotta act quickly, Citi. And this info only stays between you and me."

"Of course."

Soon, the visit was over, and Citi was hugging her brother good-bye. She didn't want to leave his side, but it was their life now. She didn't cry as he was escorted back into lockup, but the minute he was out of sight, the tears started falling.

The next day, Citi went down to Wells Fargo in lower Manhattan. With the accurate information, along with the key and PIN, she was ushered into the secured room and given privacy to access the boxes.

Citi was astounded when she opened all three boxes and saw three hundred grand and four kilos in the boxes. *Leave it to Chris to hide drugs and money in a bank*, she thought. Citi cleaned out everything and made her exit. It was time to get the wheels turning on her and her family's survival.

CHAPTER 30

With Cane down in Miami, Citi stayed in New York and continued to run the family business. Her family had built their empire through blood, sweat, and tears, and she refused to see it crumble to nothing. In fact, she was determined to make what her father and brothers had created much stronger. She was forced into the driver's seat.

Citi entrusted L to take over her brothers' organization with her, and the two started to become large. She had to travel to Washington Heights to meet with the Dominicans. With Chris being incarcerated, the Dominicans feared he might become a snitch. Citi couldn't allow that pipeline of hard white to dry up, nor for her brother's name to be tarnished. She met with Paso's partner Victor personally and had a sit-down with him.

"I assure you, my brother is no snitch. You know the bloodline we come from and what we're about, and with me in charge, business will continue as usual—even greater than before. You have my word on that."

"Chris is a good man, a good hustler. You, I barely know."

"Well, you know me now. I'm my father's daughter, and I'm not a bitch to fuck with. Check my pedigree. These streets don't lie."

Victor, a hardcore hustler, always had respect for the Byrnes. He sized Citi up, asked her a few questions, and decided to continue to do business with the Byrne family via Citi. She was elated, but didn't show it. The two shook hands.

"Don't fuck this up, and don't fuck with me, Citi. I'm not a man to take lightly."

Citi nodded. "And I'm not a bitch to be caught slippin'. I'm gonna handle my business on my end, and you make sure you continue to handle it on your end. We get this money, and there will always be that mutual respect."

Victor smiled. "I like how you think."

"Then you gonna love how I do business."

Citi realized that the first priority was to get the business end of the game straightened out. She had to solidify her source of income, and make her connect happy and trustful of her. After that was taken care of, she had to confront the dirty side of the business next—Get at the wolves before they got at her. And she knew it was only a matter of time before they came ready to bite.

With Maino still MIA and Emanuel back in Harlem, the threat was real. She couldn't dwell on it, though. She had a business to run and was determined to run it with an iron fist. With Chris and Cane gone, she had to hire a few ruthless goons for her muscle, and L also had a few tricks up his sleeves.

Day by day, and month by month, with L by her side, the organization kept growing. She was making millions trafficking narcotics in several different states, and had three lavish homes—in New Jersey, upstate New York, and North Carolina—and a fleet of cars. She moved with security at all times.

▲

Citi walked through Short Hills Mall in New Jersey enjoying the shopping spree. Everything was now within reach, and she had it all—Gucci, Prada, Chanel, Louis Vuitton—so she no longer needed to shoplift. Life was good to her, even though there was still danger lurking in the streets. She continued with her business and lived her life like she was one of the rich and famous, traveling extensively and shopping at the finest stores.

However, Emanuel Martinez was becoming a serious threat, and since his return to New York, the body count had shot up, making the game even tenser. It was clear on the streets that he had a beef with Citi and her family, but Citi refused to be discouraged by the foreign thug. New York was her home, and she was going to continue running her family's empire by any means necessary.

Citi went in and out of posh stores, her security playing her close. L was out of town on business, and she just wanted to get away from the streets and have a personal day for herself, which included spa treatments, shopping, and dinner at a five-star restaurant later in the evening.

Short Hills Mall was Citi's place of escape. It was far away from the hood and the city, all the way in the boondocks. She felt safe there and moved through the shopping complex freely. Derrick was her shadow. Wherever she went, he followed. He stood six-three, weighed over two hundred pounds, and carried around a holstered Desert Eagle under his coat.

Citi exited the mall with a few shopping bags in hand. Derrick was walking right behind her. Clad in a mink coat and stylish knee-high boots and looking like a diva, she walked briskly toward her gleaming Escalade.

"Citi!"

She spun around to see who had called out her name. Derrick, his hand near his weapon, moved closer to her, but before he could shield her from any harm, two goons hemmed him up between two parked cars. Citi was ready to reach for the gun in her purse, but seeing Maino put hesitation in her action.

"Citi, I just wanna talk to you," Maino said coolly.

"Maino, what the fuck is goin' on?" she barked. "How did you find me? Get the fuck away from me."

"Just fuckin' hear me out."

"No, not after what you did to my brother."

"We need to talk." Maino grabbed Citi aggressively by her arm and pulled her away.

"Get off me!"

"Look, I didn't have shit to do wit' your brother gettin' shot."

"Why are you here? It's been months since I've seen you, and now you come back from nowhere and expect me to believe that?"

"Look, I had to go on the lam. Feds were closing in on me. Shit got hot, so I had to be out. But I didn't gun down Cane. Yeah, he pulled that gun out on me, but he let me live. Your brothers are like sons to me."

Citi was having a hard time believing him. Soon after her brother was shot, Maino had disappeared. She looked over at Derrick.

"Ya boy is a'ight. We ain't gonna kill him."

Citi was fuming. "What do you want from me, Maino?"

"Look, I came to give you some news. I'm gonna be straightforward wit' you. The reason Emanuel is comin' at you is because he believes your father murdered Alonzo."

"What? You're fuckin' lying. My father and Alonzo had love for each other. They were like brothers. All of y'all were like brothers."

"Listen, Curtis and Alonzo had tension. It was over a woman. He was the one that robbed Alonzo of his stash. Now Alonzo's old crew is comin' at you. They're the ones that shot up Cane. I thought you should know the truth."

Shocked, Citi glared at him. He hadn't changed. She couldn't believe she used to be in love with him. Now, he repulsed her. Maino's words felt like poison being shoved down her throat. But then suddenly she remembered what Chris had said to her a while back—*"The one individual that comes to you with this information I'm giving to you now is the nigga you definitely can't trust."*

Citi then thought that if Maino knew her father had murdered Alonzo for his stash, then it was likely that he'd murdered her father for that same stash. Finally, the pieces were coming together. She remembered the look on her father's face when he saw the jewels she and Cane were sporting. Then there was the lengthy speech that came from him right before his murder. Maino was the only one who could have gotten close enough to her father and strike him down. And then he became the boss. He had blown up financially and didn't have the decency to pay for the whole funeral.

"I just came to warn you," Maino said. "I still care for you, Citi, and I love your family."

Citi became enraged that she'd fucked him—the man who'd killed her father. The rage inside her exploded, and she rose up and spat in Maino's face. "You son of a bitch!" she screamed. "It was you! You killed him!"

"What?"

Suddenly, gunshots rang out, and before Citi knew it, one of Maino's goons was dead, and Derrick and an accomplice were aiming for Maino, who barely escaped with his life.

"Citi, you okay?" Derrick asked.

Citi was in too much shock to answer. For a long time, she had been sleeping with the enemy. She wanted to throw up. She felt like she had betrayed her father.

How didn't I see it? The evidence was directly in my face.

CHAPTER
31

It seemed like the world was against the Byrnes, and everywhere they turned, there was some enemy trying to gun them down and take away everything the family had built.

The word on the streets was, Curtis had murdered Alonzo and Juliette, and now Citi and her brothers had to pay for their father's actions. Juliette's brothers from the Bronx wanted to tear her apart, Emanuel wanted to decapitate her, and Maino wanted to skin her alive. The pressure against her was building, and building fast. Citi tried keeping a cool head, but the odds were stacked against her to continue to run her business and go to war with three different drug crews.

Citi and L rode in the backseat of the SUV in silence. The killings were becoming extensive, and Emanuel Martinez made it clear that he was headhunting for Citi and her family. He'd put a bounty on Citi's head: one million dollars to anyone who killed that bitch and her man. So Citi made it her business to pay Emanuel a personal visit. She wanted to see the face of the enemy up close and look into his eyes. She wanted to have a few words with him. L was against it. He tried to persuade her to stay away from the man, but Citi was adamant about walking into the lion's den.

"Citi, you sure you wanna do this? Think about it. He got a bounty on your head. It's crazy to just walk into the man's business like that. It's just fuckin' crazy."

"I guess I'm a crazy bitch then. But ain't no man gonna scare me out what is mine and what I got goin' on. I can swing my dick too. Fuck Emanuel. He wants war, and he wanna come at me, then I'm gonna see the face of the man I'm fighting."

L sighed. No matter what happened, he was always going to have her back. He loved her, and had always proved it with his actions. He had killed for her, and would continue to do so.

They drove to Emanuel's establishment in Harlem two trucks deep with armed thugs ready for anything. The Escalade came to a stop in front of Emanuel's restaurant on Convent Avenue, a quaint spot well known for harboring gangsters and drug dealers. Emanuel had owned it for years. Citi had gotten wind of his location through L's sources in Harlem.

Citi stepped out the Escalade looking like the baddest bitch in the game, clad in tight jeans, a leather jacket, and leather boots. L was by her side, and four goons, armed like soldiers in Iraq, were behind the couple.

She burst into the eatery, surprising Emanuel and his goons. "You were lookin' for me, muthafucka?" she shouted. "Here I am."

Guns quickly came out, both sides ready to react.

Emanuel was seated at a table having dinner with a friend. "Bitch, who the fuck you think you are coming into my place of business like that?" he shouted.

"I'm in ya fuckin' face, you bitch," she retorted. "You put a bounty on my head. Fuck you!"

"Watch how you talk to me, little girl. I'll rip your tits off and feed them to my dogs."

"I'm not scared of you. My father wasn't, and I'm not."

Emanuel was dressed in Armani and looked more like a Wall Street tycoon than a gangster.

"This is a grown man's game, little girl, far out of your league. I warn you, by week's end, I'll have your head and tits in two separate boxes," he said through clenched teeth. "What your father did to my brother, you and your family will pay dearly with slow and agonizing deaths."

Citi didn't flinch. She stared at him. "Fuck you! I'm gonna finish what my father started wit' ya fuckin' family."

"You will die, Citi."

L stepped forward, ready to defend his woman's honor. "Fuck you, nigga! We got guns too!"

Emanuel laughed. "My men missed once, but I'll guarantee that they will not disappoint me again."

"And we won't miss either," L spat back.

"Let me shoot this *puta*!" Hector shouted, raising his weapon at L and Citi.

There was a deep chill in the room. One word, and the men were ready to wipe each other out.

But Emanuel didn't want any bloodshed in his eatery. He said to Hector, "Not in here! This is my grandmother's place, and no blood will be spilled in here."

Hector lowered his weapon.

"Leave here, you little bitch! But we will see each other again."

"You look at me. I'm my father, so remember that, Emanuel, when I cut ya dick off. Because I will kill you."

Citi and L started to make their exit.

"You got balls, bitch, coming up in here like that," Emanuel shouted. "The bogeyman is coming for you, bitch. This is a man's world, and pussy is meant to be fucked. And before you die, I'm going to fuck you till your pussy falls off and then tear you and your friend apart bit by bit."

Citi didn't reply. The crew walked out, and she hopped back into the backseat of the truck with L by her side, and they took off.

L sighed with relief. He looked at Citi and said, "They ain't gonna stop coming."

"I know."

"We gotta definitely arm ourselves heavily." L was trying to come up with a game plan to get at all their enemies, but it was like a village going against Rome.

"I'm gonna kill 'em in my father's name. I just gotta find a way."

Citi got quiet. She had a lot on her mind. She refused to be bullied, no matter how powerful Emanuel was. She had her goons, but between Maino, Juliette's brothers in the Bronx, and Emanuel, the odds of surviving the war were stacked against them. But she refused to let her enemies see her worry and sweat. She was a Byrne, and a Byrne always found a way to stay on top and survive.

CHAPTER 32

MIAMI, FLORIDA

Cane watched the group of men leaving the notorious King of Diamonds nighclub. It was four in the morning as the crowd began to disperse with laughter and loud chatter. Cane was dressed in all black and waiting for the right opportunity to strike at his targets as he sat in a black Lexus, smoking a cigarette and holding on to the .50 Desert Eagle, his favorite toy. Once it hit a man, he wasn't getting back up.

The four men got into a white Range Rover and sped away, and Cane followed them. The Range Rover jumped on I-95 and headed south. They traveled for a few miles, and were in North Miami.

When the Range Rover came to a stop at a red light on a desolate street, Cane decided it was the perfect time to attack. He leaped from his car with the gun in his hand and trotted toward the driver's side. The driver had his window down completely and was downing a flask filled with liquor, music playing loudly. Before the driver could react, Cane leaped like a predator out of the dark and opened fired into the truck.

Boom! Boom! Boom! Boom! Boom! Boom! Boom!

The muzzle flash lit up the night, and the bullets tore into soft flesh. Cane made sure to kill everyone in the truck. He smiled at his handiwork and then retreated back to his car, leaving Miami-Dade to clean up his mess once again.

▲

Miami had been Cane's home for a few months, and he had fully recuperated and was back to his old ways. He missed New York, but he had built a strong family in Miami. He missed his brother and sister, but unbeknownst to them, he had linked up with Ashanti, and they'd reconciled their differences.

Ashanti had become a major figure in Miami when she started to date Marcus Dashwood, AKA Black Mamba. He ran Miami. His empire had an estimated worth of two hundred million. Black Mamba had connections throughout the world, from war tyrants in Africa, to drug cartels in Mexico, to the Senate in D.C., to the shot-callers on Wall Street. Soon, the two got married, and Ashanti was by her husband's side helping him run and control all of Miami. Being with Curtis for so many years, she proved useful to a man like Marcus, who was dazzled by not just her beauty, but her brains too.

Cane had inadvertently reconnected with his mother when he and a friend of his got into an altercation at one of Black Mamba's nightclubs. There was an argument, and a fight ensued. Cane smashed a champagne bottle over the head of one of the thugs. Gunfire erupted. Cane shot one goon in the stomach, crippling him.

It so happened that the thug Cane shot was connected to Black Mamba, and there was a bounty on his head. When Ashanti saw that it was her son they were about to kill, she quickly intervened and persuaded her husband not to take her son's life. For the love of his wife, Marcus spared Cane, but with stipulations. He had to prove his worth in Miami, and Cane did so. He started to kill for his stepfather, and he did it so well, Marcus made him a lieutenant in his organization.

Cane and Ashanti had South Beach on lockdown. Miami became Cane's playground. He had money, cars, women, and power. But the one thing Cane didn't have was his brother and sister. He was worried about them. Word had gotten to him about Citi's troubles in New York, and he was dying to go up there and wipe all her enemies out. It hurt Cane to be apart from his family, even though he was with his mother.

▲

Cane went to have a talk with Ashanti. He wanted to go back to New York and protect his baby sister. He had the killer crew that could paint the streets of New York red with blood.

Ashanti was ready to help her son with his wishes. Despite being out of her children's lives for so many years, she loved them and was ready to do whatever she needed to protect them. She'd never disclosed to Cane what motivated Curtis to kill his best friend Alonzo. She knew she was the one that caused that ripple between their friendship, and she felt guilty about her actions. She planned to take that secret to her grave. She knew her children would never forgive her and would probably attempt to kill her if they knew the truth, especially Citi and Cane. All the same, the guilt of Curtis' murder made her want to be a better mother and protect her kids.

Ashanti stared at her son. "I loved your father very much, Cane. He was my world. When I look at you, I see him in you."

Cane nodded as he listened.

"Your father's death was tragic, but I promise to make things right with my children. I'm sorry for my long absence from the family, but from this day forward, I'm here for every one of y'all."

"Then get Black Mamba to destroy Emanuel, 'cuz he's tryin' to destroy my sister. I can handle those bitch-ass brothers from the Bronx and Maino. I plan to finish what I started wit' that snake muthafucka."

With a man like Black Mamba in his corner, Cane knew even a powerful man like Emanuel Martinez was as good as dead. Emanuel was nothing compared to Marcus Dashwood; it was like a tomcat trying to go against a lion. Emanuel was a gangster with money, but Marcus was an entity with influences all throughout the world.

Ashanti went to her husband and persuaded him to help her children win a war in New York, and out of respect for his wife and her son, he sanctioned the hit on Emanuel Martinez. The man was already dead; he just didn't know it yet.

EPILOGUE

The reunion was bittersweet. Citi and Ashanti in the same room together could prove disastrous, but Cane was there to smooth things over between mother and daughter. The two arrived in New York via Learjet and immediately went to see Citi at her undisclosed location in New Jersey.

Citi was ecstatic to see her brother again, but when Ashanti emerged from behind Cane, she had a few harsh words to say to her mother.

Ashanti apologized to her daughter for her absence, but Citi didn't want to hear anything her mother had to say.

"Where were you when we needed you? When I needed you? When I needed my mother to hold me and comfort me?" Tears streamed down her face. "I just wanted you around at one time in my life."

It was painful for Ashanti to hear, but she stood there and took the berating. "I know, baby, but I wasn't the woman I am today. I admit, I was selfish, left y'all with Curtis to raise, but I knew he would do a wonderful job with y'all. And I stand by my decision today. But I promise you, I'm here for my little girl now."

"I'm not a little girl anymore, Ashanti."

"I know. You have grown to become such a beautiful woman—smart and feisty. You did very well for yourself, Citi. I'm proud of you, and I know he would be too. His children are guarding the throne. He did so well with y'all."

Citi wiped the tears from her eyes. The unkind words to her mother needed to be said. She needed to release the pain she'd been feeling all those years.

L, standing next to his woman's side, was astounded by the resemblance between Citi and her mother. They were both stunning.

"We a family again. Fuck that," Cane said.

Ashanti and Citi stared at each other for a moment. Then, out of the blue, Citi, tears trickling down her cheeks, ran into her mother's arms.

Ashanti embraced her daughter lovingly. "I'm here for you, Citi. We gonna make things right. Not a soul will harm my little girl. I promise."

Cane watched the reunion between them silently. He was ready to put in work. He had a few scores to settle. He had missed New York, but now with all of them together, the Byrne family was untouchable, except for Chris, who had received a mandatory fifteen years in prison.

▲

Cane and his Miami crew gunned down Juliette's two brothers in cold blood in front of a popular nightclub in the South Bronx, leaving their blood-splattered and bullet-riddled bodies in a gruesome display as a warning.

Maino was next on their hit list. Cane had caught him slipping at his bitch's crib in Mt. Vernon, New York. Maino had become weak with the feds investigating him, and his empire had crumbled. He had been moving from borough to borough and state to state, trying to remain incognito, but with enough money spread around for information, his own men turned against him and snitched him out.

Cane crept into the dark room and stared down at Maino asleep and hugged up with some light-skinned bitch. He and his partner, a young thug named Kong, smirked at the sight. It was a golden moment for him. Maino had killed his father. Now he had the chance to extract revenge. It was making his dick hard.

He walked over to Maino and knocked him across the head with the butt of his pistol. "Wake ya bitch ass up, muthafucka!"

The light-skinned bitch screamed when she awoke and saw two armed men in her in the bedroom. Kong had her at gunpoint.

"What the fuck!" Maino screamed, holding his bleeding head. His eyes widened with fear when he saw Cane towering over him. "Cane, what the fuck is ya problem?"

"You my problem, bitch!"

"Yo, we can work somethin' out."

Cane barked, "Work somethin' out? Nigga, you must be out ya fuckin' mind. You killed my father, fucked my sister, and then tried to kill me. It's too fuckin' late to work somethin' out."

"It wasn't me, man. I ain't had shit to do wit' Curtis' death or you. I was family to you, Cane. I loved all y'all. Don't do this to me."

"Nigga, save all that pleading shit until you meet the devil soon, 'cuz I ain't hearin' shit ya sayin' right now." Cane pointed the pistol at Maino's head.

"Cane, don't do this."

"Fuck you!"

Cane fired his pistol into Maino's face at point-blank range, and the hot shells tore his flesh apart. It was ugly. Kong followed suit and killed the woman Maino was lying with. The bed became soaked in their blood. Cane smiled. Killing Maino was like busting a nut. He felt relieved, having avenged his father's death.

Cane and his vicious Miami crew put a hurting on New York City like it hadn't seen since the crack era of the '80s. They had bodies dropping everywhere. Cane and Citi was showing the underworld that a new force was reigning supreme in the city's criminal world, and they had the money, the muscle, and the influence to become number one. Now, the Byrne throne was stronger than ever.

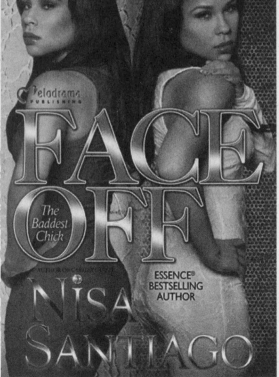

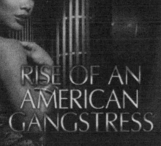

Follow

Melodrama Publishing

www.twitter.com/Team_Melodrama

www.facebook.com/MelodramaPublishing

Order online at
bn.com, amazon.com, and
MelodramaPublishing.com